CAROLINA CRUEL

CAROLINA CRUEL

Cindi,

Thanks for reading!

Enjoy!

a novel by

LAWRENCE THACKSTON

RIVERS TURN
P R E S S

Rivers Turn Press
617 Rivers Turn Road
Orangeburg, SC 29115

First edition, first printing May 2017

Book Design by Holly Holladay and Major Graphics
Author photo by Joni Thackston

Manufactured in the United States of America

Library of Congress CN: 2017932288

Hardback edition ISBN 978-0-9985755-1-3

Trade Paperback edition ISBN 978-0-9985755-0-6

Advance Praise for *Carolina Cruel*

Praise for Lawrence Thackston's *Tidal Pools* and *The Devil's Courthouse*

"Omnes enim ex infirmitate feritas est."

"All cruelty springs from weakness."

—Seneca

Seneca's Morals: Of a Happy Life, Benefits, Anger and Clemency

In Memory of:
The Emanuel Church Nine
Charleston, SC

"There's nothing that evil fears more than love."

OCTOBER 11, 1962

10:41 PM

Trina blew out a deep breath and leaned forward in the driver's seat. She grabbed the keys dangling from the ignition, made the sign of the cross over her chest with her left hand, and said a hurried Hail Mary. She pumped the gas pedal as she tried the starter once more. The engine of the black 1960 Lincoln Continental coughed and spit but then died into silence just as it had done the past twenty times.

She gazed out of the window. The moon, peeking through moving clouds, lent a bluish tint to the night, and she could make out the woods and open fields around her. She turned to her right and caught Sara Beth's nervous smile in the glow of the dashboard. "I don't know anything about engines," Sara Beth admitted. "Do you?"

"Only that they run on gas. And I know that the tank was full when we left Orangeburg." Trina tapped on the gas gauge with her index finger. She then frowned and slumped in her seat. "We should have never taken my uncle's car. We should have ridden with Amy and the rest of the girls. We could have all squeezed in."

Sara Beth knew it was futile to second guess their actions at this point. "Where are we exactly?"

"I saw a sign not too long ago. We're halfway between Columbia and Charleston – near some place called Macinaw." She scanned the darkness again. "Great short-cut, huh?"

"Maybe we should walk to Macinaw. See if they have a station or someone who can help us."

Trina eyed the road ahead of them. It had been a lonesome highway to this point, meandering through the quiet towns, swamps and cotton fields of the South Carolina Lowcountry. "It

1

may be a couple more miles. And then there may not be anything open once we're there."

Sara Beth shrugged. "Beats sitting here though, right?"

Trina agreed with a tepid smile. But as she reached over to unlock the door, a figure appeared next to her window. She screamed and practically leapt into Sara Beth's lap. Both girls latched onto one another as they watched the shadowy stranger move slightly from side to side.

The figure hunched over, pressed up against the window and then banged on the glass with a fist.

"What do you want?" Trina yelled.

"Y'all okay? Y'all need some help?" a man answered. Though muted by the glass, Trina could pick up on the man's high-pitched, Southern voice.

Trina gathered herself enough to respond. "Can you...? Will you call someone for us, please? Our car has engine problems."

"Ain't got no phone," the man replied. "But I can drive you two into town. My truck's up yonder at my farm, 'bout half-a-mile." He waited through their silence, "It's eight more miles to Macinaw."

Trina looked at Sara Beth who discretely shook her head *no*. "I think we better go with him," Trina whispered harshly. "Unless you want to stay here all night."

"But we don't know anything about this guy. He could be one of those weirdoes we're always hearing about."

"Don't be paranoid. He's probably just a local farmer."

"Walking all alone out here so late?"

"I don't see that we have much of a choice, do you? I think we'll have to trust him."

Sara Beth bit down on her lip and eyed the figure through the window. "Well... okay, I guess," she relented.

Trina leaned forward, popped the lock, and eased the door open. She instantly regretted it as she took in the man before her. He was razor thin—skin and bones wrapped in a long-sleeved blue shirt and baggy jeans. The in-and-out moonlight revealed his severely angular facial features, causing Trina to gasp. His skin seemed translucent—as if someone had taken a thin sheet of cellophane and simply wrapped it around the man's skull. His eyes bulged out like a rabbit's, and he was bald except for long thin patches of hair that hung like rat-tails off the back.

He smiled as he stuck his head in the door to look at the girls. Both were wearing skirts, and his eyes lingered on their young, shapely legs. "Havin' some problems, is ya?"

Trina tried to muster a smile. "Something with the engine. It won't turn over."

He smiled wickedly. "Transmission maybe. That could do it. Why don't y'all follow me to my farm? It's right up there." He pointed down the road with a long, boney finger. "I can take ya to town. Find ya some help." He smiled again—all jagged teeth and cheek bones.

Both girls eased out of the car, grabbing their purses. As Trina locked the doors, Sara Beth stood completely still, eyeing the man guardedly.

Trina turned to face him, interlocking her arm with her friend's. "So, how far is it to your farm?"

"Just up the road a piece."

They fell in behind the man as he walked along the shoulder of the road. The night air was cool and the girls, still arm in arm, kept close behind. They felt the long, wet highway grass brush up against their ankles as they walked further into the darkness. Soon, they were no longer able to look back and see the car.

"Where you ladies headed?" the man asked, keeping his back to them as he marched on.

"Charleston," Sara Beth volunteered. "A friend's parents have a place down there. We're going to hang out at their house for the weekend."

The man nodded and turned slightly toward them. "Sounds real nice." He pronounced the word "nice" slowly so that he made a hissing sound like a snake.

"You girls look kinda young. Y'all still in school?"

"We're freshmen at Winthrop College," Trina said. "Do you know Winthrop?"

He wheezed a little laugh. "Don't know too much 'bout schoolin'. But I'm sure it's real nice." He hissed the word again.

The girls eyed each other as he turned around. They walked in silence for a few more minutes, branching off the road and deeper into the woods.

"How much longer until we get there?" Sara Beth asked. "We've been walking for a while now, and I don't see any lights ahead."

"Depends…" the man said.

"On what?"

He stopped and turned to face them. His smiled widened. "On whether you girls is good girls or bad girls?"

Sara Beth squeezed down on Trina's arm tightly. Trina's heart raced and she felt weak in the knees. She wanted to turn and run but could not move. "Sir?"

"Good or bad. I've got to know if the good Lord has forsaken you. Will you fight for the kingdom of heaven or spend the eternal war in hell? It's a simple matter really."

"What do you mean?" Sara Beth protested. "We're both good…."

"Hold it now," he said interrupting and raising his hand. "I can't depend on your words. Many is the time the devil has protested his innocence. We should let the angels decide."

"Angels? What are you talking about?" Trina demanded.

The thin man drew an eight-inch pointed boar dagger from his pocket with his right hand and held it up in the moonlight. "This is Michael—the good angel of death." He then transferred the knife to his left hand. "And this is Abaddon—the destroyer—

4

an angel of Satan. They will decide who is good and who is bad. And then one will call you home tonight."

Trina threw her pocketbook at the man's feet, and then did the same with Sara Beth's. "Please, sir, don't hurt us. Take our money, if that's what you want. You can have it all. The car too." Unable to speak, Sara Beth only rapidly nodded her head in agreement—tears in her eyes.

The man took a step forward, passing the knife back between his hands. He whispered a few words—a conversation with himself. "No. We ain't interested in your money, little ones." He reached out his left hand and held Trina's face while using his right to bring the knife's point under her chin. "Congratulations," he said before plunging the knife in her throat, "The angel of the Lord desires you in heaven."

SEPTEMBER 28, 2016

6:46 PM

Greyson Bledsoe stepped cautiously around the knotty cypress tree. The move failed to disperse his 230 pounds evenly, and his Kevlar snake boots sunk several inches into the bordering pluff of the Edisto River. He took another wary step, his boot sucking free from the muck before sinking again into the black, watery ooze that crept past the boot's rim and sought out his rubbed-raw ankles.

Bledsoe, decked out in his favorite camo fatigues, looked like a tight-rope artist as he balanced himself, arms out, his right hand clutching his prized crossbow. With one false move, he could wind up with his backside soaked, or with his face planted in the thick, soupy chunk. Neither option especially appealed to him.

He made several more laborious moves toward another clump of trees. Moving ten feet felt like walking ten miles. His calf muscles had tightened into knots, and he felt shooting pain working into his fifty-year-old hip-joints and knees.

He arrived at the little hump of an island and found solid ground at the base. *This is far enough*, he figured. He turned his back to the Edisto and scanned the dark forest on the riverbank in front of him. A steep hill hidden in mounds of kudzu climbed beyond towering trees dressed in thorny vines and poison ivy.

He was now safely in the honey-hole, a thin strip of land that was the headway to a heavily-trafficked deer trail. Previous hunts there had taught him that as the day drew to a close, white tails wandered down the trail and out into the inlet to drink from the cool run-off of the twisty Edisto.

He positioned himself by leaning his meaty shoulder against the centermost tree—an old walnut, gray and disfigured; animal

6

burrows littered its rotting trunk. The hardwood had shed its last leaf and wouldn't last many more seasons out in the swamp.

Bledsoe put his foot in the bow's cocking stirrup and locked it into position. He then raised it to shoulder height. It was a new model crossbow, a Barnett Ghost 410 from Cabela's—a bit pricey, but coin well-spent in his mind. He knew he could hold his position for several hours, supporting its light weight. He slipped an arrow from the quiver mounted underneath and lashed it into the bow's arm. He counted the yards between him and the water's edge. He was far enough away to keep his *stink* from reaching a deer's nose but close enough to bring a ten-pointer to its knees should the situation arise.

With the safety on, he settled closer to the dead tree, focused on his target area, and waited.

Time passed like the pour from a bottle of Carolina cane syrup, but eventually his patience paid off. From the darkness of the wooded path, a young buck emerged. It was big one, 170 pounds or so, with six perfectly spaced points on its titillating rack.

The animal hesitated a few yards out, eyeing its surroundings warily. But after a twitch of its pink ears, it moved again toward the river.

Bledsoe leveled the bow, disengaged the safety, and locked in on his target. He hoped for a perfect strike into the animal's meaty throat or chest. The great hunter eased out the last of his held breath and steadied his aim. The deer dropped its head to drink and then quickly bobbed back up, looking directly across the water to where Bledsoe was hidden.

Hold still, ol' buddy. Bledsoe felt the pressure of his finger on the trigger and heard anticipation buzzing in his ears. It was now or never.

But in the quiet moment before the kill, an electronic squelch rang out, echoing across the swamp.

The noise shocked both hunter and prey. The deer leapt backwards and then turned to dart back toward the woods. Bledsoe took a hurried step from the islet and lunged into the cold river. Knee-deep now in the black water, he took a desperate shot at his prey. The arrow whizzed far off the mark and into the kudzu-filled hill behind the trees.

"Dammit!"

By the time he could even think about reloading, the deer had scampered off into the forest—a golden opportunity lost.

Bledsoe stared at the deserted trail and then glanced down at the walkie-talkie attached to his belt. An orange signal light winked back at him.

He had left it on. All that preparation, all that hard work, and he had simply forgotten to turn off the radio. He grabbed it in disgust as he sloshed his way to the bank.

"Whatcha want, Billy?" Bledsoe said into the device.

"I'm done. Ain't seen nothing over here. Where you at, Grey?" Billy's voice crackled back.

"I'm in the hole. Watching a buck give me the sideways smile."

"Do what?"

"Never mind. Get down here and help me find my arrow. I can't afford to lose another." Bledsoe plopped down on the bank and drained the slush from his boots.

By the time his anger had whittled into mild disappointment, Billy Horton, his hunting partner, had arrived. Horton was a mirror image of Bledsoe, same heavy build, same scruffy beard, even the same style of camo fatigues. He looked down at his partner on the ground and saw that Bledsoe's pants were soaked.

"Go swimming?" Horton asked with a slight laugh.

"Wouldn't had to if it hadn't been for your perfect timing," Bledsoe said, a bit of the anger's heat returning.

"Don't blame me if you can't shoot worth a shit." Horton chuckled and looked around. "Where were you aiming at?"

Bledsoe hopped up and pointed. "That hill over yonder. Missed him by an inch."

"Yeah, right. Yellow and red? Or blue and purple?"

"Yellow and red," Bledsoe said, confirming the arrow's colors.

Both men waded through the underbrush and squeezed past the tall pines and oaks until they faced the waves of kudzu. A Southern curse of epic proportions, kudzu was a vine-filled mess that sprouted without much prompting and grew heartily with little inhibition. This strand had enveloped the fifty-yard hill in a looping bed of tangled misery.

"It went in here?" Horton asked.

"Here or about," Bledsoe said.

"Shoot, you ain't gonna find anything in here."

"Just help me look for a minute. I done lost three arrows since the season started."

"All right, all right, don't get your panties in a wad. I'll help you look." He hesitated for a moment. "But you ain't never gonna find it."

Bledsoe smirked. "C'mon."

They fanned out, each walking from the center of the mass of the perennial vine toward the outer edges. Both men periodically brushed at the offshoots in a vain attempt to see anything yellow or red.

They searched for what felt like forever, and Bledsoe was ready to give up when Horton shouted out, "Over here! I found it!"

Bledsoe ran over and stood next to Horton. A little lower than waist high, the yellow and red feathered end of the sixteen-inch arrow was peeking out from under the vines. Horton had reached in to pull it out. "It's wedged into something," he said as he struggled to loosen it.

"Let me try," Bledsoe said. He moved in and grabbed hold but felt resistance, too. He gave it several hard jerks but with no success. "Take your knife to it, Billy."

Horton pulled a six-inch, serrated hunter's knife from a belt sheath and hacked through the kudzu. After a few minutes, he had cleaned out a couple of inches of its depth. He looked in and laughed.

"What?" Bledsoe asked.

"Looks like you bagged yourself a Goodyear, Grey. It's wedged into an old tire."

"A tire?"

"Yeah, somebody must have dumped..." Horton's voice trailed off as he continued to hack at the vines.

"What is it?"

"It ain't just a tire. I'm hitting against metal now." He rapped the blade hard against the object so that Bledsoe could hear. "Might be a whole car or truck under here."

Bledsoe joined Horton and helped to tear away the vines. Within minutes, they cleared enough to expose the smashed front end of the driver's side of the auto—the tire with the arrow included. They began to tear the kudzu away quickly now. Both men felt a sudden urgency in their discovery.

After ten minutes of pulling and chopping, they had exposed the driver's side dirt-encrusted door, sitting at a downward angle—the car having plowed nose first into the bottom of the hill.

Kneeling, the two men dug at the remaining stubborn vines and brushed away the dirt with their hunting knives and hands. Bledsoe stood and read the rust-covered insignia on the door. "Macinaw County Sheriff's Department," he said, pronouncing each word with deliberation. He stared at Horton. "You don't reckon..."

"Gotta be...."

The two men continued to free the smashed patrol car from its entanglements. Mounds of vines, leaves, and dirt covered the wreck inside and out, darkening the driver's side window which was rolled down several inches and had spider web cracks throughout the glass.

"I can't believe this," Horton added. "Do you know how many people have been looking for this?" His voice rose with excitement.

"This is huge, Billy. The find of the century kinda thing," Bledsoe confirmed. "Should we open it? Get a look inside?"

The door was pinched in on the sides; the handle rusty and broken.

"I don't know," Horton said. "Maybe we should get the police down here first. What do you think?"

"Do that, and *we'll* never get to see what's inside," Bledsoe argued.

"True that."

Horton moved to the door and grabbed the handle. He eyed Bledsoe, and then gave the old door a pull. It cracked open; rust and black dirt poured like a giant hourglass from the angled bottom.

Horton continued to pull, but the door refused to open any further. Bledsoe stepped in and worked his fingers into the inside of the door. Both men put their weight behind the pull, even going to a timed jerking motion like a two-man tug-of-war.

The door of the old patrol car finally gave way, flying off its hinges and sending Horton and Bledsoe tumbling to the ground.

Horton brushed his fatigues as he got up, alternating a laugh with gasps for air. "Man, that was one tough door." He fell silent as he took in Bledsoe's stare. He followed his friend's line of vision, suddenly mesmerized.

Released from the packed dirt, clay and leaves, the men eyed a set of bones intact, still seated behind the wheel. Exposure and time had eaten away the muscle and tissue leaving only skeletal remains amid tattered clothes. Pinned against the wheel with a hole the size of a quarter in the left temple was a skull, the jaw gaped open and twisted.

Horton and Bledsoe remained on the ground unsure of what to say or do. They just continued to stare—certain only in that what they had unearthed from the mud and kudzu today would become the latest chapter in the greatest unsolved mystery in the history of South Carolina.

JUNE 16, 1976

As he slowed to exit US 301, Chandler Adams hung his long arm out of his mint-green, '68 Ford Torino, Lynyrd Skynyrd's *Free Bird* blasting from the eight-track tape deck. He flicked the ash from his Marlboro Light onto the hot, black pavement below. The summer heat rose in shimmering sheets—the Carolina sun cooking the landscape until all around him seemed a well-done brown.

He felt welcomed relief from the heat as he made his way onto the Lowcountry highway, a towering pine and shady oak-lined road that would take him the rest of the way into town. The road cut through the Edisto Basin—swampland mostly—with the moss-drenched forest encroaching the thin road, threatening to swallow it altogether.

Chan slowed as he reached the highway's first sign of civilization. He gazed out through his rolled-down window and read the sign before him: *Welcome to Macinaw, the Heart of South Carolina*. Under the words was a county map of the palmetto state. Macinaw was indeed at the center, highlighted as the town seat in the middle of Macinaw County, right between the counties of Orangeburg and Colleton.

He soon entered the outskirts of the town. The swampy woods gave way to open, dead areas of sandy turf dotted with trailers and small houses. Pinned to one squiggly maple tree were two homemade signs—scribbled in the worst handwriting—advertising bait for sale and a tree stump removal service. Junk cars on blocks, trash-filled ditches and knee-high grass lawns didn't help in forming Chan's first impression. He shook his head. Having driven four hundred straight miles, he seemed to have arrived in the middle of nowhere.

Great choice, Chan.

He eventually came within the city limits and stopped at the first traffic light. A mom-and-pop convenience store anchored it on his left. He leaned out the window to talk to a fat, sweaty man propped up in a folding chair next to the store's open door. The man was using a newspaper to fan bugs and heat from his jowly face.

"Looking for Marshall Street," Chan said.

"Two blocks down, take a left at the light and then go through three stop signs. Marshall runs both ways," the man said gruffly.

Chan gave him a nod of thanks and then pulled away. The fat man closed his eyes, leaned back in his chair, and resumed his fanning.

Chan followed the given directions, then took a chance and made a right onto Marshall. Turning into an old subdivision lined with huge, moss-covered oaks. Chan swore the temperature dropped yet another ten degrees as he rode along under the shade of those giant oaks.

The houses on Marshall were extraordinarily huge as well, with extended wrap-around porches and spacious yards with mature azalea and hydrangea bushes sprouting from every fence line. Wisps of wisteria hung in the trees like purple puffs of smoke. But the houses were mostly old and in ill-repair. Many sat vacant. Throughout the neighborhood, signs of simpler, happier times remained: porch swings, hammocks, and hand-cranked wishing wells. But like the homes, they seemed old, abandoned, forgotten. Chan likened it to traveling through a ghost town.

He checked the address again on his notepad: 617 Marshall Street. The house numbers indicated his destination would be on the left.

He finally steered the Torino down a short drive to a worn-grass parking pad in front of the house. Compared to the neighbors', the home was a bit smaller, around 1,800 square feet.

But it still had one of those over-sized porches of which the Macinaw townsfolk seemed fond—a pair of wooden rocking chairs included.

Chan hopped out and grabbed a duffel bag and a suit hanger from the backseat and then went to the front door. He dropped his bags and knocked several times, noting the creaking floor boards beneath his feet as he waited.

The door opened quickly. A woman of sixty with frightful, red hair dressed in a flowery bath robe peered out from behind the door. "Yeah?"

"Mrs. Hallman? My name's Adams. I'm here about the apartment."

She gave him the one-eyed look-over, taking note of Chan's six-foot frame and momentarily admiring his boyish good looks. Her eyes narrowed in on his blond hair, which he kept parted down the middle—the length drifting over his ears and below the collar of the back of his shirt. "You some kinda hippie?"

"Ma'am? No, ma'am, I'm a reporter. I called about the..."

"Key's in the box by the door. Take the stairs behind the house. Leave your deposit and first month's rent in my mailbox." She noticed his shirt pocket. "And I don't allow no smoking round here." She slammed the door.

Chan turned to look out into the front yard and sighed. He popped another Marlboro Light into his mouth and brought it to life.

Yeah, helluva move coming here.

6:20 PM

Chan moped around his one-room apartment for a while and after hanging up a few shirts and ties decided he had been confined long enough. He got back in his car and found his way onto Macinaw's Main Street.

The street, like most of the downtown, was decked out in red, white, and blue for the nation's upcoming Bicentennial—

flags and banners hung from nearly every building. In passing, he encountered several banks, two pharmacies, an office supply store, a few garages and salons, law offices, churches, the county courthouse and even a sizable Piggly Wiggly. On the square at the end of Main Street was the building that housed *The Macinaw Republic*, the local newspaper and Chan's new employer.

Chan pulled into a street parking space, ignored the meter, and headed toward *The Republic's* front entrance. It was a red brick building with stacks of old newspapers piled next to the door.

With the front-office unattended, Chan moved into the newsroom, his eyes darting about. The room was empty of people as well except for one black lady in her mid-thirties with closely cropped hair. She was sitting at a desk—her eyes were closed—a pencil hung from her partially opened mouth.

"Excuse me," Chan started. "I'm looking for Dennis Darby?"

The woman cocked open one eye then the other. The pencil rolled to her lap as she yawned and stretched, pointing in the direction behind her.

"You can try his office. He may not have left yet."

Chan smiled and then followed her direction across the newsroom. He came to an unmarked glass-paned door and gave it a single knock.

"Come," a voice said from inside.

Dennis Darby stood behind his cluttered desk as Chan entered. Dennis was in his late fifties—completely bald, with a heavy belly that was accented by his short, wide tie. He had narrow brown eyes and his slight nose seemed partially lost atop his bushy moustache. Chan thought he looked somewhat cartoonish—like the guy on the Monopoly game, minus the monocle and top hat.

"Mr. Darby?"

"Yeah, that's right. You Adams? Wasn't expecting you until tomorrow."

"Yes, sir. I just thought I'd drop by and introduce myself."

"Have a seat." Darby indicated the chair in front of his desk. He went to a file cabinet as Chan sat. The editor-in-chief flipped through files as Chan drummed his fingers along the arm rest. Darby found the file, closed the drawer, and returned to his desk.

"Let's see now," Darby began as he flipped through Chan's application. "Says here you graduated from the University of Georgia just this past month."

"Yes, sir."

"And you wanted to start your journalism career here with us?"

Chan smiled. "Yes, I know most of my fellow graduates wanted positions with larger publications: *The Journal-Constitution*, the *Times*, *Washington Post*; but I wanted to start smaller. Find a nice hometown paper where…"

"Cut the bullshit, Adams. I've got your grades right here in front of me. None of those big rags would have anything to do with the likes of you. You're damn lucky you even graduated with grades like these. You should be pushing a broom across these floors instead of making copy, am I right?"

Chan lost his smile and his eyes found the floor. He looked back up and tried the smile again. "Sir, now I know my grades weren't the best, but if you'll give me a chance…"

"Let me tell you how things run around here, Adams. Although I had zero to do with your hiring, you work for *me* now. You will report to this office every morning by six, and you will stay until the daily is put to bed, whether that's seven, nine, or midnight. You will get an assignment each day, which may or may not involve writing copy, but probably will involve you getting me a cup of coffee and maybe even picking up my dry cleaning. It's my job to do whatever is necessary to get this

17

paper out, correct and on time, and it's your job to do whatever the hell I say, *comprende*?"

Chan shifted in his chair. "Yes, of course, but..."

"How many words can you type a minute?"

"A hundred," Chan said, although it sounded more like a guess.

"Do you know anything about us locally?"

"Certainly, I reviewed most of the..."

"How many counties do we have here in South Carolina?"

"Counties? Well..."

"Who's our state's lieutenant governor?"

"Well, let's see. The lieutenant..."

"How many school districts do we have in our county?"

"Um... I think it's..."

"Who is the chief of police in Macinaw? How does our crime rate compare to the national average? What's our primary industry? What's the ratio of blacks to whites in this town? What percentage of our people depends on government assistance?"

Chan was now perfectly still and mute—Darby's point having been well-made.

"Be back here in my office at six in the morning, Adams."

Chan nodded and got up from his seat. He opened the office door.

"And don't forget my coffee," he heard as he closed the door behind him.

The black woman from the newsroom was waiting for him just outside the office door. She chuckled at Chan's startled look.

"Sorry, honey, I should have warned you."

8:47 PM

Tyrell James pulled his blue truck to a stop under the sycamore tree that he used as his carport and eased his aching body out of the old Chevy. His ten-hour workday had turned into thirteen, and he was feeling every second of overtime as he labored across his yard to his trailer. A machinist by trade, the twenty-seven-year-old black man worked for Olsen Tools, one of Macinaw's few industries and its biggest employer.

Tyrell lived on the North Fork of the Edisto River on the outskirts of Macinaw—far enough away to have an isolated place of his own but only a ten-minute drive across the river from his momma's house. His momma often worried about him living alone out there in the swamp, but he never felt scared living by himself. Besides, Tyrell James was a good-sized man who had grown up on the black side of town—he knew how to take care of himself.

"Kean!" he shouted toward the trailer. A brown, German shorthaired pointer came from around the back of the trailer and met Tyrell on the front stoop. They played their daily ritual of *good-to-see-you* with Tyrell admonishing Kean not to jump up with his big paws.

Tyrell fished the key to the trailer from his pants' pocket and soon he and his dog were making their way inside. Kean went to his bowl where Tyrell poured a cup of his favorite dog chow mix. Tyrell then stood in front of the icebox mulling over the turkey or meatloaf TV dinners.

Kean stopped digging into his late supper and scampered to the trailer's back door, whimpering a bit to get out.

"What is it, boy? You want out already?" Tyrell did a double-take at the dog's half-eaten bowl of food. He shrugged, unlocked the back door, and let Kean out.

Tyrell stepped one foot onto the back wooden deck and watched Kean bound down the steps and onto the riverbank that served as his backyard. The dog hesitated a bit before running off into the darkness. The hinge on the trailer's back door was broken, so Tyrell propped it open with an old broom and followed. "Kean? Kean! Come here, boy!"

Tyrell squinted his eyes as if he could see through the pitch dark; he then heard a solitary bark from somewhere nearby. "Kean? What is it? Kean?" Tyrell stepped further from his house and into the damp night. "Kean?!"

Now on the top of the bank with the Edisto twisting away below him, Tyrell could only make out the outlines of the monstrous trees across the river. The summer sounds of chirping crickets and buzzing mosquitoes on the deck gave way to the deep night call of frogs somewhere down river. A hot rain had fallen the night before, and Tyrell could smell the familiar pungent odor of the swamp stewing in humidity.

He followed the Edisto's edge a few more feet and came to the spot where he often played fetch with Kean, throwing sticks into the river's turn. "Kean?" he tried again. But again, the dog did not respond.

Chasing a raccoon or opossum, maybe. Tyrell shrugged and turned to head back to the house. He eyed the darkness a final time as he trudged back up the steps. When he reached the top, he noticed the trailer's back door was now closed. The broom lay inexplicably on the deck.

Tyrell picked up the broom and leaned it against the outside trailer wall. *How in the world?*

He jerked his head in the door's direction when he heard noise coming from inside. It was a thumping noise like something large had fallen. Warning bells sounded in his head.

He eased the door open and slipped inside, careful not to give himself away. He went to the kitchen cabinet over the sink, looked behind the extra place mats, and retrieved his .45 revolver. He kept his shotgun in his bedroom closet and was thankful that he kept his backup here. He checked the chamber, saw that it was loaded, and slid the safety off.

Tyrell froze when he heard another rumble coming from his bedroom. He strained to listen and within seconds he heard it again.

He made his way from the kitchen down the small hallway to the bedroom. The door was half-opened and his overhead light was on. *I know I turned that off this morning.*

Tyrell pulled back the hammer on the .45 and with his left hand, he slowly pushed the door all the way in. He inched his way over the threshold, his eyes darting back and forth, the muscles in his shoulders and neck as tight as a drum. At the sound of another slight bump, Tyrell realized that the source was coming from under his bed.

He thrust the .45 straight out and leaned over the right side of the bed. He held his breath, kneeled, and with his left hand, he grabbed the bed covers.

One...
Two...
Three!

He threw back the covers with great force, falling onto his backside as Kean came charging out at him and licked him in the face.

"Kean! You scared me to death, you rascal!"

Tyrell stayed there for a moment more, catching his breath and rubbing Kean's head. "Man, I might have killed you, charging me like that," he said with a laugh.

With his heartbeat finally slowing back to normal, Tyrell stood. He eased the hammer back down and slid the safety on.

"C'mon, boy, let's go finish our supper."

Kean's growl at the stranger emerging from the closet came too late. The knife jabbed through the back of Tyrell's neck and sliced through his carotid artery—he died before his body hit the bed.

OCTOBER 1, 2016

11:25 AM

Tindal Huddleston checked the address she had saved in her iPhone again. The numbers were correct, and she had been directed to the right spot, but the house was not at all what she was expecting: a concrete block style home, simple and non-descript—not at all like the man who supposedly resided inside.

She pulled her rental car, a light blue 2012 Buick Regal, into his drive and parked behind an automobile covered with a grey tarp. Leaves, tiny sticks, and water stains all about indicated that the vehicle underneath hadn't been used in some time.

She stepped out of her car, threw her work satchel over her shoulder and walked to the front door. Tindal was quite beautiful, but she carried herself without the vanity that sometimes goes with it. She was five feet ten inches tall, thin and had long, straight brown hair. She had green eyes that suitably matched her hair as well as that of her light-brown skin, which made her appear tan no matter the time of year. She wore 'Gigi' style sandals with her skinny jeans and white t-shirt. She didn't appear dressed for business, but business was upper most on her mind.

She knocked several times on the front door until she heard a rustling inside.

"Just a sec," a man's voice finally said.

A lock clicked, and the door opened a few inches—still held by a chain. Eyes and a scruffy, partial beard appeared from behind the door.

"Chandler Adams?" Tindal asked.

"Who wants to know?"

"Sir, my name is Tindal Huddleston. I'm an investigative reporter for Reuters News Agency. I'd like to talk to you about the recent discovery of the patrol car on the Brooks property."

The door closed for a second, and Tindal heard the chain being worked loose. When he reopened it, she had a better look at the man behind it.

The years had worked their toll on Chandler Adams. His hair was still as long as it had been forty years before, but the color had darkened from blond to a light brown sprinkled with grey. His goatee was multidimensional like his hair, deepening his wizened look. Tindal noticed his gaunt cheeks and the red eyes which she recognized as signs of a person who lived from bottle to bottle.

"I've called several times now and left dozens of messages about coming to see you," Tindal continued. "Do you not answer your phone?"

Chan half-glanced into the dark room behind him and then said, "Not sure where it is." He smiled sheepishly. "You're from Reuters?" He held his hand up to block the near noon sun from his eyes.

"That's right. I'm here to do a feature on the patrol car. I was told you might be able to help fill in the gaps, so to speak."

Chan looked at her sourly. "I dunno. That's been over forty years. My memory has been a sieve of late."

Tindal smiled briefly. "Please, sir, this story has generated a great deal of interest around the country—speculation is high. And you had a front row seat to what went down back then. What you have to add could really help bring this story together."

Chan stood for a moment contemplating before meeting Tindal's green-eyed gaze. "Oh, uh, forgive me. Come in, please." He backed into his house and led her through the door.

"Thanks," she said, making quick observations as she entered. Although it was technically the house's living room, Tindal thought it was anything but. The shades were pulled on the windows, so it was dark. There was a stuffiness to the room as well, as if fresh air hadn't been allowed in for months. A TV sat in the corner, but it looked old and had a thin layer of dust across the screen. The room was devoid of pictures or decorations. An opened fifth of Jack Daniels sat on a cabinet top near the TV.

"So, how'd my name come up?" Chan asked, as he sat on the couch and directed Tindal to the worn recliner.

"A quick Google search of the case..."

"No, I guess what I meant was, who told you I was here... in Macinaw? I thought I had effectively dropped off the planet."

"Sheriff Monroe told me your address. I hope you don't mind."

Chan shook his head, indicating that he didn't mind. He thought about it for a second. "Ironic they found the patrol car out there on the old Brooks property, huh? Have you been to the site?"

"Law enforcement won't allow anyone near it. From what I understand, they haven't even touched the car yet."

"Monroe's handling it?"

"The sheriff and his deputies are serving as the blockade to any interested passers-by, but I get the feeling others are in charge."

"Probably SLED, the South Carolina Law Enforcement Division," Chan offered.

"Yes, perhaps even the FBI. It's a big case."

"It was huge then, too," Chan confirmed, which gave Tindal her opening.

"That's why I'm here. I need you to tell me what happened forty years ago. What do you remember about that night? What happened to Sheriff Crawford and the others? Or we could start with the Macinaw Seven. The Dover murder? Henry Brooks?"

Chan sighed and rubbed his hands on his jeans as he thought about the magnitude of all that she was asking. "That's gonna take some time. Obviously. And I hate to come off as a complete ass, but what's in this for me? As you might imagine, I've gone down this road several times."

Tindal forced a smile, a bit disappointed. "What do you want?" She glanced around his sad little house. "We could offer you an information fee. Or perhaps you want story credit? I know you've been out of the game..."

Chan waved her off. "No. I don't need any of that. Writers who seek fame and fortune are either hacks or fools—usually both."

This time, Tindal agreed with a genuine smile. "So, what is it that you want?"

Chan rubbed his hands again and bent his head as if prayer. He sighed again and then looked back up. "You hungry?"

Tindal thought about the yogurt she had had at the airport in Columbia at 5:30 a.m. and the hunger pains rumbling in her stomach. "Sure."

"Me, too."

"Okay then, let's get something to eat. How about you pick the spot, and I'll pick up the tab? Deal?"

"I like the way you think, Ms. Huddleston. It's a deal."

"Good. And you can call me Tindal."

Chan stood and offered his hand. "Only if you call me Chan."

Tindal rose from her chair and shook it. "Agreed. So, where are we going, Chan?"

"The only place worth going to in Macinaw."

"It's that good?"

He smiled. "Oh, yes. Good enough to make the poets weep and the angels sing."

12: 36 PM

"What's this?" Tindal asked with a slight frown.

Chan sat down across from her at the picnic-style table with the exact same plate. He had placed her change on her tray. "It's called 'the Large.' Your only other choice here is 'the Small.'"

"Large what though?"

"Barbeque. The best in the state. Some say the entire Southeast."

"Oh, I guess the pig sign out front should have given me the hint, huh?" Tindal said playfully. "The thing is, I don't eat meat. Especially meats that once walked around the barnyard and had adorable faces." She took her plastic fork and pushed at the cut meat covered in golden mustard sauce. She then pointed to another divider in her plate. "And what's this?"

"It's hash on top of rice."

"And what goes in the hash exactly?"

Chan laughed, ignoring the question. He pointed to another divider. "And that's coleslaw. Surely, you have coleslaw where you come from."

Tindal dug through the slaw and brought a scoopful under her nose. "Yeah, but not dripping in liquid lard like this stuff."

25

Chan smiled and picked up the slice of white bread from his tray and pointed to it.

Tindal shook her head. "Do you know how many preservatives they put in white bread these days?"

"C'mon. Give it a go, Tindal." He took a bite of his barbeque. He then indicated the Styrofoam cups on the table. "Hell, the sweet tea will kill you. Why do you think the lifespan down South is so short?"

Tindal laughed and looked around at the others who had come to dine in Lulu's. A variety of folks had gathered, a mix of blacks and whites with many sharing the same waistline problem. She then looked toward the serving counter. A large African-American woman, whom she assumed was Lulu, was working the register, while several other staff filtered in and out of the open kitchen behind her. A brick smokehouse a few yards behind the building could be seen through a kitchen window.

She then zeroed back in on Chan. He seemed to be enjoying his plate. He was handsome in a way, or perhaps once was. The lines in his face were minimal for a man over sixty, but he did have pronounced crow's feet around his eyes whenever he smiled at her—which is what he was doing now—having caught her stare. She smiled back but turned her head slightly in embarrassment.

"I know that Reuters is a net news organization that covers the globe," he finally said. "So what city do you work out of?"

"New York."

"Is that where you're from?"

"Seattle, originally. I moved all over as a kid. My dad was an executive with Sears. My family lived in Chicago during my high school years. I went to Northwestern after. Worked at the Tribune my first year out."

"Impressive."

"Thanks. I've been with Reuters for the past four years. I used to do the one-minute news video pieces you see on AOL and elsewhere, but just this past month I decided to move to their investigative print division. Cold cases like this have always fascinated me." She paused and then asked, "So what about you? What's your background?"

26

"I'm a Georgia kid, grew up in a sweet little place called Villa Rica—about an hour away from Atlanta on the Bama side. My parents split early, so it was just me and my mom."

"And you started working for the Macinaw Republic in '76, right?"

"Yeah. Moved here right after college. Didn't know a soul."

"Things must've happened quickly as far as the case goes."

Chan smiled as he remembered. "First day on the job actually."

"Baptism by fire."

"Most definitely."

Tindal pulled out a notebook and a recorder from her satchel. She pointed at the recorder. Chan gave his approval with a simple shrug.

"So where do we start?" Tindal asked

"What do you know?"

"The basic facts leading up to that night. I skimmed through your book, *Chasing Henry Brooks' Ghost* on the flight into South Carolina—quickly skimmed it, truth be told. I guess I picked up on few things, but I'd still like you to walk me through all of the details."

Chan nodded thoughtfully as he took a drink of sweet tea. "There are so many pieces and parts to this story. And they're perpetually in motion. Even in today's world." Chan wiped his mouth with a paper napkin. "I know it sounds cliché, but if you really want to know what happened, we should start at the beginning. Before I got involved."

"Robert Dover?"

"Before that even. 1968—the Orangeburg Massacre."

Tindal leaned forward and lifted an inquisitive eyebrow. "Okay, I'm all ears."

"Our sister county to the north, Orangeburg, is home to South Carolina State, a historically black college—the first of its kind in South Carolina. On February 6 of 1968, some of the students from State went to the local bowling alley but were denied access by the white owner. The students continued to gather at the bowling alley and tensions rose over the course of the next two days. As part of their protest, the students staged a rally around a bonfire on a street in front of the campus. A fire truck was called in to douse the fire, and state troopers were assigned to protect the firemen. Things get out of hand quickly. One of the kids threw a banister rail from a campus building and struck a trooper in the face. Five minutes later, you had nearly seventy officers lining the campus with weapons. Apparently one of them fired a warning shot to get the students back and then all hell broke loose. The other officers thought they were being fired upon and opened-up on the crowd. In the span of about ten seconds, thirty of the students had been shot, three fatally."

"Jesus...."

"Yeah. It was the first such tragedy on any American campus. In fact, it was two years before the Kent State killings in Ohio."

Tindal leaned back in her chair. "For someone who wasn't there, sounds like you know all about it."

Chan shook his head. "No, I'm no expert on it. Bass and Nelson were the men who wrote the definitive account. The two Jack's, I call them. After what happened in Macinaw, I tracked them down and interviewed both."

"What happened to the troopers who fired?"

"They were acquitted a year later in federal court." He paused, noting the concern on her face. "This was the late '60s, Tindal, in South Carolina. Civil rights, protests, and marches had reached their apex. The media and the politicians only shrugged, buoyed by a public malaise with the whole thing."

"But surely the African-American community..."

"When the societal deck is stacked against you," he interrupted, "voices fall quiet quickly."

"So, no coming together, no organized reaction—like what was done after the Charleston shootings last year?"

"No, believe me when I say a lot has changed in our state and in our country in the last fifty years. It was a different time."

"They did nothing then?"

"It was buried. People moved on," Chan said and then caught himself. "Well, most moved on."

"Most? So, this does tie in to the Dover murder? How?"

"Two of the Macinaw Seven had been on State's campus the day of the Massacre. At the time, it was believed that they went after the Dover boy as retaliation for the troopers being acquitted."

Tindal sipped at her tea. "I see what you mean by all the moving parts." She pushed her tray away, placed her elbows on the table, and clasped her hands, interlocking her fingers. "I obviously came to the right source. But before we continue, I really need to know what is that you want? What can I give you for your help in all of this?"

Chan took another swallow of tea and cleared his throat. He took his time with his words. "Whatever they find in that patrol car could possibly tie all of this together. The Orangeburg Massacre, Dover's murder, the Macinaw Seven, Henry Brooks— it all made a compelling story back in the day, but a story without an ending. I want to know, Tindal. I've got to know. My price for my help is for you to keep me informed...of everything. I've got to be in on all the details. I've got to know what you find. Before you let anyone else know. Agreed?"

Tindal nodded her agreement. "This one was personal for you, wasn't it, Chan?"

Chan looked beyond her shoulder as if he was staring off into the past. "You have no idea."

JUNE 17, 1976

The break room at *The Macinaw Republic* was known as the *bullpen* to the reporters. It was where they gathered each morning to scour their work from the day before and to summon enough courage from their coffee and cigarettes before meeting with Darby. It seemed that Chan's one-way-street experience with the editor the day prior was a common occurrence shared by most of the staff.

Chan sat next to Norma Wiles, the black woman he had met when he came to introduce himself. She was the only African-American in the group but did not seem stymied by that fact. As she greeted her co-workers that morning, Chan noticed Norma was not only well-received by them, but she also had a mothering way about her that they all appreciated. And now she had a new bird under her wing.

"Don't let him get under your skin, Chan. He can be a bit abrasive, but he's not a bad guy at all. He just wants what's best for the paper." Norma leaned over and doused her cigarette in an overflowing tray on the coffee table. "He'll take a little getting used to."

Chan nodded as he continued his smoke, the ash falling between the couch and the table.

Norma looked over to a square, breakfast-style table where two men were sitting and scanning the paper. She caught the eye of the man closest to her. "You're covering civil court this week, Hal?"

The thin, dark haired man shook his head. "No, Judge Bair is out this week. But hopefully Boss will send me to the courthouse anyway. See what I can stir up."

"Maybe Chan can tag along," Norma said, indicating the cub reporter with her thumb. "It would be a good place to get his feet wet."

Hal made an unenthusiastic nod to the suggestion and then went back to reading the paper. Norma turned back to Chan.

"Whatever Darby gives you—school board, market report, city government, kid's birthday party—take it without hesitation and work on your article like it's a Pulitzer. And before you submit it, let me take a look."

Before Chan could respond, there was a knock on the frame of the break room door. Darby stuck his round head in. "Let's go, people. Assignment time."

6:02 AM

The conference room was adjacent to the break room, so all were seated quite quickly. Chan watched and listened as the day's assignments were handed out and discussed. The staff then departed after receiving their marching orders. Within fifteen minutes, everyone was gone except for Norma and Chan. Darby fished some papers around at the head of the conference table.

"Still working the Main Street drainage issue, Norma?" Darby asked.

"Yes. I still want to get feedback from some of the store owners on that end and check with the mayor's office again before I submit the final. We can definitely go with it in tomorrow's edition."

Darby shook his head. "Yeah, okay, but it may have to wait." He then hesitated, which got Norma's attention. "Before I came to work this morning, I got a call from Pebo over at the Sheriff's office. There was a murder last night off the Edisto. Tyrell James."

"Tyrell James?"

"Yep. One and the same."

Chan glanced back and forth at them—confusion on his brow.

Norma leaned back into the couch. "My God, I know his momma well. This is going to break her heart." She then sat upright, back in reporter mode. "Is there a suspect?"

"Nothing yet. Pebo said he was stabbed in the neck."

"And you want me over there?" she asked even though she already knew his answer. Norma was always given stories that dealt directly with Macinaw's African-American community. She was well-aware of how life in a Southern town worked and was acutely knowledgeable about her role in it.

31

"Yes, and you can take the kid there with you," Darby said. He then pointed at Chan. "You okay with that, Adams?"

Chan stood, smiling. "Yes, sir. I'll be happy to help investigate, flesh out leads...."

"Nobody said anything about you investigating, Adams. You go with Norma. Watch and learn. Keep your mouth shut and stay out of her way. Got it?"

Chan's smile faded. "Yes, sir."

"Good." Darby looked back at Norma. "Deputy Haskit is at the scene. You can start there."

Norma stood, nodding at Darby and slinging her pocketbook on her shoulder. She walked past the editor, and Chan began to follow. Darby stopped him by grabbing his arm.

"You didn't get me my coffee this morning, Adams."

Chan looked over at Darby's empty coffee mug on the conference table and then back to his boss. "I didn't know how you take it," Chan said, an iciness enveloping his words.

"Black. Think you can remember that?"

"Yes, sir," Chan said breaking from his grip and heading out the door. "I'll remember."

6:27 AM

Norma and Chan were both working on their second cigarette of the morning as they rode down Main Street. Chan had offered to drive his car, and Norma took him up on it, figuring it would do him good to learn the roads first hand.

"So, who's this James fellow that was killed?" Chan asked. "His name seemed to get your attention."

"Take a right up here," Norma said, indicating the next street. She waited as they turned and then responded, "Tyrell James has a history here in Macinaw—and it's a rather uncomfortable one."

"Uncomfortable for him or for Macinaw?"

Norma took a drag and blew the smoke out the window. "Both. He was one of the Seven—what some people called the Macinaw Seven. Have you heard about them?"

Chan turned down the corners of his mouth. "No. Who were they?"

"They were seven local black males, kids mostly, who were arrested for the murder of Robert Dover back in 1969. Dover was the son of Ellis Dover, a prominent farmer and political big-wig in this area." She paused before adding, "And yes, the Dovers are white."

"So, racial issues?"

Norma nodded. "At every turn. A powder-keg-waiting-to-explode kind of situation, if you know what I mean."

"The seven weren't convicted?"

"No, acquitted—which is amazing in itself considering the courts down here. But it was an uneasy acquittal. Things really never settled after the trial."

"And the murder?"

"Unsolved to this day. But to be honest, I don't know if the cops really looked too hard after the acquittal. They were certain the Seven had done it."

"How so?"

"They were seen coming from the barn where Robert was found—his body hanging in the hayloft—a rope around his neck."

"Hanging? Did the police ever consider it a suicide?" Chan asked.

"Not when they had seven blacks witnessed running from the barn. And they had motive some say. Many believed they killed Robert in retaliation for the Orangeburg Massacre."

"The what?"

"Don't they teach social studies over there in Georgia?" Norma asked lightly.

"Must've overslept that day," Chan quipped.

Norma hesitated as she looked up at the road ahead. "Take the first left after the bridge." She refocused on Chan. "I'm afraid the story gets more complex the more I tell. Suffice it to say, the Seven may have had cause."

Chan nodded as he thought about it. "So how were the Seven acquitted if the cops were so convinced?"

"Sonny Watts—their lawyer. He found a lot of holes to loop in the investigation. The case against them fell apart during the trial."

"But not according to the cops, right?"

"Right. The cops, the Dovers, and many other people to this day still believe that the Macinaw Seven got away with killing Robert."

Chan tapped his fingers atop the steering wheel. "Intriguing. And now one of them is dead."

"Murdered," Norma clarified.

"Right, murdered. I imagine this is going to be hard on the town, raising all those ill feelings again."

Norma sighed. "I'm afraid that is a definite possibility." She turned to look out of her rolled-down window and away from the glare of the rising sun. "Welcome to Macinaw, Mr. Adams."

7:02 AM

Norma had Chan park the car down the dirt road from the crime scene so that they could approach discreetly. They walked toward the house side by side.

"Take it slow," Norma said. "Cops don't like it when you rush a crime scene. They get all closed-mouthed and protective. And let me initiate the conversation. I know how these guys think."

As they stepped onto the dirt driveway, they were met by two Macinaw sheriff deputies who were leaning against their patrol cars, blocking the entrance. Both deputies were tall, close to six feet, although Chief Deputy Bobby Haskit, the lankier of the two, may have been an inch taller. Deputy Jimmy Evans with his broad shoulders and crew cut was more intimidating to Chan. Both lawmen looked alert despite the early morning hour.

"Hello, there, Miss Norma," Haskit began. "How're you?"

"Morning, Bobby," she said. "Too early in the day for all this."

The deputies agreed with a nod.

Norma pointed behind her. "This is Chan Adams. He's with the paper now." She turned to Chan and indicated the two men. "Deputies Haskit and Evans."

Chan reached beyond Norma and shook both of their hands. Bobby Haskit smiled at the young reporter—Jimmy Evans did not.

"So, what's the situation?" Norma asked

Haskit looked back at the house, caught Deputy Evans' wary expression, and then refocused on Norma. "This is strictly off the record, Norma, but it's a bad scene. Somebody got to Tyrell last night. Jabbed him in the neck. Left a ton of blood inside."

"Forced entry?"

"Not that we can tell."

"Anything stolen?"

"He lived alone, so it's gonna be hard to say—although his TV, stereo, and guns are still inside. Nothing else appeared disturbed."

"Drugs?"

"I never knew Tyrell to run with that crew, but anything is possible at this point."

Norma paused and then added, "You said a ton of blood. Which room?"

"Back bedroom. His bedroom. We found him on the bed. We think the assailant surprised him there."

"Can we take a look?" Chan blurted out.

Norma shot a stern look at Chan.

Haskit smiled at the young reporter. "Not yet. We have more investigative procedures to follow." He looked back at the house before adding, "Could be several hours yet."

"Next of kin notified?" Norma asked.

Haskit nodded in the affirmative. "His momma is at the station now. In fact, she was the one who called Tyrell last night to check on him. When she didn't get an answer, she sent her brother over to find out why. He discovered the body."

"And what time did she make the call?" Chan asked.

Instead of admonishing Chan, Norma stayed focused on the deputy as she knew his question was appropriate.

"Around nine, I think. He had been working late yesterday."

Norma moved slightly forward and lowered her voice a bit. "And what of the other six, Bobby? Has anyone checked on them?"

Haskit hesitated to answer. "I'm sorry, Norma. I've said too much already. We're just working this crime scene. You need to ask the sheriff about all that."

4:45 PM

Sheriff Justin Crawford's office was what Chan had imagined a small county sheriff's office to be: twelve square feet, cramped and clipped, with a singular window—the shade drawn shut. A distinctive combination of cheap cigars, gun oil and old leather smells permeated the room.

Chan sat quietly with Norma in visitor chairs across from the sheriff's desk waiting on his return, eyes drifting about the room. He noted scattered documents and folders of all kinds as if a huge file cabinet had suddenly exploded, raining paper down on everything.

He was drawn to the faux wood walls where he saw plaques, medals, and citations jammed against various pictures of the sheriff—some with fellow lawmen, others with certain dignitaries. A personalized autographed picture of President Nixon was lost amid the clutter. A locked gun rack was placed prominently on the wall below the photographs.

The sheriff's desk was also a testament to an overworked man. Beside the obligatory wife and kids' photo, the desk held a filled ash tray, two coffee cups overflowing with pens, a multi-function phone with messages taped to the receiver, in-out boxes filled with assorted papers, and a desk calendar littered with personal reminders scribbled in red ink.

The office door swung open, and Sheriff Crawford stormed in. He was authority and assurance wrapped in a tan sheriff's uniform. A huge presence, Crawford maintained an athletic build on his five-eleven frame despite being well past the age of fifty. His head was still covered with a chock full of black hair although time had tempered the edges to a snowy grey. He had a prominent nose and strong jaw on his clean-shaven face. And his eyes, like his hair, were the color of night. He cast them upon his visitors as he made his way around his desk.

As he sat, he spread out the desk clutter with his hands and then leaned back in his leather chair. "Always a pleasure to talk to the fourth estate, Norma, but we're a little busy today, as you might imagine."

"We're busy, too, Sheriff, with deadlines looming," Norma said. "We need to know of any progress on the investigation."

Crawford shrugged. "All dead-ends so far. We'll continue to work the case, obviously, but we really have nothing to report right now."

"No prints? No leads? Nothing?"

"The investigation continues, but no, there is nothing so far."

"Could this have something to do with Tyrell's past?" Chan blurted out. "Specifically, his involvement with the Macinaw Seven?"

Crawford frowned and set his eyes on Chan. "And who are you, sir?"

Norma leaned forward, "This...."

"I'm Chan Adams, with *The Macinaw Republic*," Chan said, jumping the introduction. He looked down at his open notepad and then back up. "In 1969, Tyrell James and six others were charged with the murder of Robert Dover...."

"I'm well-aware of the Macinaw Seven, young man. I was sheriff then, too."

"So then, you would also know that their acquittal left many in this town with feelings of an unsatisfied need for justice."

Crawford almost laughed. "You don't have to connect the dots for me, Mr. Adams. As I said, I was sheriff then. I was the one who arrested the seven men. I lived through the trial and the fallout."

"Have you contacted the others involved?" Chan asked.

Crawford dismissed the notion with a quick shake of his head.

"That would seem a logical move. If nothing else, to check on their safety."

"No need to jump the gun, Mr. Adams. We have the situation under control. This appears to be an isolated attack. We have no reason to believe others are involved or that anyone else is in danger."

"But how do you...?"

Crawford pressed his hands down on his desk as he stood. "As I said, it's under control, sir. Now if you and Miss Norma will excuse me, I have other business that I really do need to take care of." He shot a look directly at Norma.

Norma rose without hesitation. "You will keep us apprised, Sheriff?"

"Of course," he said. "As soon as we know anything."

Norma headed out without another word—Chan right on her heels.

Crawford waited for their stir to dissipate and then grabbed his phone. "Deputy, get in here."

Within seconds, Bobby Haskit appeared in the door to the office, a somber look on his face.

"Did you check with the coroner's office?" Crawford asked.

"Yes, sir, and you were right. The exact same as Henry Brooks."

6:47 PM

Chan wheeled the Torino into the employee parking spaces behind *The Macinaw Republic*. He pulled his car to a stop, but kept the engine running. Norma grabbed a Hardee's bag from the floorboard and cracked open her door.

"See what you can find out from Luther Jennings." She handed him directions written on a napkin. "This is the latest address I have on him. See if he's heard anything from the other five. And ask him when he contacted Tyrell last."

"He may be more inclined to talk with you," Chan said.

"Yeah, but I've got to finish my article on the drainage issue and get our preliminary on Tyrell ready for tomorrow's edition. You can do it—you have good instincts. Just be direct like you were with Crawford. He'll respect that. Swing back by here later, and let me know what he said."

"Okay. Cover for me with Darby."

"Will do."

Norma stepped out and headed toward the building.

Chan drove back onto Main Street, following Norma's directions. He rubbed at his tired eyes and felt the day's tension in his shoulders. He'd had a rough start, but he was at least thankful to have had Norma as a partner for the day. Although their investigation into Tyrell James's death had been rather fruitless so far, it had given him time to hear much of the back-story on the Macinaw Seven and the Robert Dover murder.

Luther Jennings, as he was told, was the other member of the Macinaw Seven who had been on the South Carolina State campus the day of the Orangeburg Massacre. He and Tyrell were juniors at State in 1968 and became swept up in the fervor leading up to that fateful night in February. They befriended Cleveland Sellers, the civil rights activist and program director for the Student Nonviolent Coordinating Committee, who helped stage the protests at the bowling alley. According to Norma, after everything was over, Sellers was forced to take the fall for the riot, which angered Luther and Tyrell. And the following year, after the patrolmen were acquitted in the deaths of the three students killed on State's campus, the two went out on their own and vowed to get even with the system. They returned to Macinaw and, with five other recruited locals, went looking for trouble.

Trouble. That's exactly where Chan thought he was headed as he crossed the railroad tracks and into Macinaw's black section of town. A small town divided along racial lines was almost cliché, but he recognized that was a reality across much of the South, including his home in Georgia. Economic and social factors drew most of the dividing lines, and Chan knew that people were people no matter their side of the track. But the world loved to point out the obvious, and race was always the first thing people noticed.

Chan parked on the street in front of Luther's modest home and hopped out. He crossed the sidewalk to the sound of a dog barking a few houses down. He went through a chain-link fence gate—a cement path led to a covered porch and the front door.

The house was dark, but Chan thought he heard movement inside. He knocked twice.

"Mr. Jennings?" He waited and then, "Luther Jennings?"

Chan peeked inside a front window, waited a few seconds, and then banged against the door. "Mr. Jennings?"

"Get the hell outta here, Henry Brooks!" a deep voice called out from within the dark house.

Chan hesitated in confusion. "Sir? My name is Chan Adams. I'm a reporter." He waited and then tried, "I just want to talk with Mr. Luther Jennings."

"Go away! I ain't said nothing about nobody! Get the hell away from me!"

"Sir? I don't understand...."

Chan heard stomping coming toward the door. "I say I ain't said nothing! Do you hear? Now leave me alone!"

Chan leaned his head against the door. "Sir, I just have a few...."

The door swung open, and Chan nearly fell into the barrel of the pointed shotgun. Luther Jennings had a desperate, wild look in his eyes. He was a young and strong man, but his youthful appearance was belied by the fear etched in every line of his face.

Chan ducked and spun his body before the first shot blasted by his head. He felt the heat of the blast and sensed pellets fire past the back of his neck and left ear. Within a solitary second, he had leaped down the entire stairs leading to the porch and was stumbling toward the gate. In two giant strides, Chan was at the end of the yard. He sensed the shotgun being leveled at him again and dove over the fence. The second blast caught him in mid-air, tearing cloth and skin away from his backside. He landed face first on the sidewalk, breaking his nose and skinning his hands and forearms.

Chan heard footsteps pounding behind him, and he managed to pull himself up and blindly jump into his Torino. The pain was excruciating, but he fumbled the keys from his pocket and started the car. Through his bloody right eye, he saw Luther coming after him with the shotgun. He slammed the accelerator and tore down the street, a third shotgun blast echoing behind him.

JUNE 18, 1976

"Mr. Adams, how're you feeling this morning?"

The woman's gentle voice woke Chan from his sleep. He was lying on his stomach in a hospital bed with bandages across his face and hands. His hospital gown was pulled up around his waist, and his exposed right bottom cheek was still throbbing in pain.

He had somehow driven to the emergency room at Macinaw General. His failed conversation with Luther Jennings seemed like a distant dream now—well, more like a nightmare. Chan had never had his life threatened like that, and his heart skipped a beat thinking about that gun barrel being leveled at his nose.

"I'm Nurse Reid. I will be taking over the next shift."

Chan picked his head off the pillow and turned slightly to look at his new nurse. He didn't remember much of his night-shift nurse except that she was a short, grey-haired woman who woke him every hour to check on his pain levels. But Nurse Reid was certainly worth remembering.

She was five and half feet tall with wavy, golden blonde hair that reached past her shoulders. She was studying his chart, but he could tell that there was something special about her— alluring certainly, but more. Her nose wasn't perfect, a little large perhaps for her slender oval face; however, everything else seemed just right. She was about his age, maybe a year or two older. She reminded him a bit of the model-actress Farrah Fawcett.

She placed the chart on the end of the bed and approached him. From his prone position, he could see that her legs were slender and well-defined despite the white nurse's tights that she wore under her uniform. She bent at the knees to be level with him—her blue eyes inquisitive yet compassionate.

She reached over and pulled aside strands of his hair hanging in his face. "Do you need anything?"

"A new nose." He paused. "Maybe a new ass."

She smiled and then took a quick glance at his backside. "No, everything looks just fine back there to me."

Chan tried to smile, although it hurt to do so. "I'm Chan Adams."

"Jean Reid."

"Nice to meet you, Jean. I'm afraid you're catching me at a bad time."

"No need to apologize. I've seen much worse."

"That's hard to believe."

"Truly. I expect you to be up and around in a few days. We've been known to work miracles in this hospital."

"Good, because it feels like I'm gonna need one." Chan's half-smile faded. "What about the guy who peppered me? Any word on him?"

"The police have the information. I'm sure they'll be contacting you sometime today. And..." she pulled a note from her uniform pocket and read, "...someone named Norma called to check on you—said she'd be here later." She looked back at Chan. "Is Norma your wife? A girlfriend?"

"Surrogate mother. Although to be honest, what kind of mother sends her child into the streets to be shot at anyway?" He winced as he finished the words.

"Do you need anything else for the pain?"

"Yes, the whole drugstore, please."

Jean smiled again and stood. "Listen. Get some rest. I'll check with the doctor about upping your meds. And I'll be back to check on you soon, okay?"

"I hope so. I've been here in this town for two days, and you're about the only person I've met who I'd care to ever see again."

She leaned back over and brushed the hair from his eyes again. "Then it's a date."

Chan watched as she left the room and then he closed his eyes. The pain was severe, and he could use some relief, but for the moment, just the thought of this angel of mercy was medicine enough.

10:11 AM

Sheriff Crawford bounded down the steps of the courthouse and headed for Chief Deputy Haskit and the waiting squad car.

"Luther in the pen?" Crawford called out.

"Yes, sir. Took three deputies and two city cops, but we managed him outta his house. He's at the complex now in the holding cell." Haskit waited until he was face to face with the sheriff. "I ain't never seen anything like it. He was completely non-compliant. You want us to stand on his head a little?"

"Standing on his head" was Macinaw police talk for roughing up a prisoner. Crawford was not above such measures, but he shook his head.

"Did he give you his whereabouts from two nights ago?" Crawford asked.

"He ain't talking, Sheriff. Least not to us. He was acting very antsy like he was high on speed or cocaine. You think he might've had something to do with Tyrell's death?"

"I don't know. But to have two of the Macinaw Seven involved in anything causes me great concern."

"Yes, sir."

"And the mark they found on Tyrell. That's just…well, that disturbs me even more."

Crawford's words sparked a recollection for Haskit. "Did you read that reporter's statement from last night's shooting?"

"Not yet. Why?"

"He said before Luther started shooting, he was shouting at him to go away. Said he called him *Henry Brooks*."

"What?!"

"Yes, sir. That reporter said Luther thought Henry Brooks was after him."

10:52 AM

Crawford proceeded down the corridor of the Macinaw Law Complex, a civic building that housed his office as well as the offices of the city police. The corridor separated those offices from the temporary holding cells in the back. He passed a deputy behind a guard desk and slipped through an open metal door, bypassing the larger drunk tank and continuing to the individual cells at the end of the hall.

Luther, in a green Macinaw prison jumpsuit, sat rigid on the edge of the wall bunk in the last cell. Crawford grabbed the bars of the cell and leaned his head near an opening. He took a moment and looked around the cramped quarters.

"Beats the hell outta the old jail, don't it, Luther? New walls. Paint. Clean sheets."

He waited, but Luther remained quiet.

"Smells better anyway," the sheriff said. "They say they're gonna tear down the old jail. Maybe put up a shopping mall. Can you imagine?"

Luther did not react.

Crawford pulled the key from his belt and unlocked the cell door. He stepped in, closed the door until it locked, and moved in front of Luther. Under the cell's florescent light, Luther's eyes looked a dull yellow.

"So, what'd you go and shoot that white boy for, Luther? What'd he do to you?"

Luther angled his yellow eyes to meet the sheriff's but said nothing.

"He must've really pissed you off about something, huh? Good thing it was just bird shot, or that boy mighta woke up in the morgue."

Luther held his peace, but his right leg started to bounce.

"Truth of the matter is, I don't care much for reporters myself—they can be irritating as hell—sometimes I feel like shooting 'em myself," Crawford joked. He then looked toward the hallway and lowered his voice. "But I've got to know something, Luther. Why Henry Brooks? I know you've grown up in these parts, and I know you know all about that son of a bitch. But why call his name? Why think he's gonna show up at your door? He's been dead now for years."

Luther maintained his stare, but his bouncing leg picked up speed.

"Maybe the reporter misunderstood you? Or maybe there's another Henry Brooks I'm not aware of, huh?" More silence greeted Crawford. He straightened up again. "Listen. Your buddy, Tyrell, is dead. I don't know who got to him, but maybe you do. If you two were into something, you need to tell me. I can protect you, but you've gotta trust me." He waited and then said, "C'mon, Luther. Think about your life outside these walls."

Luther dropped his stare and hung his head. The cell light above him hummed through the silence until the sheriff sighed.

"Okay, okay, you win. But remember, cooperation will get you outta here sooner." Crawford exited the cell and slammed the door shut to lock it. He held up for a moment—waiting, hoping for a change of heart.

But the sheriff would get nothing from Luther Jennings.

3:47 PM

Norma sat in a chair next to Chan's hospital bed as Chan paced the small strip between her and the door. He looked pathetic hobbling along in a hospital gown, covered with scrapes and bruises, and with black eyes developing above his nose bandage.

"Are you sure you don't want me to call your mother for you?" Norma asked.

"God, no. She would freak out—insist that I come back to Georgia. Better to keep this from her."

"But how will you manage?"

"I'm fine, Norma," he said. "Just give me a few days, and I'll be good to go."

Norma stared at him for a bit, broke into a smile, and then covered her mouth to muffle a laugh.

"What?"

"Nothing." She paused and then added, "Except that you look like a blonde-headed raccoon that didn't quite make it to the other side of the road." She laughed aloud.

"Glad my injuries can bring you some joy, Norma."

She held out her hand as if to beg forgiveness. "I'm sorry, really."

"You should be. It's your damn fault I was there in the first place," Chan said, unable to suppress his own grin.

"Welcome to the newspaper game," she said. "I'll bet they didn't teach you how to dodge bullets in your advanced journalism classes, did they?"

"Must be the 'on-the-job training' they kept talking about."

A single knock on the door interrupted them and Sheriff Crawford stuck his head in the room. "Sorry if I'm barging in. Just wanted to know if you had a little time to talk."

"Of course, Sheriff. Come in," Chan said.

He backed up and Norma rose from her chair as Sheriff Crawford entered.

"Recovering okay?" The sheriff's words sounded appropriate, if not entirely sincere.

Chan nodded.

"Would you care to sit?" Crawford offered.

Chan shared a smile with Norma. "No, I'm okay standing."

"Fine then," Crawford said. He looked in Norma's direction. "I'm sorry, Norma, but would you excuse us for a few minutes?"

"Of course," she said. "I need to be getting back to the paper anyway."

Norma glanced at Chan before heading out. He assured her with a knowing look.

Crawford shut the door as she left and turned to Chan. "We wanted to let you know that Luther Jennings has been arrested for his assault on you. We have him at our law complex awaiting arraignment."

"Thank you, Sheriff. It was scary as hell, but the truth is, I don't think he knew who I was. I got the feeling that it may have been some manner of mistaken identity."

"Oh?" Crawford feigned surprise. "And what makes you say that?"

"He thought I was somebody else. In his rage, he called out another name: Henry Brooks."

"Are you sure of the name?"

"Well, Luther was inside the house, and it was a bit muffled, but that's what it sounded like to me."

Crawford nodded thoughtfully as he paused. "What else did he say to you?"

"To go away—to get away from him."

"Is that it?"

Chan pursed his lips. "Yeah, mainly. He was acting wild—crazy." Chan gave it a moment's more thought. "He also yelled that he told 'nobody nothing.'"

"Nobody nothing? Nothing about what?

Chan frowned and gestured with his palms turned up. "I have no clue. But that's what he was yelling."

"I see." Crawford said, as he sat on the edge of the bed.

Chan could tell the wheels in Crawford's head were spinning. "So, should I be aware of this Henry Brooks?"

"Actually, I'm surprised that you aren't. He's a fairly notorious figure around here."

"Who is he?"

"A cold-blooded killer, Mr. Adams. One of South Carolina's worse."

AUGUST 6, 1963

6:47 PM

Sheriff Marion Newton's patrol car bounced up and down the deep washed-out areas of the dirt road he traveled. He continued to follow the clay-bound road as he passed abandoned plows, rusty irrigation wheel lines and dried corn fields, which even the starving crows dared not approach.

When his term expired with the upcoming election, the sixty-eight-year-old sheriff planned to retire, move with his wife Alice to Florida, take up golf, and end his days in tropical sunshine. But a heavy cloud hung over Macinaw's popular constable. Death had come to his small county in an unimaginable way, and he had made a vow to the populace to stop the madness before he left.

He drove by a ramshackle house and assorted clapboard pot sheds until he saw the man outside an old barn—it, too, grey and worn—a strong wind away from collapsing. He pulled the patrol car next to an empty hog pen and came to a stop.

Sheriff Newton sat inside the patrol car and watched his target digging a pail into a feed bin. The man was thin, too thin, even frightfully so. He had on a blue work shirt that seemed to swallow his upper torso. His jeans were dirty and saggy, held up by twine instead of a belt. His head was small and mostly bald, save the clumps of stringy hair that hung down the back. He appeared sub-human, and it gave Newton chills just to be watching him.

Newton grabbed his wide-brimmed sheriff's hat and got out of the patrol car. As he neared the feed bin, he detected the man's faint voice—he was whispering, talking to himself.

"Henry..." Newton called out.

Henry Brooks jumped a bit, turned toward the sheriff, and smiled. "Sheriff Newton, didn't hear ya coming up."

"Didn't mean to scare you, Henry. I just wanted to speak with you for a few minutes." Newton stood in front of the man and rubbed his lower back. "You really need to work on that road of yours. You've got some real kidney busters out there."

"Yessah, I'll get right on that. Been meaning to do that for a while."

"And your fields, Henry," Newton said. "They're in bad shape. They need some attention right quick like—before the weeds come calling."

"Yessah, I'll get on that, too. Damn tractor been broke now for weeks."

Newton saw through the man's hideous appearance and felt a twinge of pity. "You need to take better care of your place and yourself, Henry. It's what men do. It's the right thing to do."

"Yessah, yessah, I know. I know." He paused to eye the sheriff and then asked, "Is that what you come all the way out here for, Sheriff Newton? Ask about my fields and welfare?"

"Well, no, Henry. I was headed home to grab some supper, and I just decided to stop by. I thought you and I might have us a little chat about what's been happening lately in Macinaw. You know, with the people disappearing and then their bodies turning up with them weird marks on 'em."

"I sure don't know nothing 'bout that, Sheriff. Nosah, I surely don't. I told Deputy Crawford the same thing a couple of months ago."

"Yes, I know. But maybe I could just ask you a few more things about it and see if it stirs your thinking some."

Henry Brooks hesitated and then looked at the pail of grain at his feet. "I got my hogs to feed, Sheriff. If I don't feed 'em on time, they'll cause a ruckus and a half."

"Go on about your chores then," Newton said. "I'll just follow behind you. That is, if you don't mind."

Henry smiled—a skull full of yellowed and crooked teeth. He struggled to pick up his pail and then entered the old barn— Sheriff Newton directly behind him.

"This used to be my daddy's cow barn, but now I keep my hogs in it," Henry announced.

The potent smell hit the sheriff as soon as he entered. It smelled like death. It was dark too, unkempt with hay and farm tools strewn all about. Little light streamed through the roof and illuminated a series of pulleys and hooks hanging from the rafters. Newton nearly tripped over long, thick ropes and leather straps that were lying on the barn floor, and he stepped carefully around them. He didn't think much about the riggings, as he assumed they were a way for Henry to move around hay bales or heavy livestock.

Henry stopped at the first stall and poured the pail into a trough at the stall's head. Newton heard the grunting hogs moving about in the dark, positioning for their grub.

"So, what is it you wanna know, Sheriff?"

Newton leaned back against an empty stall opposite of Henry and eyed the little man the best he could. "Like I said, Henry, it's about those murders we've had over the past few months. I was hoping you might be able to shed some light on a few things."

"Like what?"

"Well, like Catfish Jones for instance. You did know him, right?"

"Yessah, me and him was good friends," he said, "despite the fact he was a colored boy. Me and Catfish would hunt and fish together sometimes."

"And you don't know who got to him—stuck him in the throat and then left him to die on the banks of the Edisto? Carved that weird mark on him?"

"Nosah, don't know who would do that to ol' Catfish." Henry moved from the first stall to a second and again poured from his pail. More grotesque snarling and bumping came from this hog bin as well.

"How about the two college girls then? The ones traveling from Winthrop."

Henry shook his head. "Nosah, don't know nothing 'bout that neither."

"They found their car only a mile from your farm, Henry— their bodies in a field just up the road from Watkins Bridge. You sure you didn't hear or see anything that night?"

"No, like I said, Deputy Crawford done come out here 'bout that. He already done asked me a million questions. I told him like I tell you, Sheriff, I don't know nothing about it." Henry continued to move back and forth between the stalls as he talked.

"Twelve people, Henry. Twelve have been murdered over the past year and a half. All lived on this side of the river—

except them girls—and their car broke down near here. You must know or have heard something about it."

"I don't know nothing," Henry said. He bent over and fiddled with something in the dark. "But...but I might know someone who does."

Newton perked up. "You do? Who, Henry? Tell me."

Henry Brooks moved to the center post between the stalls directly across from the sheriff. Two hand cranks were attached to either side of the post. He grabbed both handles and turned them in opposite ways.

"Now if you really know something...." Newton stopped mid-thought as he heard something drag across the floor. "What's that? What're you doing there, Henry?"

But Henry said nothing and turned the cranks even faster. Sheriff Newton felt something whip against his lower legs and heard the pulleys squeak above him. "What the hell?"

The rope ends reeled into two collection wheels in the rafters and stretched the ropes tight, pinning Sheriff Newton. Before he knew it, the sheriff was caught against the empty stall's door—unable to move his arms or legs.

"Jesus, Henry! I'm trapped! Stop this! Stop this now!"

Henry spun the spools with frantic energy. The sheriff cried out in pain as the rope tightened around his midsection—his hat tumbled to the barn floor. The bindings dug into the exposed skin on his arms until they ripped and bled—the pressure continued to build until one of his ribs cracked.

"For God's sake, Henry! I can't breathe! Cut me loose!" He struggled with all the strength he had left but to no avail. He spat blood. "Henry!"

Moments from passing out, Newton could make out Henry's outline in the dark. The madman had pulled an eight-inch knife from the pocket of his baggy jeans. He passed the knife back and forth between his hands, mumbling to himself. He then stood face to face with Newton.

"Wherefore the seal of God upon your head, Sheriff? You claim authority of the people and much righteousness, but you betray the cross when no one watches. A sinful heart hides not in one's chest but is a banner for all the world to see." He leaned over and whispered in Newton's ear. "The king of locusts awaits you. Abaddon calls you to the fiery pits of hell—to lead his charge." Henry raised the knife with his left hand and placed it at Newton's throat.

"Henry, no! Don't...!"

Sheriff Marion Newton's life came to a sudden end, not in the joyous Florida sun as he had hoped and dreamed, but in a foul-smelling barn, tied to an old stall door, under the cold hand of the angel of destruction.

OCTOBER 2, 2016

October arrived with a noticeable seasonal shift in the Carolina morning. The summer's heat had finally released its grip, and the sky seemed to stretch forever in the early light—kissed with the golds and purples of the autumn to come.

Chan stood in front of the old Brooks house with his hands in his pockets. He still had on the same jeans from the day before but had changed from yesterday's t-shirt to a fresh, white button-down.

He eyed the old place as if he half-expected it to break free from its foundation and chase him down in the fields behind him. It amazed him that whoever owned the property now had not taken the eye-sore down. Every single pane of glass in the windows was either cracked or missing. Full blown brush and weeds of enormous height had popped through the front porch, snarled around the broken floorboards and blocked the front door. Holes in the rusty roof were large enough to encourage nesting birds and the side brick chimney seemed to teeter under its own weight.

He heard Tindal's rental car coming down the dirt road behind the house and he walked in that direction. The car pulled to a stop in front of him and Tindal hopped out. She had on black boots, dark leggings and an oversized cowl-necked burgundy sweater that reached down to mid-thigh. Chan figured no matter what the young woman wore, she would look like she just stepped out of the pages of some fashion magazine.

"Good morning, Chan. Thanks for meeting me here."

"How goes it down the road?" Chan asked.

"Still heavily blocked. Looks like all manners of law enforcement have made their way to Macinaw—SLED, ATF, FBI."

"Still no reporters allowed?"

Tindal smiled. "No, but your Sheriff Monroe promised me I would get access the moment he got the word."

"That's good," Chan said. "Have they extracted the body yet?"

"*Bodies*," She said. "And no not yet. Evidently, they have forensic teams and engineers down there trying to decide how to get to them out without disturbing evidence. I also hear they may be bringing a crane down later to pull the patrol car out."

"I understand it's quite a drop from the old farm road to the swamp."

"Monroe said the patrol car may have tumbled fifty yards or so down the embankment before it wound up in the kudzu. The river is but a short distance away from the crash site."

"Did he say anything else? You said bodies. Did they find three in the car?"

She nodded in the affirmative. "Does that add up with what you remember from that night?"

Chan put his hands on his hips and looked down the farm road as if he was watching the 1976 patrol car drive past. "Yeah, three were seen driving through Macinaw that night. It was raining hard as hell as I recall." Chan took a quick glance back at the old house. "But why come out here? This has to be more than some on-the-nose coincidence."

Tindal only shrugged and then pulled out folded documents from her satchel. "I was able to track the land's ownership last night," she said as she flipped through the pages. "Brooks had no one to leave his farm to and owed the bank quite a bit so the title passed to Macinaw National after his death. The property remained idle as the hometown bank changed hands the next few years. In 1982 the land was sold by auction to Searson-Thompson, a real-estate investment firm based in Connecticut. It's been listed in their catalogue for the last thirty years."

"No-man's land," Chan said.

"Exactly."

"So, the worthless property of a dead madman. What was Crawford doing here? What was he looking for?" He paused and then, "What could have happened to them?"

Tindal again had no guess. She turned and looked beyond the house to a pile of grey, rotten lumber peeking out from tall grass. "Was that the old barn area?"

"That's it," Chan said. "Henry Brooks' little shop of horrors. After they caught him, they found twenty more bodies buried in the stalls inside. They figured by the time they sent the electricity through his skull in '66, he had killed at least thirty-eight people."

"And yet he wasn't done, was he?"

Chan looked to Tindal. "Apparently, you can't keep a bad man down."

JUNE 26, 1976

6:45 AM

Chan sat alone at the coffee table in the bullpen, plunking sugar packs across the table top. He had been told to wait there by Darby while the rest of the staff got their assignments. It was his first day back at the paper since he had been shot by Luther Jennings and he was itching to get started.

Darby walked back in, took a long look at Chan, wiped his hand over his bald head, and with a sigh, plopped down on the break room's couch. "What the hell am I going to do with you?"

"Give me an assignment. Let me do a follow-up to the Tyrell James story. I'm ready."

Darby wanted to laugh but mirth went against his personality. "Ready? You almost got killed on your first day out there. I would hardly say you were ready. Maybe I can let you empty the waste baskets or clean the toilets today."

Chan drew a Marlboro Light from his shirt pocket and fired it up. He took a deep drag, blew the blue smoke to the ceiling and finally leaned in his chair toward the editor. "Look. I know you think I'm some dumb-ass hick from Georgia who doesn't know the first thing about journalism, but the truth of the matter is I'm invested in the story now."

"Invested?"

"Damn straight. And I've got the scars to prove it." He circled the wounds on his face with his cigarette hand.

Darby shook his head. "No…"

Chan moved to the couch and sat beside him. "Tyrell James. Luther Jennings. Henry Brooks even. There's a lot at play here, Mr. Darby. It's gotta be worth looking into."

"Agreed, but you don't know anything about those cases, those people. Besides, you're just out of the womb in this business."

"Norma has been filling me in. I spent the last few days in the hospital reading all about the Macinaw Seven and their acquittal. And my God, seemingly half of Macinaw wanted those black men dead. This is all anyone in this town is talking about."

56

"Exactly. And I'm not gonna just hand a prime story like this to some rookie. There's a lot of history involved."

"I know," Chan said. "And I'm the only one around here *not* prejudiced by that history. I can give you a fresh perspective on the whole thing." He paused. "Let Norma and I work the angles on this together. She has the knowledge, the background and an ear to the people."

"And what do you have beside a broken nose and an ass full of birdshot?"

Chan grinned. "Isn't that enough?"

Darby sighed again, this time deeper and more prolonged. "I'd be lying to you, Adams, if I didn't say those were the exact sentiments Norma used to try and convince me to give you a shot at this as well. If nothing else, you seemed to have made an impression on her." He leaned his heavy frame back into the couch and then looked at Chan. "Are you sure about the name Luther called you? Are you sure it was Henry Brooks?"

"Like I told Sheriff Crawford, it sure sounded like it. But what would Henry Brooks have to do with Luther or the Macinaw Seven anyway?"

Darby smoothed out his thick mustache with his thumb and forefinger. "Lord knows. It's not like we're known for a lot of positives in Macinaw. But Henry Brooks...." His voice trailed off.

"He was a monster. I know that. A mass murderer who killed thirty-eight people. What else can you tell me?"

"You believe in the devil, Adams?"

"Not pitch forks and flames, but I know evil exists in our world."

"Yeah, well, he was evil personified. A crazed killer with no conscience, no morals, no guilt."

"How did he get away with it for so long?"

"The devil wore grey flannel, I suppose, or maybe I should say blue overalls. No one suspected him. No one knew that side of him. He was a poor, dirt farmer. He lived alone out there on his daddy's farm, trying to make a go of it. Most people who knew him felt sorry for him, but he was just crazy, you know? The worst case of Carolina cruel I ever saw."

"Carolina cruel?"

Darby mused on the question. "Poverty. Racism. Abuse. Ignorance. Carolina cruel is our state's local affliction—the palmetto psychosis. You see it in people's eyes when they've fallen too far—reached rock bottom. Anybody can get it. The destitute woman with a trailer full of kids—no husband, no paycheck, no hope. The businessman mortgaged to the eyeballs, his wife screwing the neighbor, government after his land. Those subjugated to the cruel often turn to booze or pills or some other vice—keeps the fire burning inside of them until it finally fries their brains. That's when they do their greatest harm." He looked over at Chan. "It can be anything that sets them off: the heat, the humidity, buzzing mosquitoes. Henry Brooks' brain was certainly fried, blurring reality and the world he lived in. Too much time looking at dead fields. Too much plow dust up his nose. He tortured and killed his victims in the most savage way. I have a dossier on him in my office—you should take a look sometime."

"Does that mean I can work on the story?" Chan asked tentatively.

"Listen, the Macinaw Seven and Henry Brooks were two of the biggest stories to ever come out of the Lowcountry, tragic as they were. Everybody and their brother have an opinion on what happened so of course we're gonna follow this up. But Norma gets the lead. You can help out, just don't dare step over your bounds or it's your ass, got it?"

Chan squashed his cigarette in the ash tray and hopped off the couch. "Thanks, boss." He headed out the door. "I promise you won't regret it."

Dennis Darby remained on the couch and shook his head. "I already do," he sighed.

9:38 AM

Norma sat across the table from Chan in the Palm Leaf Café in downtown Macinaw. The Leaf was a typical small town greasy spoon—easy on the wallet, a little harder on the digestive system. The breakfast menu offered the basics with a few specialties including the local favorite of grits and gravy over egg and sausage patties in cheese biscuits. For Norma and Chan, the café had the sole benefit of being next door to the offices of

The Republic. Other customers that morning continued to come and go, but the two reporters seemed not to notice as they were deep into their planning.

Norma pushed an open folder across the orange Formica table top so that Chan could see. "This is the file I kept on the Dovers. Ellis Dover is the one on the left." She tapped her finger on Dover's face in the Polaroid.

Chan took a hard look at the snapshot. It was a family picture; Dover hovering behind his progeny on the expansive steps of what Chan figured to be the Dover home. Ellis Dover was a handsome man in many ways with a thick head of auburn hair, piercing blue eyes and radiant smile. But he also had age lines and weathered skin that tempered his good looks. Chan had known many farmers growing up in rural Georgia and knew how working under the sun for a living could change a man in more ways than one. "Which one is Robert?" Chan asked.

"Far left. The one looking away from the camera."

Chan focused on the youngest of the Dover clan. He was handsome like his father, thinner, a bit less dynamic in his appearance. It seemed strange to Chan that Robert, who was close to Chan's age at the time of the picture, was dead and had been for some six years. "Who are the others?" Chan asked.

"That's Phil, Chris and Kevin," Norma said as she traced her finger down the line. "Robert's older brothers." Handsome athletic types all.

"Where's the mother?"

"She died years before the picture was taken—car accident. She and her sister, Andrea, were killed coming back from their beach home in Litchfield."

Chan looked up at Norma. "So, I get the Dovers?"

"See if you can get an interview with Mr. Dover. We need to know his reaction to Tyrell's death."

"Thought you already tried him?"

"He wouldn't take my calls. You might do better with a face to face."

"Because I'm white?"

"If we're going to get anywhere with this, Chan, we're going to have to take advantage where we can."

"Understood. What's my approach?"

Norma picked up her coffee cup and rubbed the side as if conjuring a genie from the lamp. "Politics. Ever since Governor Russell appointed him to fill the commissioner of agriculture's term in '63, Dover has thought himself God's gift to the political arena. He has thrown his weight behind candidates from local to state to national and most all with positive results."

"Republican or Democrat?"

"Like most politicians, he can talk out of both sides of his mouth when he needs to—liberal and free-wheeling in some circles, conservative Bible-thumper to the home crowd. But he's a true Dixiecrat at heart. He counts Senators Thurmond and Hollings among his friends. Presently he's backing newcomer Trey Richards, a friend of the family, who's running for one of Macinaw's state senate seats. You can start with questions about that."

"How deep is Dover's influence?"

Norma took another sip. "He was the agricultural king around here for many years. He has more money than God, a grand home for formal parties, tons of land for political outings—dove shoots, barbeques, et cetera. The old saying is the road to Washington goes through Ellis Dover's backyard."

"Okay, So I start off with some bullshit questions about the next election and then try to steer him towards Tyrell James?"

"Just gauge his reaction. Even a no comment can be very telling."

Chan rubbed his hands together. "Okay. And what's on your plate for the day?"

"Luther's out on bail, waiting for his evidentiary hearing. Crawford thinks he may end up doing a little time since having a weapon is a probation no-no, much less firing it at someone. I'll go pay him a visit and see if I can't crack his wall of silence."

Chan nodded as he hopped up from the table. "Sounds about right. I'll contact you this afternoon. Hopefully I'll have something for you by then." He threw a dollar on the table for his coffee as he headed out.

"I'll be sure to give Luther your regards," Norma called out.

Chan smiled as he threw on his shades. "Yeah, tell him I think about him every time I pull up a chair."

12:09 PM

"Ellis Dover?" Chan asked.

The man was seated comfortably in a barber chair. He had a striped smock covering most of his dark blue business suit. Expensive-looking cowboy boots shot out on the footrest. Buddy, the silver-headed proprietor and head barber, who was standing behind him, had momentarily stopped with the clippers when Chan entered.

Dover had his eyes closed but batted them open upon hearing his name. "Yes, sir. I'm Ellis Dover. Can I help you with something?"

Chan smiled. "You're a hard man to track down, Mr. Dover. I'm Chan Adams with *The Macinaw Republic*."

Dover wrinkled a concerned brow but kept his eyes on Chan.

"I'd just like a moment of your time, sir. I have a few questions...."

Dover cut his eyes left and right. Besides Buddy and one man who sat in a corner chair reading the paper, he and Chan were alone.

Dover smiled. "Of course. Buddy, give us a few minutes please."

Buddy excused himself and walked to the rear of the small establishment.

"Now, what's this all about?" Dover asked as he sat up a little in the chair.

Chan took a seat in the waiting chair directly across from Dover. "I understand you're supporting Trey Richards for the state senate this November."

Dover's face lit up. "Yes, Trey's family and I go way back. I was very proud that he took the Democratic primary several weeks ago. He's smart, energetic and dedicated to improvements in his district. I believe the young man will go very far."

"Can you speak to any specifics? What's he targeting in the election?"

"Well, education is an overriding concern. Mr. Richards knows the value of a solid education and wants all of District 47 to be on par with the rest of South Carolina. And then on par nationally, of course."

"Will he increase taxes to get the district on par?"

"Increase taxes? Now, why would you go and use such dirty words?" He laughed then leaned forward in his chair. "We need not break the backs of the good people of Macinaw to improve their quality of life. Sometimes, Mr. Adams, the grease can come from other fry pans."

"Then how is Richards going to get his district's schools up to speed?"

"Rob from the rich and give to the poor." He smiled at his own words. "What I mean is, it would be to our advantage, along with Orangeburg, Colleton, Jasper and other rural counties, to have financial backing from all the districts of South Carolina. We are but poor farmland, Mr. Adams—goat fields and swamps. We have no industry to speak of. We have no commerce. It's Trey's plan, by virtue of legislation, that all counties share from the same pie."

"Interesting," Chan said. "Do you think the richer counties will go for it?"

Dover crossed his legs at the ankles. "They sure asked us to participate in that de-segregation of the schools a couple of years back, didn't they? Now, how is everyone supposed to be equal if the finances aren't there?"

"You were against de-segregation?"

"Personally, I have never seen anything wrong with separate schools for the races, but if we must send our children to schools with the colored folk, then at least we should have the finances to deal with their special problems."

"Special problems?"

Dover laughed acerbically. "I don't think I'm telling you anything you don't know, Mr. Adams. Blacks don't think like whites. They don't take to our society. They're of a different ilk."

"In what ways?"

"Their lack of intelligence. Their demeaning way of life. For goodness sakes, some of 'em act closer to barnyard animals than actual people."

"Like the Macinaw Seven?"

Dover dropped his smile, his face immediately flushed blood-red, and his hands coiled and uncoiled. "Exactly. Like the Macinaw Seven."

"Are you aware, Mr. Dover, that someone killed Tyrell James, one of the Macinaw Seven, just a few days ago?"

Dover bit down on his bottom lip—his blue eyes inflamed. He then lifted his chin in defiance and tried to steady himself. He uncrossed his legs, stood, removed the barber smock and tossed it in the chair. He walked up to Chan, looked down on him and seethed out the words, "Yes, Mr. Adams, I am well-aware of that *nigger's* death."

Ellis Dover marched out the door leaving Chan sinking in his chair. Chan turned and caught the stare of the man who had been reading the paper. The man made a snide grin, popped the paper in front of his face and kept reading.

1:33 PM

Norma used the back of her hand to rap on the door at Luther's house. "Luther?" she called out. She noticed the door was slightly ajar and pushed it open a tad more. "Luther? It's Norma Wiles."

She continued to swing the door open until she had a good look at the small foyer that led into his house. A few lights showed into the hallway, and she heard music coming from the back. It sounded like gospel music.

Norma entered cautiously not wanting to share the same experience that Chan had had with the man. "Luther? Are you home?" She methodically put one foot in front of the other. Despite her soft approach, her heels could still be heard on the wooden floorboards.

The music gained strength in her ears as she continued to the back. Norma recognized it, Mahalia Jackson's *Move On Up A Little Higher*. It had a grainy tone like it was coming from a radio. "Luther, it's Norma Wiles. I'd like to talk...."

Norma stopped at the end of the hall. From her vantage point she could see the dark, pooling substance on the yellow linoleum floor of the kitchen. She knew right away, but forced herself to take the remaining few steps.

63

Norma gasped at the sight, covering her mouth with her hand. There on the kitchen floor, shirtless and splayed out on his back was Luther Jennings. He had several stab wounds to his neck and chest which had pumped blood to all corners of the room.

Norma resisted the urge to flee and swallowed her nausea. She stepped further into kitchen, careful to avoid contaminating the scene. The room seemed undisturbed otherwise. The radio was on the kitchen table—Mahalia still wailing away.

Then she saw something on Luther that she thought was not possible. "No…it can't be."

She moved closer and took a good look at the killer's work to make sure. "It is… my God… Henry Brooks."

2:34 PM

Chan flew down the street—his bandaged wounds throbbed as his feet pounded underneath him. He never dreamed he would be back in this neighborhood so soon.

He waved his press badge at the Macinaw policemen who had cornered off a section of Luther's street and hustled beyond the flashing lights of the gathered emergency vehicles. He saw Norma alone, smoking a cigarette, on the sidewalk out in front of Luther's house.

"Are you all right?" Chan asked.

"I'll be okay," Norma said. "But it looks like you and I are two for two at this address."

"It was Luther?"

"Yes."

"Killed in the same manner as Tyrell?"

"I'm afraid so. And perhaps in more ways than one."

"What do you mean?"

Norma did not answer and instead looked to Luther's porch as Sheriff Crawford and Chief Deputy Haskit emerged through the front door. Chief of Macinaw Police, Aaron Stodges, a short, wiry man with wavy brown hair, followed close behind with two of his officers. Norma tossed her cigarette, broke past the police line, hustled to the foot of the stairs and blocked their exit.

"Now, hold on, Norma," Crawford said. "We're not in a position to discuss this with the press just yet."

"Too bad," Norma said. "You're gonna have to discuss this whether you like it or not."

"Tomorrow, I promise. Chief Stodges and I will hold a joint press conference...."

"Bullshit, Justin. You're not going anywhere until we get some answers. Now, c'mon, you know how much this means. I saw what he cut into Luther's chest. Was the same done to Tyrell?"

Crawford hesitated. He looked at Haskit and then turned to glance at the chief. Stodges shrugged and then nodded the go-ahead. Crawford turned back to Norma. "Yes."

"Jesus... and which mark did he leave on Tyrell? Michael or Abaddon?"

Crawford hesitated again, putting his hands on his hips. "The Michael symbol was carved into Tyrell."

"Wait a minute," Chan interjected. "What do you mean carved into Tyrell? And what or who is Abaddon?"

Crawford drew his large hand across his face as he eyed the two reporters. "Why don't we let the detectives and deputies do their job here. We can go back to my office. If you promise to sit on the details until we can make sense of all this, I'll share with you what I know."

5:33 PM

Norma and Chan found themselves back in Crawford's office in the same chairs as before. Deputy Haskit was leaning up against the gun rack—weariness etched into his face. Sheriff Crawford was at his desk signing papers. He finished and handed the papers to a waiting Deputy Evans who then exited the office.

Crawford took an unlit, half-smoked cigar from the ashtray, popped it in his mouth and chewed on the end. He looked up at his visitors. "Y'all look as confused as I feel."

"Why didn't you tell us about the mark on Tyrell?" Norma asked—her tone blistering and direct.

"You know why, Norma. It was bad enough that Tyrell was dead. Just having one of the Macinaw Seven murdered was enough of a problem, but then throw in Henry Brooks...."

"The people have a right to know."

"The right to know what?" Crawford asked. "That the crazy man who scared this community to death years ago is back? That we have another Henry Brooks on our hands? To be honest, Norma, I didn't know what to do with the information. I'm still trying to wrap my head around it. Besides, everything is case-sensitive right now. I don't want anyone blabbing any of this to the public."

"Explain more to me about these angel tattoos," Chan interrupted. "You and Norma both said that Brooks carved them into his victims."

"That's right. Henry Brooks was a psychotic killer who used the demonic angel Abaddon, and Michael, the archangel of the Lord, as a means to separate his victims."

"What do you mean separate?"

"Those who were good would go to heaven and serve God," Norma stated. "And those who weren't would spend an eternity in a fiery abyss, tolling for Satan."

Crawford nodded. "Exactly. According to Henry, the two angels resided in him and were in a constant struggle with each other, vying for people's souls to add to their mounting armies."

"Mounting armies?"

"For Armageddon," Crawford said. "Henry believed a war of souls was coming and that he was the chosen device in which heaven and hell divided these souls." Crawford shook his head at the absurdity. "Pretty screwed up, huh?"

"To say the least," Chan said. "How did he decide the fate of his victims?"

"Don't know, really. It seemed a fairly random selection— any fly in the web so to speak. It's hard to understand a mind as warped as Henry Brooks' that's for damn sure." Crawford leaned back in his chair and momentarily looked to the ceiling as he tried to recall some of the victims, "Walker Stevens, Ancil Tucker, George Garrick, Esther Jefferson... all locals with little to no connection... besides living on the same side of the Edisto as Brooks."

"Esther Jefferson," Norma repeated. "Sweet lady. She lived alone out there off Watkins Bridge Road—she had been recently widowed. Friends saw her at church that morning, doing as she had always done, going through her normal routines." She looked over at Chan. "They found her tied to a tree behind her house—butchered like some animal."

"Many of his victims he lured to his home and killed them out there. We found several in that old barn of his," Crawford said.

"Once he selected a victim," Norma added. "He would kill them with his right hand if the soul was destined for Michael and used his left hand for Abaddon."

"Right. They say he was ambidextrous," Deputy Haskit said, raising both his hands.

"Tell me about the tattoos," Chan said.

"Sigils," Crawford corrected. "It's the signature or mark of the angel. Abaddon had one as did Michael." Crawford looked at Haskit. "Did you get Henry Brooks's file?"

Haskit leaned up off the gun rack and pointed. "There on your desk, Sheriff."

Crawford scanned his messy desk. He found a yellowed folder jammed with documents. He pulled off a rubber band used to hold the folder together and flipped through the papers. "Here." He pulled a page and turned it so that Chan could see.

It was the sigil for Michael. A long fluid line adorned with loops and sharp angles. Chan traced the sigil with his finger. "Looks like the number *two* with a cross on the bottom and then a series of scribbled peaks and valleys."

"It's an ancient sigil," Norma stated. "They have found it on the walls of tombs, churches. It was even tattooed on several preserved bodies that were unearthed in Turkey in the 1950s."

"Supposedly, the sigil contains the essence of the angel or demon in question and gives the bearer the power to summon it when needed," Crawford said. He pointed to indicate Norma and his deputy. "We were all schooled on this stuff years ago. Though to be honest, I never thought we would have to talk about it again."

"And this Abaddon, the demon angel, had one as well?" Chan asked.

Crawford pulled another paper from the file and showed it to Chan. "Henry used a pentagram-like emblem to indicate Abaddon—the encircled star there. Generally, he would carve these sigils into his victim's chest after stabbing them in the throat."

Chan looked up from the drawing and caught everyone's eye. "So now someone is using Henry Brooks' methods again. To murder two of the Macinaw Seven."

Crawford blew out a held breath. "It appears so. Crazy as it sounds."

"And what of the other five men?" Norma asked. "I know of at least three that still live in Macinaw."

"We've got patrols out already on the known addresses, monitoring their homes and streets," Crawford confirmed.

"It's gotta be just a scare tactic," Haskit said. "Get inside those boys' heads."

"It's working," Chan chimed back in. "Somehow Luther knew that Henry Brooks had gotten to Tyrell and believed that he would be coming after him. The night he shot at me he was scared to death."

"And now he *is* dead," Norma said.

Deputy Evans appeared at the door and interrupted. "Sheriff, phone call for you. Line three."

"Okay. Thanks." Crawford focused on the reporters. "Look, I better take this. I've got a long night ahead of me, and I've told you all that I know to this point. We will set up some kind of press conference when we know more."

Norma and Chan rose, thanked the sheriff and left.

Outside the law enforcement complex, the sun was still high in the Macinaw sky and the temperature still hovered near ninety degrees.

"What now?" Chan asked

"I'll head back to the paper, get started on our story. You hang out around here in case we need to squeeze out any more information from Crawford," Norma said as she walked to her car.

"Norma," Chan called out. "Not to make assumptions, but Ellis Dover still harbors a lot of hate for the Seven."

Norma came to a stop. "How much hate?"

Chan thought for a moment and then said, "Enough hate to raise the dead."

JUNE 27, 1976

7:56 AM

Chan followed the Lowcountry highway out of the city as he headed south. The morning edition of *The Macinaw Republic* lay on the passenger seat—its headline screamed: SECOND MACINAW SEVEN MURDERED. The associated article on the front page was just as provocative: HENRY BROOKS' METHODS USED.

As unfortunate as the subjects of the articles were, Chan couldn't help but feel a bit of pride that his name was added to the byline alongside Norma's. It was his first article ever and it was front page news. It had been picked up by *The State* and *The Post and Courier*, two of South Carolina's largest papers. The story was so hot that Darby ordered two additional printings to keep up with demand. Chan laughed to himself when he thought of how earlier in the morning Darby had congratulated Norma on the articles but then had completely snubbed him, only demanding that Chan get his coffee. *Keeping me humble, I guess.*

It had been decided that Chan would continue to highlight the Brooks angle in the paper for the next few days, and so he was first instructed to interview the psychiatrist that had done the final analysis of the madman before his execution. Chan protested, thinking that his time would be better spent on gathering information on the recent killings, but Norma convinced him that a look into the past may help clear up things in the present. Besides, any article on Brooks was a sure-fire seller for *The Republic*.

Chan passed the hospital on his way out of Macinaw. He thought about taking five minutes and wheeling in to say hi to Jean, but he wasn't sure if she would be working today. Closer to the truth, he didn't want to look like a fool and get shot down by a woman he barely knew as he feared he may have read too much into their moment they had shared days ago. So he rolled down the window, fired up a Marlboro Light, slipped *Toys in the Attic* in the eight-track tape deck, grinning as he joined Steven

Tyler's bellow, "...talk about something you can sure understand. 'Cause a month on the road and I'll be eatin' from your hand." He and Mr. Tyler met the morning journey head-on.

11:33 AM

Chan maneuvered down Lighthouse Road on Hilton Head Island until he reached the Harbor Town Yacht Club in the Sea Pines Resort. He had been to the coast before but had never spent any time this far south of Charleston. He thought the drive into Sea Pines was especially appealing with its oak-lined streets, exquisite homes and manicured lawns.

Boat traffic was already picking up as dozens of vessels pushed wakes along the Intracoastal Waterway and headed to the open ocean. Chan parked, passed the marina's series of shops, and crossed a walking bridge to the semi-circular dock area. The morning heat was on the rise, and so was the smell, a mixture of the harbor's pleasant and unpleasant aromas.

As he continued down the wooden planks, he glanced at the numerous yachts and sport fishing boats resting comfortably in their slips. The names ran from the grand: *Nautilus*, *Poseidon*, and *Liberty* to the sublime: *Fishful Thinking*, *Meals on Reels* and *Lobster Mobster*.

On the fourth to the last slip, Chan came to a 1972 fifty-three-foot Hatteras fishing boat called *Whaleman*. It was stark-white fiberglass, scrubbed clean from top to bottom. The fly bridge stretched well into the island's blue sky—a tower Bimini Top blocking the sun. The *Whaleman* had polished teak wood on the deck and cabin door. The door was latched open and Chan heard noises coming from the galley.

"Hello? Dr. Barron?" Chan called out.

Dr. Cliffe Barron appeared in the doorway holding two heavy fishing rods. He was an older man in his mid-seventies, a pleasant face under choppy white hair and beard. He narrowed his eyes at his visitor. "Are you the reporter?"

"Yes, sir. I'm Chan Adams with *The Macinaw Republic*."

He motioned with a wave of one of the expensive rods. "Well, come aboard, then." He waited as Chan leaped onto the deck. "Give me a few minutes to put these away, and I'll join you up top."

Chan nodded as he passed the galley door and continued around to the bow. He bypassed two cushioned lounge chairs and made his way to the very end of the Hatteras. He scanned the Calibogue Sound as the warm, summer sun sprinkled diamond patterns off the quiet waters. Having been sequestered in the swamplands of Macinaw for the past two weeks, a touch of the coast was just what Chan needed. He closed his eyes and soaked it in.

"Beautiful day, isn't it?"

Chan spun around. Dr. Barron had returned. He was wearing shorts, flip-flops, and a baggy shirt—the uniform of man who no longer had pressing engagements. He had also donned a floppy hat and aviator-style Ray-Bans to protect his eyes.

"Yes, it is," Chan replied. "I imagine you have quite a few beautiful days down here, Doctor."

He smiled. "Oh, yes. When God gets tired of heaven, he comes down here and stays with us for long weekends."

Chan laughed and then glanced around the vessel. "Not a bad looking boat either. You keep her in tip-top condition, I see."

"My home away from home," Barron said. "And no pesky grass to cut."

Chan nodded but then cut the pleasantries short. "I appreciate you seeing me today. I have a lot of questions regarding Henry Brooks. My editor said you wouldn't mind."

Barron frowned a bit but then shook his head. "Not the avenues I care to travel down much these days. As a psychiatrist, I don't generally discuss patients with reporters, even deceased patients, out of privacy and confidentiality concerns, of course. However, I am willing to talk about the part of Henry's case that I know is already part of the official forensic record—if you think it's important...." He gestured to the two lounge chairs and they both sat. "They tell me you have a copycat of sorts up there in Macinaw. Is that right?

"Two victims in a week, Dr. Barron. Both were stabbed in the neck and both had angel sigils carved into them."

"Sounds like our boy, Henry. The victims were local?"

"Yes," Chan said simply. He started to say more but thought it best not to get into all the Macinaw Seven details with the doctor at this time.

"Well, how is it that I can help you?"

Chan pulled out his notebook and pen. "First, can you tell me how you got involved with Henry Brooks?"

Barron placed his hands over his chest and interlocked his fingers. "I was with the South Carolina State Hospital in Columbia at the time. I worked with many of the patients housed in the maximum detention buildings. I guess I had developed a bit of a reputation for analyzing some of our more difficult patients. I wasn't subspecialty trained as a forensic psychiatrist, but let's just say I had a knack for it. Henry was ordered by the court to undergo extensive evaluation upon his arrest in the fall of 1963, and I drew the lucky straw."

"What were your first impressions?"

"I'd be lying if I said the hairs on the back of my neck didn't stand on end the moment he was brought into the observation room. He was a thin man, perhaps the thinnest I have ever known. His skin seemed only window dressing for his skeletal structure. Completely emaciated." Barron gritted his teeth as he remembered. "His eyes seemed close to bursting right out of his head as if the slightest pressure would pop them out completely."

"And your professional opinion?"

"Henry was... well, a difficult patient to precisely diagnose. As we shrinks sometimes say, 'He didn't read the DSM'—that's the psychiatrists' diagnostic manual. I don't recall all the details about most of my patients, but Henry was different—I could never forget *his* details. Without question, Henry was psychotic. Clinically, he met the diagnostic criteria for paranoid schizophrenia. He experienced auditory hallucinations and he had a well-formed system of bizarre religious delusions. Those angels of his, Abaddon and Michael, were a core part of his religious delusions. But it's important to understand that paranoid schizophrenics with religious delusions are a dime a dozen. Most are only harmful to themselves. They scare the hell out of people because they're strange, but most are as dangerous as kittens. There was more to Henry than his psychosis, or to be precise, there was less to Henry..."

"Less of him? What do you mean?"

"Henry lacked a conscience. He lacked remorse. He lacked empathy. He lacked that part of the human mind that allows most of us to behave as safe, polite neighbors—that part of each of us that allows our species to get along without killing each other. Henry lacked that vital part of being human. And because of that, he enjoyed killing people. Most psychiatrists would describe Henry as having a psychopathic or sociopathic personality. The technical term now is antisocial personality disorder, but I prefer psychopath... less clinical, more evocative, don't you think? In addition to being a paranoid schizophrenic, Henry was a psychopath and that's what set Henry apart. And he was smart—very smart—and malicious as hell. That is a very dangerous combination, my friend. Those were the special snips and snails that this serial killer was made of. As interesting patients go, he was a once in a lifetime case. I suppose Henry was the pinnacle of my career; but he gave me many of these white hairs on my head."

"And what got Henry Brooks to that point, Doctor?"

Barron wiped a bead of sweat that ran from his forehead and looked over at the reporter. "That's a long story, my friend, and I'm feeling a little famished. Can you stay for lunch?"

12:22 PM

They sat outside the Quarterdeck Restaurant overlooking the harbor and its famed red and white striped-tower lighthouse. Chan had a go with the restaurant's double-cheeseburger and onion rings while Cliffe Barron enjoyed their celebrated blackened jumbo shrimp. Both complimented their lunch choices with Budweiser drafts.

"So, about Henry's background?" Chan asked.

"Sad, to be honest, but also wickedly fascinating at the same time. Whenever I could get him to talk about his family he spoke about them fondly, but, God, what a complete can of worms...."

Chan took a drink of beer. "What was the root of his delusions? Why angels?"

"In addition to his pig farm, Henry's father was a well-oiled Pentecostal preacher. In the 1930's, he came to Macinaw from Western North Carolina, the Appalachian Mountains, and began his own church. They were bizarre believers—snake handlers—fire eaters. They put their faith against any and all tests. I'm afraid Henry was subjected to the worse of his father's stringent beliefs."

"Like what?"

Barron wiped his mouth with a paper napkin. "He often took young Henry to his barn out behind their house. It was where he kept his snakes for church handling. The father would release two rattlesnakes from their cages onto the floor and put Henry on a stool in his bare feet. The father stood on a broad, sturdy wooden box and beat him severely with a belt, taunting him to jump onto the floor if he had enough faith in God."

Chan blew out of breath of disbelief.

"As you can imagine, Henry developed a fascination with right and wrong. Over the years, he manifested these beliefs into the two representing angels, Michael and Abaddon. He believed to the very end that the two angels resided inside of him, waging a war for lost souls."

"What happened to his family?"

"His mother died in '32—snake poisoning—can you imagine? The father disappeared around '38. The neighbors reportedly stopped seeing him around the farm. Henry claimed he went back to North Carolina, back to the Smokies. But my guess is he was among the scattered bones found buried in that old barn of his."

"So, Henry remained alone afterwards?"

"He was about twenty years old by then, but yes, that left him in charge of the farm which he ran by himself. He had only one other sibling, a brother, who died of the 1918 flu pandemic before Henry was born. He had no wife. No other relatives."

"Isolated, confused, severely damaged. Did anyone ever try to reach out to him?"

"He indicated to me that the voices kept him company. The angels. He sought no help because they told him all he needed to know."

"Including when and who to kill."

"Yes."

"He was obviously unstable, Doctor. Surely the courts saw this."

Barron nodded as he drained his draft beer. "At his trial, Henry was represented by Crane and Campbell, an ambulance chasing group out of Columbia. They really didn't try too hard to put up a defense as I recall—completely out of their league. Many people believed they represented the man just for the free publicity." Barron threw his napkin on his plate. "It was the 1960s and South Carolina at the time was a state of agitation, separation, and execution. So, on the fifteenth of March, 1966, they squeezed every bit out of Ol' Sparky's electrodes to rid us of one Mr. Henry Brooks."

4:39 PM

Norma raced up the church steps, opened the doors of the vestibule and immediately felt cold air rush out to greet her. She came inside and paused for a moment as her eyes adjusted from the bright Carolina sun.

She made her way into the large sanctuary of Northfork Chapel, an African Methodist Episcopal church, and scanned the interior. A custodian was sweeping the carpet in front of the altar.

"Sir, excuse me, but can you tell me if Reverend Anderson is here today?"

"Yessum," the old man said. "He back there in his office." He pointed the direction with the end of his broom. "At the end of the hall."

Norma thanked the man and followed through the door to the right of the choir loft. She followed the mauve-colored hallway past several empty offices until she reached the last one—the closed door adorned with the moniker: Associate Pastor. Norma knocked gently.

There was a momentary pause and then the door opened. "Well, hello there, Sister Wiles, how are you today?" William Anderson asked. The portly clergyman backed up and welcomed her in to his office.

"I'm fine, William. Glad to see you're doing okay," Norma said as she entered and took a seat opposite Anderson's desk.

"Yes, ma'am. I'm well...despite all that's happened." Anderson sat behind his desk.

Norma pulled out her notepad and took a good look at Anderson. He was dark skinned and even though he was close to thirty years of age, he still had a round, cherub-like baby-face. "Of course, that's why I'm here, William."

"I'm sure you have questions, Norma, but I'm afraid I have few answers. I'm as puzzled about Tyrell's and Luther's deaths as anyone."

Norma nodded as she wrote. "Had you spoken with them recently? Had any contact?"

Anderson shook his head. "No, of course Luther was a member here, but he had not been to church in weeks. Any contact I had with him before was only for church related business." He lowered his voice. "We never spoke about our past."

"And Tyrell?"

He shook his head again. "Nothing. I knew he was here in Macinaw. But through the years, I may have seen him only three or four times. We acknowledged one another but that was it."

"What about the other members of the Seven? Deonte Johnson, Ja'Len Wells, Darius Grimes or Brandon Cheeseboro?"

"After the trial, we went our separate ways. I haven't seen or spoken to them in years."

"I see." Norma scanned her notepad. "William, did the Macinaw Seven have anything to do with Henry Brooks?"

Anderson's eyes widened. "No, of course not. I read that in the paper too. Very strange, isn't it?"

Norma tried reading through Anderson's poker face. "Are you sure, William? Nothing from the Orangeburg Massacre? Nothing from the day of the Dover boy's murder? Nothing from the trial?"

Anderson smiled half-heartedly. "Henry Brooks had been dead for years before any of that, Norma. We were just a bunch of kids at the wrong place at the wrong time. Our trial proved that. We had nothing to do with the death of that white boy. And we certainly had nothing to do with Henry Brooks."

"What did happen that day, William? How did you seven end up at Ellis Dover's barn?"

William shrugged his round shoulders. "You know the story as well as I, Miss Norma. We were just out walking. We came up the hill out there, saw that big red barn of his and wanted to take a look. Just curiosity really." Norma squinted her eyes with doubt, but William continued. "We peeked inside and saw him hanging there… that rope around his neck… my God, it was awful. We all just freaked out and ran away as fast as we could."

Norma sat in silence for a moment hoping for more. She then tapped her pen on the pad. "Okay," she finally said. "Well, I've got addresses for Johnson and Wells and I'll check with them. See if they have anything to add. Do you know the whereabouts of the other two?"

"No. Like I said, we went our separate ways. I don't know where they are now."

Norma stood. "All right, then, I thank you for your time." She slipped him her card. "Please call me at this number if you think of anything else."

She paused before turning to go. "You know I'm just trying to help, William. The last thing I want is more of our people dead."

"Of course," he said. "A pleasure to see you again, Sister."

The conversation ended and Norma left. Anderson held his position for a few moments staring at the closed door.

"All right. She's gone now."

A closet door to Anderson's right opened. Four black men, the remaining members of the Seven, stepped out from hiding. They huddled in front of the desk as Anderson gathered them in with his eyes.

"Like we agreed years ago—not a word about any of this. Do you understand? Keep quiet and keep low. Or sure as hell, we'll all be facing Henry Brooks."

OCTOBER 2, 2016

12:56 PM

After the morning investigation at Henry Brooks' farm, Tindal and Chan returned to Chan's house. Tindal wanted to see all of Chan's old notes and articles from the forty years before. She had pulled her boots off and was sitting cross-legged on his floor—mounds of notebooks, newspapers and documents surrounded her.

Chan walked over from his bar and handed her a glass. "What's this?" she asked.

"Whiskey. On the rocks."

"Isn't it a bit early for cocktails?"

Chan frowned and looked at a wall clock. "You're a writer, Tindal. I'd say we're about an hour late as it is."

Tindal smiled but sat the glass down beside her without taking a sip. Chan shrugged and drained his glass.

"None of this makes sense," Tindal said as she directed her attention back to the paper pile.

"Murder rarely does."

"I know, but what would anyone have to gain by knocking off the Macinaw Seven?"

"Revenge," Chan said. "Especially if you think that they had something to do with your son's death."

"Still think it was Ellis Dover?"

Chan sat down on the floor next to Tindal. She smiled again as he exaggerated the ache of crossing his sixty-two-year-old legs. "Sure. Why not? He had motive and the resources to get it done. It made sense then; it makes sense now."

"But your investigation turned up nothing on him. He had alibis in all but two of the murders. Even if he had hired someone like you theorized, why wait so long? He had ample opportunity before. And another thing: Would a man like Dover risk everything that he had built in his life to kill seven people? It just doesn't seem plausible to me."

"Perhaps he was biding his time, waiting for the right moment. I don't know. But there was little else to go on. And there were no other suspects, unless you want to believe it really was the ghost of Henry Brooks."

Tindal held up an old copy of the Macinaw Republic and pointed to the headline: VANISHED. It described the night of Sheriff Crawford's disappearance. "You said it yourself; you thought Crawford was on to something. Who else was in that squad car with him?"

"Witnesses said there were three people in the car that night. Two up front and one in the back. We can assume the other one up front was Deputy Haskit as he's been reported missing since that night as well."

"And in the back?"

"No one was sure. It was at night, and it was raining. But the FBI will do a DNA test on the corpse, so we should have a positive ID soon."

"What was Crawford working on at that point?"

Chan shook his head. "He kept everything close to the vest. At the time, he was being hounded by civil rights groups, the FBI, everybody. And he saw us, the press, as a nuisance, always kept us at arm's length. By that point I'm sure he was sick of seeing me around the station."

"Didn't the feds have a theory?"

Chan shook his head. "Too much ego on their part. That group never much likes to admit defeat. They left it as on-going."

Tindal mulled it over and then asked, "Do you think Crawford's disappearance was tied into the murders of the Macinaw Seven?"

"That's the million-dollar question, isn't it? What if Crawford and Haskit had picked up the killer? What if he was that third person in the squad car? Why did they end up at Henry Brooks' farm? And how did all three end up dead at the bottom of that hill?"

Tindal bit down on her lip. "It is crazy. So many pieces to this puzzle."

"And none fit." He paused as he crunched an ice cube from his glass. "Now you know why I drink so early in the day."

Tindal smiled at Chan's light-hearted comment although she knew there was more to his dependency than the puzzling mystery. She then ran her hand through the slush pile of papers. "Okay. That part of the story has to be the end game anyway. I think we may be rushing things here. Take me back to the last week of June, after Luther's murder. Macinaw was in an uproar. You and Norma Wiles were checking leads. What happened next?"

JUNE 28, 1976

5:07 AM

Chan hopped out of the shower and dressed quickly. Although he usually woke around five thirty, he couldn't sleep and was anxious to get to work to continue processing the story. His tie-in article on the history of Henry Brooks had won the approval of his editor (Darby actually patted his shoulder slightly) and was running in the morning edition.

He arrived at *The Republic* in short order, grabbed a copy of the paper and sat down alone in the bullpen. After reading his own contribution, he read Norma's article on the fallout over the deaths of Tyrell James and Luther Jennings. He thought about the impact their deaths were having on Macinaw. He had heard the whispers in the black and white communities. Talk of fear ran rampant on the one side, while the talk of justice permeated the other. It was the same old story. No matter how much progress was seemingly made in racial matters, something was sure to come along and split the harmony right down the middle.

Chan stood to fix a cup of coffee when the realization hit him: What was happening now had the potential to be devastating to Macinaw. Left unsolved, the deaths of Tyrell James and Luther Jennings would eat away at the stability of the town until those *train tracks*, both real and imagined, would no longer keep the townsfolk from tearing each other apart. He resolved then and there that he would not let that happen. He would stop this Henry Brooks "wannabe" before it was too late, before the town fell into complete chaos.

9:08 AM

Chan was back on the road heading down the Lowcountry highway again. He would next interview Sonny Watts, the lawyer who had taken up the case for the Macinaw Seven and did the near impossible job of convincing a mostly white jury to acquit them in the murder of Robert Dover. It seemed a good idea to pick his brain over the case and glean as many details from the past as possible. Perhaps Watts would even be aware of a connection that existed between his clients and Henry Brooks.

Darby and Norma warned Chan of Watts's somewhat eccentric nature, and he got a first-hand look at that eccentricity as he pulled up in front of his sprawling place in the southern tip of Macinaw County.

Watts was standing above a forty by twenty-five-foot excavation to the right of his white columned house. Piles of rich, black earth formed the perimeter of the dig. The man was an interesting sight standing there in muddy boots and covered by a royal purple robe. A cigarette dangled from his mouth. He held a rolled-up paper in his right hand and was instructing several Mexican laborers who were toiling down in the pit.

As Chan parked and made his way over, he saw that Watts was a man of some forty-plus years, solidly built. He had light brown hair that fell over his ears and into his eyes. He kept swooshing his hair back with his free hand so that he could see. He greeted Chan with a partial grin.

"You must be Chan Adams." He maintained the cigarette in his mouth—blinking the exhaled smoke from his eyes.

Chan took his outstretched hand. "Yes, and you are Mr. Sonny Watts."

"Correct. Forgive our bit of construction here. I have long dreamed of adding a pool to my compound—for cooling off on days such as this." He swooshed his hair again, flicked sweat from his nose and then discarded the cig in the open pit.

Chan nodded, admiring the work. "I'm sure it will be nice, Mr. Watts."

"Call me, Sonny, please. I hear Mr. Watts all day long in the courthouse."

"Very well, Sonny. Thanks for agreeing to see me."

"I have a deposition today in Summerville at 2:00 p.m. Until then, I'm at your disposal. But let's go inside—get out of this heat, shall we?"

Chan followed the man up the brick steps of his home. Watts kicked off his boots at the entrance and led Chan through black double-doors and into the foyer. A wooden staircase stretched high to a balcony on the second floor overlooking the foyer. Chan was immediately taken to the animal heads on the walls of the room—an impressive selection of African springbok, blue wildebeest, gazelles and a massive Cape buffalo.

Watts then led Chan into a study just off the foyer. It too was handsome and maintained the same safari theme. More exotic animal heads poked through the wall behind a grand black oak desk on which Watts placed the plans for his pool. A side wall contained bookshelves lined with stuffy-looking law books. "My favorite room in the house," Watts announced. "I bought the house eight years ago when I moved here. Belonged to a local doctor who had just passed. I wanted this place to represent who I am." He moved behind the desk and patted the long, furry neck of an African Impala. "Brought all my darlings with me."

"It's very impressive. Does your wife approve?" Chan asked innocently.

Watts laughed. "No. And that's why they're here and she's long since gone."

Chan grinned at the cavalier comment.

"Please, have a seat," Watts said with a wave of his hand.

As Chan sat in one of the plush reading chairs, Watts backtracked to the study's entrance. "Ximina! Ximinia, come here, please."

Within seconds an older Mexican woman in a simple smock appeared at the entrance. She handed Watts a starched white shirt.

"Ximina, bring us two lemonades." He held up two fingers. The woman nodded and disappeared to the back of the house.

Watts returned to his desk. Before sitting, he removed his robe, revealing a pair of pinstriped grey slacks. He slipped the white shirt over his undershirt and then sat without buttoning it. He offered Chan an odd-looking cigarette from a silver case on his desk.

"It's a *Kretek*," Watts said. "From Indonesia."

Chan fired up the clove cigarette, a crackling sound followed. He then inhaled deeply. "Interesting flavor. From Indonesia, did you say?"

Watts nodded as he lit his and blew the sweet-smelling smoke. "A friend of mine works in shipping in Charleston. He gets me a case every now and then."

Chan placed the smoke in an ashtray on a small circular table next to his chair. "So, Mr. Watts, I mean, Sonny…"

"You want to know about the Macinaw Seven," Watts surmised. "You want to know about the court case, how I got involved, how they were acquitted that year, the fallout after the trial." Watts stood and slipped on a pair of black loafers that were behind his desk. He began to button his shirt. He eyed Chan with the *Kretek* hanging from his mouth. "And you want to know if there was some connection with the mass murderer, Henry Brooks."

Chan nodded. "Macinaw, the whole state of South Carolina rather, is understandably curious."

Watts opened the top drawer to his desk, pulled out a pair of silver cufflinks and ran them through the eyes on his shirt sleeves. "Well, let me answer the last one first. There was absolutely no connection to Henry Brooks. Those kids were frightened when they were brought in that day. Crawford and his boys had roughed them up pretty good; I managed to calm them down. But from that initial meeting to preparation for the trial to the days in court to the acquittal, none of those kids said anything about Henry Brooks."

"Might *you* or your firm have mentioned something to them about Henry Brooks? Even in the most obscure context?"

"No. At the time I didn't even know who Henry Brooks was. There was never any mention of him. And nothing since I became involved."

Chan jotted his words down in his notebook. "And how did you get involved exactly?"

Watts smiled and brushed back his hair. "Well, I've always been a bit of a crusader. I got wind of what was happening that day and rushed down to the jailhouse before they could railroad those kids."

"You volunteered to represent them? You weren't in the public defender's office, were you?"

"No, but if they didn't have quality representation they could have ended up paying the price for the Dover murder. I just didn't think it was right. I may have been brash, idealistic… maybe a bit naïve, but I didn't want what happened in Orangeburg to happen here. I didn't want a Macinaw Massacre."

Ximina appeared at the study entrance holding a tray with two lemonades and a folded black tie. Watts grabbed the tray from her and slid it on his desk as he dismissed her. He then handed Chan one of the glasses.

"Made with real lemons. Enjoy," Watts said.

As Chan took a quick sip, Watts grabbed the tie and, as if done a thousand times before, expertly tied it around his neck within seconds.

"No compensation for your efforts?" Chan continued the inquiry.

"Their families paid bare minimums. But what was more important was seeing justice done. Check with my office and you'll see that is not a rarity for me. Sometimes I can't help myself in pulling for the underdog. It's part of my nature."

Watts sat on his desk and drank his lemonade. As he did, Chan scanned the trophy heads behind him and wondered if Watts' nature included underdog status for those animals as well.

"Very open-minded of you," Chan said. "I'll bet there aren't that many lawyers around here who would have done the same for those kids."

"Well, if you're hinting at the racial differences, I'd like to think I am a representative of the new South, Mr. Adams. A South without the old barriers, the old clichés. Take Ximina and my pool crew for example," Watts continued. He then put his hand to his mouth as if he were whispering the words. "They're here in South Carolina illegally."

"Oh?"

"Yes. But I give them odd jobs to do around here. I even let them camp in one of the fields behind my place. Soon they'll have enough *dinero* to have their families move here, get nationalized and be a part of the Macinaw community." Watts smiled but then quickly said, "You won't print that about them being illegals, will you?"

Chan dismissed the thought with a shake of his head and moved on. "Tell me about the acquittal. I read you were able to conflict the prosecution's star witness."

Watts drew down the corners of his mouth as he thought about it. "She conflicted herself, really. Mrs. Teresa Glazer—a widow who lived near the Dover estate. She has since passed away. Anyway, the police had the seven kids who ran from the Dover barn that day, and it was Mrs. Glazer's testimony that she witnessed the seven running from the barn—identified them all. But on the stand, under cross examination, and with the Bible underhand, she swore that she had initially counted *eight* young men running down the road. And later I showed her pictures of the seven and she swore that it was them, but I had replaced two of the seven with pictures of different black kids. It wasn't much, but it was enough to cast some doubt on her testimony." Watts brushed back his hair from his eyes and laughed. "Roy Todd, the state's prosecutor at the time, was so mad that he could spit fire. He spent all that time building the case, tying those kids to the Orangeburg Massacre, making it a case of vengeance against the troopers' acquittal in that case. He thought he had it all locked up. But the reality was that there was no evidence against the Macinaw Seven—except for the fact they were there in the vicinity."

"And why were they there?"

Watts took a drag from his crackling *Kretek* and smiled. "No law against walking down a country road, is there?"

Chan smirked and then looked at his notes. "I also read that as part of the defense you pushed the suicide theory—a hanging not a lynching."

"Yes. To me it was obvious. I believe the poor Dover boy hung himself."

Chan furled his brow. "Why would he do that?"

Watts threw his hands in the air. "I'm not sure, but have you met his father yet? A man like that could do a lot of damage to a kid's psyche."

Chan nodded as he recalled his meeting with Ellis Dover. "So, the jury comes back and acquits the Seven. What happened after?"

"I'd like to say we all lived happily ever after, but this is Macinaw, so no such luck. To say things were tense between the white and black communities is putting it mildly. Crawford and the police continued to harass my clients. They trumped up charges of larceny and drug use against the Seven to the point where it ran a few of them out of the county. But to be honest, life does move on and I've had little contact with any of the Seven since the trial."

Chan continued to prod Watts for the next twenty minutes, but basically, they rehashed most of what was already well-known. After mutual pleasantries were offered, Watts led Chan out of his house and back to the front lawn where they first met.

"If you think of anything else that might be useful, please call me at the paper or at my home," Chan said. "Anything at all."

Watts nodded. "I will. Good luck with the story. I sincerely hope the police can stop this new Henry Brooks. It's high time we put all this madness behind us."

As Chan made his way to his car, Watts moved back to the pool dig and stood over his workers. Chan drove away from the house down its old plantation-style road lined with mature Magnolia trees. It struck him how this new South was not so far removed from the old one. And he wondered if the irony of that fact had been completely lost on someone like Mr. Sonny Watts.

2:11 PM

Sheriff Justin Crawford sat alone in the Palm Leaf Café. Lunch this week had been late every day, if at all, and Crawford just wanted thirty minutes of peace to enjoy his turkey sandwich and iced tea.

But as the café's door swung open, Crawford knew the growls in his stomach would have to wait.

Ellis Dover with a scowl and sullen eyes slid his big frame into the booth seat opposite the sheriff. He dropped a copy of *The Macinaw Republic* on the table top.

"You seen this?" Dover said tetchily.

Crawford glanced at the headlines. "I've seen it."

"Goddamn witch hunt," Dover said. "And they're making *me* the goddamn witch."

"It doesn't go that far, Ellis—although you would be well-advised to watch your mouth around the press from now on."

Dover scanned the headlines again himself. "Little mutt of a dog, comes barking at me in the barber shop. Catches me off-guard." Dover re-focused on Crawford. "Everybody in this town can read between the lines, Sheriff. They have a helluva nerve thinking I'd even care to knock off those black sons-a-bitches."

Crawford glanced around and then brought his hands down close to the table signaling Dover to lower his voice.

"I don't give a damn who hears me, Justin. I just need you to handle this."

"I have no power over the press," Crawford said.

"And I'm not gonna be the punching bag for *The Macinaw Republic*, the NAACP and any two-bit porch monkey who thinks it's a good time to get at the man. I need to be cleared of all this."

Crawford shrugged. "You're not a suspect, if that's what you're getting at?"

Dover feigned surprise and put his hand over his heart. "I'm not? Well, la-dee-da. That's mighty white of you, Sheriff."

Crawford frowned and leaned over the table. "Listen, Ellis, I don't pretend to deny that you've had my back in every election since Newton's death, but I can't steer a murder investigation anyway you want it to go just because of that fact. You just need to sit tight and shut that big mouth of yours. We'll catch this killer soon enough."

"Like you did for my son's murder?"

Crawford pounded the table with his left hand. "Goddamn it, Ellis. We arrested the Seven. I collected every bit of evidence I could find on those boys. It was circumstantial at best. It didn't hold up."

"They were radicals for God's sake! Probably members of the goddamn Black Panthers. They were on a mission that day to come take what was most precious from me. And they did, Justin. They found my boy and strung him up. Took the life right outta him and me!" His voice quivered with rage.

Crawford caught the furtive glances and worried faces of the other customers in the café. "I know, Ellis. I know," he said calmly. "I'm sorry about Robert. I'm sorry for your loss. It's just that evidence went against us that day. It happens."

Dover quieted in response as well, to the point of being strangely stoical. He sat for a moment in thought and then, "The paper said Henry Brooks' methods were used on the two colored boys, James and Jennings."

"That's right," Crawford said. "The sigils and everything."

Dover nodded again. "The death angels. I remember that so vividly. During those terrible months, I never let my boys go outside to play. They lost a part of their childhood because of that monster. And now it's happening again. Interesting."

The sheriff eyed Dover as he solemnly got up from the booth. The man, whom many considered the most powerful person in Macinaw, then walked out of the café without another word.

Justin Crawford looked down at his plate and the waiting sandwich, but the sheriff's appetite was long gone.

4:44 PM

At *The Macinaw Republic*, Chan sat at the desk he shared with Norma. He stared at his typewriter—his piece on Sonny Watts was nearly complete. He would give it another run-through and then pass it to Norma before submitting it to Darby and his critical eye. But he realized the article, like everything else he had submitted to this point, was raising more questions than answers. Watts didn't know of a connection of his clients to Henry Brooks, yet the sigils and Luther's vocal belief that Brooks was after him indicated there was. But it couldn't be Brooks. *That's not a possibility.*

Chan went to Darby's office and asked for the file on the deceased killer. Like the one that Crawford had, Darby's file on Brooks was thick, yellowed and filled with dog-eared documents. The editor turned it over to his rookie without comment and Chan didn't know if that was a sign of respect or indifference—although he wouldn't bet against the latter.

Chan took the file to the bullpen and spread it out on the table. Every news article on the disappearances and killings, every op-ed piece during those years, every photograph of the atrocities, every police report, medical analysis and court document on the case was seemingly jammed in there. Chan felt well-versed on the story so he focused more on Darby's copies of the police and medical reports.

As he scanned the 1962 coroner's analyses of several of the victims, he became intrigued by the language dealing with the "sharp force injuries" or stab wounds. Specifically, Chan learned that the "Abaddon" victim had small skin tags or abrasions on the left side of the penetrations and especially on the sigil. The "Michael" wounds had them on the right side. These minute, jagged cuts indicated direction of the entry into and away from the victims' flesh. This led investigators to the theory of a right handed and left handed killer. It was no surprise then when they finally arrested Henry Brooks that he was ambidextrous. His divided mind had truly split him down the middle—the two angels vying for control—occupied his left and right side respectively.

Chan picked up the phone in the bullpen and called the sheriff's office. After several minutes of waiting and transfers, Deputy Jimmy Evans picked up.

"What do you want, Adams? We're busy down here," Evans said.

"Put me through to the sheriff, Deputy."

"He's busy. What do you want?"

Chan was a bit put off by Evans' brusqueness, but he kept his focus. "Have you seen the coroner's reports on James and Jennings?"

"Yeah. What about it?"

"Have you looked at the details, Deputy Evans?"

"I told you I've seen it, Adams."

"The cuts. The sigils. Did they have the same small abrasions, the same skin tags as the ones Henry Brooks left in his victims? The ones that indicated if he used his left hand or his right hand?"

There was a brief pause on Evans part and then, "If I speak to you Adams, you keep my name out of this. You understand me?"

"Yes, of course," Chan readily agreed.

"I mean it now. If I see my name in the paper, I'm gonna come over there and stomp your ass."

Chan rolled his eyes but kept the same tone in his voice. "It will be an undisclosed source. I promise."

"Well, okay then. It was the first thing we looked for after Luther was killed and marked with the Abaddon sigil. It had the left-sided abrasions whereas Tyrell's marks had the right indicators. And one other thing, Adams, back in the day, they never found the knife that Brooks used on his victims. The wounds on these two colored boys look identical in shape and depth to those made in the early sixties."

"So, exactly the same as Henry Brooks' knife?" Chan questioned.

"That's right. But again, you didn't hear any of this from me."

Before Chan could thank him, Evans hung up. Chan lit another cigarette and then picked up an old photograph showing one of the past victims with the Michael sigil carved into his chest. He then picked up a photo of one with Abaddon's mark and compared the two. He shook his head as the cigarette smoke wafted past the photos.

"Exactly the same," he said to himself.

9:18 PM

The Lakeside Motor Court on the east side of Macinaw County near Interstate 95 was curiously named as there wasn't a lake within thirty miles of the place. It was a shabby, one level motel with only twenty-five units available. It had a twenty-two dollar a night rate, but one could finagle an hourly price if needed. It was next to an oily Shell station which saw heavy, constant traffic from I-95. And Dolly's Dollies, a hole-in-the-wall strip club, was right down the road.

Sheriff Crawford pulled his cruiser into the parking lot with his lights flashing and joined Deputies Haskit and Evans. An ambulance was also parked near the deputies' squad car. Two paramedics waited outside the vehicle.

"Two more of the Macinaw Seven?" Crawford asked Haskit.

"I'm afraid so, Sheriff. Grimes and Cheeseboro. Both moved out of South Carolina years ago, but here they are in this place— dead as doornails."

"Who made the call?"

Haskit pointed to a large woman in a floral moo-moo and tennis shoes who was leaning against the wall of the motor court's office and sucking down a cigarette. "Miss Taylor, the manager," Haskit said.

"She witness anything?"

Deputy Evans shook his head. "Just made the discovery. And there was only one other guest here at Lakeside and he didn't hear or see anything either. He's been ordered to stand-by."

"How long ago did this happen?" Crawford asked.

Haskit shrugged his tired shoulders. "The medics think within the past few hours, but can't be sure. You want to talk to 'em?"

"Not yet. Payton on his way?" Crawford asked, referencing Payton Medlin, the county coroner.

"He's been notified."

Crawford scanned the entire motor court, processing the scene. A thunderstorm had passed through there earlier in the afternoon leaving puddles and a muggy stillness to the air.

Crawford finally focused in on the manager and made his way to her.

"Evening, Miss Taylor," Crawford said. "Sorry about all this."

The woman nodded her jowly face, her eyes still big as saucers. "Liked to freak me out, Sheriff. Saw it coming out from under the door yonder. Stepped right in it." She lifted both of her feet and showed the blood stains on the rubber soles of her heel-worn shoes.

"I'll need to look at your records and ask you some follow-up questions after I check the scene. Okay?"

Taylor threw down her cigarette butt. "I ain't going nowheres."

Crawford walked back to his deputies and pointed at the unit with the open door.

"Yep, number eleven," Haskit said. "They're in there."

"It's not pretty," Evans added.

Crawford nodded. He stepped lightly around the stain and entered. Darius Grimes' naked body was curled up behind the open door. Several savage stab wounds shown on his back and neck area. His blood had not only seeped under the door, but it also soaked the cheap blue carpet from where his body lay to the bed. The sigil of Abaddon had been carved into his back.

Crawford carefully maneuvered around the body and continued to the bathroom. The door was not completely open, but Crawford could make out Brandon Cheeseboro's torso hanging out of the tub. Michael's long, flowing sigil had been carved into the inside of his left arm.

"One good. One bad. Both dead," Crawford whispered. He turned to Haskit who was watching from the door. "Bobby, get the camera from my car."

"Yes, sir."

"And while you're at it, call the station and pull all the shifts. Let's double the watch on the remaining three."

"Will do."

"And Bobby, also get Pebo to put in a call to sheriffs Vance Boone in Orangeburg and John Seigler in Colleton. They both said they would send us some of their deputies if we needed help." He blew out a long sigh as he took in the blood-stained room. "It looks like we'll need all the help we can get."

SEPTEMBER 12, 1963

With her right leg freed from the lower rope, she delivered a hard kick to the man's midsection. He dropped the long, serrated knife and doubled over in pain. In that same instant, she struggled to loosen herself from the other rope that crossed her chest. She leaned back against the stall door and felt it give a little. It wasn't much, but it was enough to allow her to slip both hands to the inside of the restraint.

The man came to his feet and grabbed the fallen knife. He growled in pain—appearing even less human than before. "God has forsaken you!" he bellowed. "You shall bear the mark of Abaddon! You shall burn as you await his beckoning!"

She tore her shirt and the skin from her back as she frantically pushed the rope away from her chest and over her head while simultaneously sliding down against the rough wooden stall door. The skeletal man grabbed her arm but she broke free of his grasp and then lunged toward the barn exit.

She stumbled and fell, twisting her knee as the door flung open. Adrenaline lifted her again and she hobbled across the barnyard toward her car. Breathless, frantic and with shaky hands, she opened the car door. But then as she looked inside, her heart sank. *Damn it! The keys!* They were in her purse which was now sitting on a table inside the madman's house. She looked up and saw him making his way toward her.

In her wildest nightmare, Lee Hill Phillips would never have dreamed such a scenario. Hired by the Department of Health, Education and Welfare only two weeks before as a medical census taker, she had been charged by the agency to spot-check the health of the populace in rural South Carolina counties as part of President Kennedy's Community Health Services Act. She had visited Allendale, Bamberg, and Orangeburg already and this was to be one of her first visits in Macinaw. She had crossed over the Edisto River on Watkins' Bridge and followed the long, meandering dirt road through the dead corn fields until she came to a worn farmhouse. She was greeted by a sickly-looking man named Henry Brooks who had invited her in, eager to comply with the survey.

He had been kind in his responses, sharing stories of his family's health and whereabouts. He told her how his brother had died as an infant and how his parents had moved back to North Carolina to be with his dying grandmother. How he was all alone, but tried his best to take care of himself and the farm. When he indicated that his animals were due their afternoon feedings, he insisted that she come along with him so that they could continue the questioning. She knew he had to be a bit lonely out there by himself, so she had agreed to keep him company. With his appearance and home life, she had felt sorry for him.

Now Lee felt nothing but fear. She breathed heavily. It was completely dark and she was bleeding. *God, what do I do?* He was coming, and he still had the knife. She looked around for something to use as a weapon, but there was nothing. He yelled at her as he neared, "You cannot escape! You have been chosen!"

She panicked and ran into the field behind her. There was no plan. No other thoughts. *Just run.*

The ground was uneven and rows of withered corn stalks shot up at different angles like tribal spears left over from an ancient war's battlefield. She felt a painful jolt in her knee every time she put pressure on it. On the soft dirt, the knee gave way and she fell again, a broken stalk jabbed into her side. She gritted her teeth, jumped up and pushed on, running haphazardly through the field.

She then remembered the highway. It was a good distance away, but that would be her goal. If only she could reach it, she might be able to flag someone down. Yet at this point, she couldn't even be sure if she was running in the right direction.

Lee kept on.

After several minutes, she fell in exhaustion between two corn rows and hid. She pulled her legs up to her chest and tried to get her breathing under control. Her eyes focused on the path she had made, watching for any movement. She rocked back and forth, whimpering, wiping tears from her eyes, ready to spring to her feet if need be.

She heard him again, somewhere in the distance. "There is no escape! The king of locusts seeks you! You will be found!" And then another menacing sound, the cold start of an engine. She saw the headlights shining into the field and heard the engine grind as he plowed toward her. She stood and saw the dried stalks fall away—wave after wave being crushed by the fast-approaching truck.

Lee took off again, heading deeper into the field. She continued to run as fast as she could. Her lungs burned and her leg muscles screamed. She would periodically fall and lay there in her exhaustion until she heard the truck nearing again. This would continue for several minutes. Each time her resting period got shorter and shorter. He was gaining on her.

She plodded on, her legs cramped, her knee beyond pain. The fields begin to spin as the engine noise grew.

Dirt flew up on her as he wheeled the truck past her. He cut a hard right and the old truck slid until its headlights now faced her. He revved the engine as Lee went to her knees too exhausted to run anymore.

"Please," she barely uttered. "Please don't do this..."

She couldn't see him at the wheel, but his window was down and she could hear. "It is your time. Tonight, you shall be marked for all eternity."

In her heart, she knew it was futile, but Lee would not give up. She yelled out at him in pain and frustration. She then stood, turned and ran as fast as she could. She heard the engine grow louder. She felt the white-hot headlights on her. She lost her balance and then felt the bone-crushing collision as the speeding two-ton truck punched her body, tossing her into the air.

Lee flew several yards from the impact, breaking both her arms and her right leg as she landed on the hard pavement of the highway and rolled to a stop. She was barely conscious. She lifted her head slightly as the headlights came into view and then stopped two feet in front of her. She heard the truck door opening and then boots on the pavement.

"No..." she whispered before passing out completely.

OCTOBER 3, 2016

Chan woke on his couch as he heard noise coming from his kitchen. He sat up and rubbed the sleep and the effects of last night's whiskey binge from his face. He scanned the den. Papers of all kinds remained scattered on the floor and an empty bottle of Wild Turkey lay on its side on the coffee table.

The morning was like the thousands of other mornings that had come before—complete with an achy head, blurred vision, little accomplished and hopes faded. For years, the Macinaw Seven case had become Chan's cross to bear—a desperate measure to find answers. He became obsessed with it and it seeped into all aspects of his life. He had maintained his job at *The Macinaw Republic* during that time, but that's all it was: a job. His journalism career took a slow, painful decline in the latter years until it came to a complete stop two years ago. And while his book about the case released in 1982 had found a modicum of success, he was often a no-show on his limited book tour, and the royalties and notoriety soon dried up.

Tindal, holding a cup of coffee, walked in from the kitchen. She grinned at Chan's condition. "Need a cup?" she asked.

"More like the whole pot, please."

Tindal laughed and walked back into the kitchen and then returned with a second cup. She handed it to him as she joined him on the couch.

"Thanks for letting me crash here last night," she said. "Very chivalrous of you to give up your bed for little ol' me."

Chan took a sip. "Chivalry aside, I probably would have ended up on the couch anyway. I sleep out here most nights."

Tindal smiled although she knew there was a great deal of pain behind the nonchalant comment. She studied his face—the age lines, the glassy red eyes, the sadness. She liked Chan and regretted his self-induced path to destruction.

Chan stifled a yawn and tried to focus on his guest. He noted that although she was still wearing the same burgundy sweater from the day before, she had removed the leggings from underneath. She crisscrossed her legs and massaged her bare feet as she drank her coffee. He thought how nice it was to have someone like Tindal around. Although she was much too young and vibrant for an old man like him, he missed having a companion, especially one as pretty, strong-willed and intelligent as her.

He stretched his arms. "So, where did we leave off last night?"

"We were talking about Henry Brooks. You were telling me how they finally caught him."

Chan nodded. "Lee Hill Phillips. She was the young woman who escaped from his barn. He tried to run her down in his cornfield—chased her for several acres. Hit her with his truck, but she survived. Luke Williams, a black farmer who lived in the area, happened to be driving by when she was thrown onto the road. He scooped her up, put her in his truck and got her to the hospital in time. The next day, Acting Sheriff Justin Crawford, the deputies, the city cops and seemingly the whole county went out to the farm and threw the cuffs on Henry. They say Henry vehemently denied any wrong-doing, but Crawford searched the barn and discovered several decaying bodies. Then they drained a small pond out there on the farm and found four of the victims' vehicles that he had hidden in there—including Sheriff Newton's patrol car. The nightmare had come to an end."

Tindal leaned back into the couch; she propped up her feet on the coffee table. "But in 1976 the nightmare returned. And yet there never was a connection made between Henry Brooks and the Macinaw Seven."

"Oh, there was a connection. And the Seven knew all about it, but they wouldn't or couldn't admit to it. I have no doubt Luther was screaming Henry's name the night he shot at me. And when they found Grimes and Cheeseboro at the Lakeside Motel, we all knew they were in on some secret connection to Henry, but they never told us or the police about it. They continued to deny it to the bitter end."

"Why? The police could have protected them, right?"

"They must not have believed so." Chan set his cup on the table. "Henry Brooks provoked fear in the people of the Lowcountry. His name alone became synonymous with the boogey-man in these parts. Even after his death it was powerful juju."

"Juju?"

Chan smiled. "Objects, talismans even names can be juju. For casting spells—witchcraft."

"You think the Seven were under a spell?"

"More or less. There is a subculture in this area that firmly believes in it. The Seven believed it, I have no doubt. They were coerced into believing that Henry Brooks would come after them, *if*...." He stressed the word.

"If what?"

"That's the part I'm not sure, but it has to have something to do with what they saw in that barn that day."

Tindal sat up too. "What they saw? As in, they did not kill Robert Dover, but maybe saw who did?"

Chan nodded but shrugged a little as well. "A theory, Ms. Huddleston, only a theory."

Tindal thought about it for a moment. "And why were they there in the first place?"

"Ellis Dover was the most prominent white man in Macinaw. And they were seven black kids, disillusioned and hostile. If I were looking to make a statement after the Orangeburg Massacre, I would go there. Destroy Dover's barn— maybe burn it to the ground."

"But once they got there, they witnessed something far worse, a suicide or murder," Tindal said.

"Exactly."

"But, Henry Brooks? How does he fit in?"

"No one knows. Well, Sonny Watts, their lawyer, might have, but we'll never know now."

"Tell me about that. What happened to Sonny Watts?"

Chan scratched at his head, retrieved his cup and took another sip of coffee. "It was three days after they found Grimes and Cheeseboro. The blacks were upset. The whites were too. Hell, everybody was. People were screaming for answers, but none were forthcoming. Norma and I were working late at *The Republic* when I got a call from Sonny."

JULY 1, 1976

7:40 PM

Sonny Watts sat in his study reviewing a copy of an old deed to a parcel of land which had become part of a contentious lawsuit between his client and the client's well-to-do family. The tract was only one acre, but it sat right dab in the middle of the most pristine stretch of Edisto Beach with a 7,500-square foot monstrosity of a beach house backing three waves of dunes, sea oats, white sand beach and a lovely view of the Atlantic.

As a third-generation member of the family and designated as benefactor in his grandfather's will, Watts' client felt the beach house was his due. But the family contended that his spending of his trust fund, which they said was quickly done like "shit through a goose," had negated his claim to granddaddy's favorite retreat—as he could not be trusted to handle such a pricey commodity.

Watts placed the copy of the deed back in the file and closed the folder for the night. This fight had little bearing on him now—he had much more pressing things on his mind. He looked over at the clock atop his bookcase. He fought the urge and then grabbed the phone.

"Yes, this is Sonny Watts. I'm trying to reach, Mr. Chan Adams, please." He waited for the transfer and then, "Mr. Adams, Sonny Watts here." He listened and then, "Yes, good to speak with you again as well. Listen, you asked me to call you if I remembered anything that might have to do with my former clients, the Macinaw Seven, and Henry Brooks. Yes, I think I may have something. Perhaps something major." He listened again. "No, I think it would be in our best interests to speak about this privately." He waited. "Yes, tonight would be fine. If you don't mind, you could come here again." He listened. "Yes, thank you. I'll be waiting."

Watts hung up the phone. He felt a twinge of nervousness and opened his case of *Kreteks*. He lit one, took a drag until it crackled and leaned back in his chair. He glanced again at the ticking clock.

8:01 PM

As the minute hand slipped past the hour, Watts stayed at his desk, flipping through journals and magazines that had piled up in his reading basket. He was just looking at the pictures; he didn't have the focus for words. Sonny Watts was not shy when it came to taking a drink, but at this moment, he passed on it for the sake of staying clear-headed.

A rapid knock came to his front door. Watts looked up from his desk, brushing his hair from his eyes. He checked the clock one more time. He knew the young reporter would not be arriving for at least another twenty minutes. He began to feel a sickening knot develop in his gut. With a key from his pocket, he opened the locked middle drawer of his desk and pulled out a Colt Cobra .38 Special snub-nose revolver. It was loaded.

He stood and, with gun in hand, walked into his foyer. He slow-footed his approach to the door. He stopped, took a deep breath and then reached for the door handle.

8:27 PM

Chan drove down the magnolia-lined drive of Watts' estate, anxious like never before. Had he heard Watts correctly? Did the man actually know of a connection between the Seven and Henry Brooks? Hopefully, this would be the news everyone had been waiting for. The missing piece.

After he relayed the astonishing news to Norma, they both raced to Darby's office and informed him. The editor took all of three seconds to call the print production manager to put the next day's edition of *The Republic* on hold and send his reporter out the door.

With the late hour, traffic had been light, but Watts lived at the southern end of Macinaw County and it still took Chan nearly thirty-five minutes to get there. He pushed the Torino to the max, emboldened by Darby's words, "Get the scoop and to hell with the speed limit!"

Chan came off the gas however as he neared the end of the drive, his car rolling to a stop. He pulled up on the steering wheel and out of his seat to give himself a better view. He could make out the outline of Watts' house against the night sky. An orange glow emanated from the roof—and it was growing. Chan floored the car again until coming to a sliding halt in front of the house. He jumped out quickly, his chest heaving with excited breath. His eyes darted back and forth between the front windows. He could see the flames eating the house from within.

Chan bound up the stairs and reached for the front door handle. He sensed the heat through the black double doors and he heard the fire popping and crackling beyond. Chan pounded on the doors. "Watts! Watts are you in there?!"

He backed back down the stairs and scanned the house again. Heated glass in the front palladium windows shattered and fell. Black smoke filtered out through every crack in the old structure. "Watts!!"

Chan took off around back of the house, keeping his eyes on the windows for any movement inside. He rounded the corner and saw a back entrance into the kitchen. He tried the door but it was locked. He then leaned into the door, pulled back and threw his shoulder against it, breaking the lock and forcing it open.

Chan ran through the kitchen, past a dining room then a sitting room until he reached the hallway that bisected the house. The smoke billowed toward the back and Chan crouched against the wall. "Watts!" he called again. "Are you in here?!" He heard no response and continued to inch down the hall to the front of the house. The heat became very intense. Chan could feel it on his face.

As Chan neared the foyer, a portion of the ceiling collapsed and he heard an increased crackling of fire gestating on wood. The old house was going up quickly.

Breathing became difficult for him, and he coughed the smoke from his lungs. He almost turned around, but figured he had a few more seconds to search. "Watts!!"

He reached the foyer. Fire had raced up the walls, engulfed all the trophy heads and extended high into the balcony and beyond. The smoke cleared for a moment, and Chan saw Watts' body on the floor of his study. Before Chan could yell out again, a support beam fell and crashed on top of the body, engulfing it in flames. Chan spun and spat smoke. He went to all fours and began to crawl away.

He made it only a few feet when the whole house seemed to shift. The balcony toppled, fire and timber came crashing down. Chan put his arm up over his head to protect himself but fragments of the burning ceiling and upstairs flooring pelted him at all angles. He lunged forward. Heat and smoke plumed down the hallway. He struggled to one knee—blood oozed from gashes to his arms and neck. Falling ash burned down his back. He tried for a desperate gulp of air, but there was none to be had. Chan took one more blind, feeble step before the wall crumbled down on top of him.

Chan remembered intense heat, pain, suffocation and then nothing more.

JULY 2, 1976

8:11 AM

"Mr. Adams? Can you hear me? Mr. Adams…?"

Chan blinked his eyes with rapidity as he came around, trying to focus on the face before him. The young, light-skinned black man smiled at him.

"I'm Dr. Hawkins, Mr. Adams. You're safe now. You're at Macinaw General."

Chan felt the bandages, the band around his wrist; saw the IV drip, bed rail, and the lime green paint on the walls. "Again?" he managed to say.

Hawkins laughed. "Yes, sir. You're lucky to be alive. Do you remember how you got here?"

"By the grace of God?"

The doctor laughed again. "Most definitely. But what exactly do you remember?"

"Fire. The Watts house collapsing on top of me."

"Considering that, it's amazing you weren't burned more than you were. And we still need to run another series of x-rays, but you apparently suffered no broken bones either. You're very lucky indeed."

Chan took a deep breath as a wave of pain came and went. "How *did* I get here, Doctor? Miracles aside."

"One of Macinaw's deputies, Haskit is his name, happened to be patrolling that side of the county and saw the flames. He arrived just in time."

"What about Watts? He was in there too."

Hawkins shook his head. "As far as I know, you were the only one he got out."

"Damn," Chan whispered. He closed his eyes and mulled all that was potentially lost.

"I'm sorry," Hawkins said.

Chan opened his eyes. "Is Deputy Haskit here? I'd like to thank him for saving me."

"We released him last night—sent him home. He had a few minor burns, but was okay otherwise. But I'm sure he'll be by to see you later."

"What about me?" Chan asked as he tried to sit up. "When can I get out of here?"

Hawkins gently put his hand on his chest to keep him from moving. "In a day or two. If all goes well. In the meantime, rest and get your strength back."

"I don't know," he said lightly. "I'm not very good at lying around doing nothing."

"Please try, Mr. Adams. I don't want Nurse Reid here to have to restrain you."

Chan looked immediately to the foot of the bed. Jean Reid had been standing there quietly—chart in hand—beautiful as he remembered. They shared a brief smile. "I won't give her any problems, Doctor. I promise," he said to Hawkins.

"Good," Hawkins said and then stood. "I'll be back to check on you later." The doctor left the room.

"You know," Jean said, a grin slowly developing, "if you really wanted to see me again, you could've just called."

"Not my style," Chan said. "I figure when I ask you to marry me, I'll have to come into the emergency room with a harpoon in my chest."

They both laughed.

Jean sat in the chair next to Chan. "So, tell me what happened."

"I went out to see the lawyer, Sonny Watts. I think he had something very important to tell me about the Macinaw Seven— about the murders. By the time I got to his place, it was on fire. I went inside thinking I might be able to save him."

"Do you think the fire was set on purpose?"

"I don't know. At this point, nothing would surprise me." He sighed and then, "I wish he had called me sooner."

"This is getting so dangerous," Jean said. "You know, I've been following your articles in the paper."

"Oh? What do you think?"

"I've lived in Macinaw my whole life, Chan. I grew up with the stories of Henry Brooks. I know all about the Dovers, the Macinaw Seven, I was part of desegregation, I went to school with Luther Jennings's little brother, Antwan. All of this is breaking Macinaw's heart. Mine too. I just want this pain to end."

"I know. I'm sorry." Chan didn't know why he apologized, but it just felt right to do so.

"There's too much madness in the world."

Chan agreed but said nothing to that. He locked eyes with Jean—their connection was deepening. Jean caught herself and rose.

"Well, if you need anything, I'll be out at the desk. Buzz me and I'll be here." She reached over and rubbed his hand.

Chan took a chance and blurted out, "How about after they let me out of here, we go out? You know, like on a real date?"

Jean smiled, put her hand over her heart and ramped-up her best Southern belle voice. "Why, Mr. Adams, I never thought you'd ask."

10:11 AM

With no fire department to speak of within several miles—not even a community volunteer unit—the eighty-year-old Watts house had incinerated in a matter of hours. Only the brick steps, columns and foundation remained.

Sheriff Justin Crawford paraded around the burnt ruins of the Watts estate like a high school coach on a Friday night sideline. He sweated in the early heat as he marched the perimeter, an unlit cigar hanging from his mouth. He kept a sharp eye on the place as if his staring power alone could ascertain clues through the smoky, charred remains. His deputies waited near the swimming pool dig, not sure if their sheriff needed or even wanted their help.

A group of other men huddled by as well, among them was Archie Howe, Macinaw's fire chief. The sixty-three-year-old chief had been summoned by Crawford to help determine the cause of the fire. With little left as evidence, determination had been problematic, yet Howe used his forty years of fire-fighting experience to garner a few insights. Waiting to be summoned by Crawford, the chief stood around joking with the others.

Another man, wearing a blue blazer and understated tie, also stood with the others. But he didn't seem interested in small talk.

His focus was on Crawford, watching his every move. After a few minutes, he emerged from the pack and approached the sheriff.

"Sheriff Crawford," the man called. Crawford stopped marching and turned to face him. The man was of average height and build. Like Crawford, he was around fifty years of age. But unlike the sheriff, he had black rimmed glasses, sharp features and thinning hair that he wore slicked back. *FBI*, Crawford immediately thought. "Special Agent Mike Dunn, FBI, Atlanta office," the man confirmed. He produced a badge and credentials from within his coat and then quickly replaced them.

Crawford put his cigar in his left hand and offered his right. "What took you so long?" he asked lightly.

"We've been watching this one closely, Sheriff. It looks like it could get outta hand."

"It already has. I have four unexplained murders, a tragic house fire, a crazed killer back from the grave and a racially divided town ready to pounce on one another. I don't see how it could get that much more outta hand."

"We're here to solve your problems. We have resources and abilities that neither your small department nor your state's law enforcement division has." Dunn meant it as condescending as it sounded and Crawford certainly took it that way. The special agent took a step closer. "You probably feel a bit in over your head, and who would blame you? We have a lot of experience in these kinds of cases—civil rights, serial killings and the like. My team just put in six weeks of work on the Bradford Bishop case in Bethesda, Maryland; you may have heard of that one." He waited and when Crawford didn't respond he stated, "We know how to approach cases like this, break them down and get to the core problem. And because the ramifications of this case are so enormous, Sheriff, we'd ask that you put this one in our hands. Let us handle it for you."

"You and your resources are welcome, Agent Dunn. In fact, y'all can all stay in my little house while you're here if you'd like. But this case is very personal to Macinaw—very personal to me. I know these people, their habits, their concerns. I have off-duty officers from three counties rotating in to help us. They report to me directly. I think it would be more upsetting at this point to bring in a new mother hen, so to speak.

"Sometimes outsiders can get done what insiders can't," Dunn quickly added in an offensive tone. "I'll be taking over this case."

"No, sir, that won't be necessary."

"Now don't be obstinate, Sheriff Crawford. The FBI can supersede when times and circumstances call for it. I'm sure you know this." Dunn pulled a small notepad from his coat pocket. "To begin, I'd like to see your files on all this: the Macinaw Seven, the Dover case, even Henry Brooks. Then I want to interview all the principals involved, one at a time. I'd also like our medical examiner, whom I brought from Atlanta, to consult with your coroner—check against his records. I'll need you to give me his number." He paused as he caught the sheriff's eye. "These are not requests; you understand?"

Crawford grinned and held comment for a moment. He then looked over to his stable of deputies. "Deputy Evans, would you come here, please sir."

Once beside him, Crawford grabbed his deputy by the shoulder and turned him towards the agent. "Deputy Evans, this is Agent Dunn of the FBI. Would you escort Agent Dunn to Macinaw and take him to my office at the complex?"

"Yes, sir."

"Show him our files on the case—all of what we got."

"Okay."

"Make sure he's given complete and total access."

"Yes, sir."

Dunn nodded pleased with the sheriff's sudden change of heart.

Crawford continued, "And while in my office, would you show him the pictures I have on the wall. Especially the one near the middle, Deputy. You know the one."

"The one of you and FBI Director Clarence Kelley, Sheriff? The one at the dove shoot from two years ago?" Evans asked, fully aware of Crawford's intent.

"That's the one, Deputy. Make sure he gets a good look at that one," Crawford said.

"Yes, sir," Evans then stated to Agent Dunn, "Right this way, sir." Evans walked toward the parked patrol cars.

Dunn held back—his hands on his hips. "Keep playing your games, Sheriff Crawford. I don't flinch that easily." Dunn turned and stomped away.

Crawford shook his head as he watched him go. "Why do all the prima donnas end up at the Bureau?" Crawford then signaled for Fire Chief Howe who made the quick jaunt over to join him. "I need some good news, Arch. I know we don't have much to work with, but give me your best guess."

Howe looked again at the remains of the house. "This was Doc Haywood's old house. The wiring had to be near a century old. Not an uncommon way for these old homes to go. It started up front, so we can eliminate any kitchen fire. They say that the Watts man was a smoker. Mighta been a tipped over ashtray."

Crawford rubbed at his chin as he thought about it. "What about a deliberately set fire?"

"No gas cans lying around, no smell of accelerants in the air, no visible pour patterns. Most arsons are usually easy to spot."

"And the body?"

"Payton said he was burned to a crisp. More ash than skin. You won't get much help out of that."

Crawford dismissed the fire chief, "Thanks, Arch."

The sheriff turned back to the smoldering foundation, stuck the unlit cigar back in his mouth and chewed its ragged end. The newspaper people said Watts had something to tell them, something that tied the Seven to Brooks. But now the potentially biggest break in the case was literally up in smoke.

1:44 PM

Norma entered Chan's hospital room with a handful of daises and her best smile.

"I get smashed by a burning house and you bring me flowers?"

Norma laughed and put the flowers on the side of his hospital tray table which was occupied with his empty lunch dishes. "I was going to get you a lighter and pack of cigarettes but that seemed a little inappropriate."

Chan smiled. "Good call." He waited until she sat next to him and then sincerely added, "Thanks."

"How are you feeling?"

"Amazing actually. Who knew I would get addicted to codeine so quickly?"

Norma smiled; she then went to her purse and pulled out her pen and notepad. "So, tell me what happened?"

"Am I to be the story now?"

"You're a part of it. Darby thinks a personal perspective will add to the readers' interest. Everybody loves a hero."

"Some hero. I didn't get there in time, Norma. Watts burned up in his house and took the information with him."

Norma bit down on her pen. "Yeah, I've been thinking about that. Awful strange for his house to go up *after* he puts in a call to you."

Chan nodded. "If someone is going through all the trouble to knock off the Macinaw Seven, then surely they wouldn't be hesitant to take out their lawyer too."

"But only after he mentions a possible tie-in to Henry Brooks."

Chan shrugged his shoulder and winced slightly at his burn wound. "Could all be one big coincidence, Norma."

"I don't believe in them, Chan," she said. "And I know you don't either."

4:32 PM

Chan lay quietly on his bed contemplating the story and his second near-death experience. With Norma back at the paper and with Jean having finished her shift and gone home for the day, Chan was anxious to leave this place and get back to work. The unsolved murders haunted his dreams. So close to the story now, he felt a personal obligation to connect the dots, end the killings and finally reveal the truth.

His medicine kicked in again and he began to drift off when another knock on the door jostled him awake.

"Come," Chan said.

Bobby Haskit, in jeans and tee shirt, entered and stood at the foot of the bed. Chan noted the white bandages wrapped around his left hand.

110

"Hey, man, thanks for dropping by," Chan said with a smile.

"Just come to check on you. You doing okay?"

"Thanks to you. You don't know how much I appreciate what you did, coming in after me like that."

Haskit shrugged, a bit embarrassed. "House went up quick, didn't it? I'd say we both were lucky to get out of there."

"Tell me how it happened. I don't remember much."

"I was just out on patrol—had the Lowcountry Highway for the evening. I was heading home when I saw it on the horizon— the flames reaching up to the sky. I called in my position and headed to the house. When I pulled in, I saw your car parked out front. As soon as I jumped out, I heard you inside calling out for Mr. Watts. I ran around the back, saw the open door to the kitchen and went inside. By the time I made it to the hallway, the upstairs caved in. The broken wall must have covered you kinda like a tent—protected you from the debris and fire. Both of your arms were sticking out in front of you. I reached in and grabbed them, and you popped out like a cork." They both laughed. "Anyway, I managed to get us both out the kitchen before the whole thing came down."

"A true miracle. Thanks again," Chan said smiling. "By the way, my car…"

"We've got it down at the complex. Not a scratch on it."

Chan breathed another sigh of relief. "Good—a lot of paper routes as a kid and late night bartending at UGA bought me that sweet little ride."

"It'll be waiting for you when you get out."

Chan's smile faded a bit. "Any progress on the Grimes and Cheeseboro murders?"

"We're still processing it. Interviewing their families, checking for other witnesses, putting their timelines together, but I can honestly tell you nothing has come up yet. Weird as hell them being in town like that."

"They all know something, Deputy. The Seven had to have had something to do with Henry Brooks."

"I reckon so. But until they talk we'll just be pissing in the wind with guesses."

Chan agreed and then said, "How old are you, Deputy?"

"Thirty-four."

111

"Were you around during the Brooks era?"

"No, I'm from over near Darlington. Never really heard much about Henry Brooks until I came down here. But the stories the people tell about him..."

"He had quite the hold on them, didn't he?"

"He still does," Haskit said.

Chan paused as Haskit's words sunk in. "I keep hearing people say that. But why? He's been dead now for ten years."

Haskit deadpanned, "Sometimes death is not the end. If the presence is strong enough—good or bad—it can live on for much longer."

Chan laughed. "C'mon, Deputy Haskit, you're starting to sound like some of the superstitious folk around here."

"There's an old saying, Mr. Adams. If you believe it, then it's so."

"Well, I don't believe a dead murderer can come back to life and kill again," Chan said adamantly.

"But those that were killed might have believed it. And that's all that matters."

6:25 PM

Deputy Jimmy Evans sat in his squad car across from a 7-11 near downtown Macinaw. The FBI agent from Atlanta had assumed authority while Crawford was out of the office, and Evans didn't care to be bossed around so he lied that he had patrol and took off.

He had his windows rolled down and was sipping on a bag beer, waiting until he was officially off the clock at seven. An old red Ford truck pulled into the 7-11 and two men got out. Evans didn't recognize either one. They were both white and both had beards and greasy, long hair. The taller of the two, Roland Wolfe, looked to be close to three hundred pounds with meaty arms that he showed off with a black tank-top tee-shirt. The other one, Terrance Orton, was smaller, thinner, wore a leather headband, but had the same kind of look of trouble about him. As a lawman through the years, Evans had gotten good at sniffing out the troublemakers and his radar went off with Wolfe and Orton.

He watched them enter the store, waited a minute, got out of his car, and followed them inside. Evans noticed the girl behind the counter: a petite, country-cute, young brunette. She stood with her arms crossed, a bit anxious. He shot her a smile and she smiled back, relaxing in his presence. The two men were in the back of the store near the beer cooler. Evans positioned himself near the magazine rack and thumbed through the latest issue of Sports Illustrated with Kansas City Royal's George Brett's smiling mug on the cover.

Each of the men grabbed a case of Stroh's Light and headed for the front. They noticed the deputy but didn't seem to care. Evans got a whiff of marijuana as they passed.

Orton threw his case of beer on the counter and eyed the girl at the cash register. "Say, darling, why don't you join us for a little party back at our place?"

"Gotta work," she said quickly.

"Aw, man, c'mon. It'll be wild. I promise you we know how to party."

The poor girl said nothing but glanced up and forced a quick smile.

"Is that a yes?" He turned to Wolfe and laughed. He then turned back to the girl, his eyes taking her all in. "What time do you get off, sweetheart?"

"Late," she said, this time with a little anger underneath.

"Well, hell, I can wait." He laughed again. The big man almost smiled.

"Sorry, not interested."

"C'mon, babe. Don't shut me out."

"She said she's not interested," Evans voiced from behind.

Orton turned slowly, met the deputy's eyes, then turned back to the girl and smiled. "So what do you say? Want to come hangout with us?"

The girl looked right past the man and pleaded with her eyes to Evans.

"Listen, sport," Evans said, leaning in. "The young lady said she's not interested. So why don't you pay for your beer and then get on outta here."

Orton and Wolfe turned to face Evans who gave them a blank stare.

"I ain't done nothing wrong. And I don't see how this is any of your damn business," Terrance Orton said.

"I'm making it my business," Evans said, tapping on his badge. "You both would be doing yourselves a big favor by paying for your stuff and getting the hell outta here like I said."

Orton inched forward and got in the deputy's face. "Watcha gonna do about it if we don't?"

"Try me," Evans said.

Orton held his look of intimidation and then grinned slightly. He turned back to the counter. He threw his hands up like he was surrendering. "Sorry, babe, some other time."

Both men left their beer on the counter and walked out. Evans followed to the door and watched them until the truck pulled out of the lot.

"Thank you so much," the young girl said, breathless and smiling.

Evans turned to her. "No, Ma'am. Thank you. You may have just given us the first lead in the biggest case we've got."

8:22 PM

Evans drove out past Macinaw city limits to the small crossroads community of Snake Creek where Sheriff Crawford lived and pulled into the drive of the sheriff's modest ranch-style home. He exited the squad car and came quickly to the front door.

"Deputy Evans," Crawford said. "Could this not wait until tomorrow?"

"No, sir. You need to hear this now."

Crawford backed up. "Come in then."

As they entered a front parlor room, Evans asked, "How's Miss Judy?"

"She has her good days and bad. More bad days then good lately though. She's been confined to her bed as of late." Judy Crawford was the sheriff's wife who had been diagnosed with amyotrophic lateral sclerosis, the so-called Lou Gehrig's disease, three years before. The once vibrant woman and mother of his two sons had been slowly wasting away. The doctors were unsure of how much time she had left. Crawford had become very protective of her and her privacy—to the point that only a few people knew the seriousness of her deteriorating condition.

"Have a seat." Crawford indicated the couch and Evans sat down. The sheriff took a chair opposite his deputy. "What's this all about?"

Evans explained the late afternoon events at the 7-11, walking the sheriff through every detail. Crawford was becoming a bit anxious until Evans got to the most important part: "And then he threw up his hands like he was giving up, and that's when I saw them."

"What?"

"Sigils, sir. On each forearm. A pentagram on his left and what looked like the beginning of Michael's mark on his right."

"Are you sure?"

"Yes, definitely," Evans said. "And I think the bigger guy had 'em too."

Crawford rubbed his hands together. "Did you get the plate numbers?"

"Already ran 'em through. Bobby is getting the info from Pebo now. He should be here shortly."

Crawford nodded. "What about the FBI man? Does he know about it?"

"No, sir. He's camped out in your office, plowing through the files. We thought it best to notify you first."

Crawford grinned. "Thanks, Jimmy. Good work so far."

Headlights soon careened through the parlor window. Both men jumped up and were quickly out the door. Deputy Haskit had arrived. He got out of his cruiser, still dressed in his civilian clothes. The three men met on the driveway in the glare of the car's headlights.

"Pebo tracked the vehicle, Sheriff," Haskit said. "It belongs to Ryan Grubbs."

"I know Grubbs," Crawford said. "He stays over in Eastland Heights."

"Yeah," Evans added. "They call him, Rhino. He's been busted a couple of times for possession and minor disturbances. Heard he's running crystal meth now. The two at the store may be part of his supply line—they could've borrowed his truck."

"Maybe it's time for another roundup at Eastland," Haskit said. "A little search and seizure—see what turns up."

Haskit and Evans looked to the sheriff who nodded then said, "Tomorrow is the fourth. Good a time as any for some fireworks."

OCTOBER 3, 2016

1:23 PM

After a quick shower and change back at her motel, Tindal returned to pick up Chan and drove them back to the Brooks property. Black clouds had rolled in during the early afternoon giving the ill-fated land and farmhouse an even more surreal quality.

Three of the Macinaw County Sheriff's Department's patrol cars remained parked behind the house guarding the cut road that led to the crime scene. The Macinaw sheriff himself, Tony Monroe, was among the group stationed out front so that SLED and the FBI could continue their investigation unimpeded.

Monroe was the first African-American to hold the office of sheriff in Macinaw County since the post-Civil War Reconstruction days. A former Macinaw High football hero, Monroe played college ball for Buddy Pough at South Carolina State and then joined the military for six years before returning to work in law enforcement for his hometown. He moved up the ranks quickly and was overwhelmingly voted in as sheriff in the last election. Although physically intimidating, he had an easy-going way about him that made him popular with both the whites and blacks. He greeted Tindal and Chan as they approached.

"Hey, folks. Out sight-seeing again?"

Tindal laughed. "That's the problem, Sheriff; there are no sights to see, unless you're willing to let us take a stroll down the road."

"Nope, can't do that," he said with a smile. "I've had to turn around dozens of reporters today—major news outlets: NBC, CNN, FOX, several local television vans from Columbia, Charleston, Florence. I even had to shoo away two helicopters circling the place."

"Can you make an exception for an old friend?" Chan asked.

"Sorry, Chan, the FBI and SLED would have my ass. They're still down there—cranes, bulldozers, trucks—must be fifty people working the scene."

"Any word on what they've found?" Chan asked.

117

"They're taking it real slow. They've excavated the patrol car from the swamp but there is a ton of dirt and sludge inside and they don't want to disrupt any possible evidence." Monroe leaned up off the vehicle and whispered to the reporters, "I did hear they found signs of gun fire."

"Were all three in the squad car shot?" Chan followed.

"Don't know that for sure."

"How about a peek inside the Brooks' house then?" Tindal asked.

Monroe shook his head. "Still off-limits too. Not until the FBI clears it." He noticed their sour looks. "I told you earlier, if and when I get the word, you guys will be the first to be notified. Okay?"

Chan and Tindal thanked Monroe and headed back to the rental car. Tindal went to start the engine but turned to Chan instead.

"So what now?"

Chan looked over at the old house. The wind from the approaching afternoon storm blew across the dead fields and rattled the rusted tin roof. A strange feeling came over him—guilt but something more. Chan could sense Henry Brooks. He was close—out in the fields—near that dilapidated barn—inside the house. He was there, all around them, laughing at them.

"What's the matter?" Tindal asked.

"I stopped, Tindal. In 1976 I stopped. I didn't finish the job. I was close, but I didn't finish. I should have kept going, should have figured it out."

"No one blames you for not solving the case, Chan. You went through hell. And as you said, it was very complicated. There are so many parts to this."

Chan stroked his grey goatee. "But only one constant."

Tindal nodded. "Henry Brooks."

"Yes, Henry Brooks."

They sat in silence for a moment. "Okay," Tindal said, "so what would you have done next? If Brooks is the key, what would have been your next move?"

3:40 PM

They arrived at the law offices of Crane and Campbell on the corner of Blanding Street and Main in Columbia. The rain storm had come and gone during the ride up from Macinaw leaving the capital city wet and sticky.

Chan and Tindal found a parking spot and hustled over to the old building that housed the law office. An empty hallway and an immediate rise of stairs greeted them as they came through the door. They stood just inside the hall and waited.

A grey-haired woman smartly dressed in long blue business skirt and matching coat approached from down the dark hall, the wooden floor boards creaking beneath her.

"Yes, may I help you?"

"I'm Tindal Huddleston with the Reuters News Agency, and this is Chan Adams. I called earlier…"

"Yes, you spoke with me. I'm Mrs. Helen Darwin. You had interest in speaking with one of our lawyers, correct?"

"We're not seeking legal advice," Tindal said. "Just information."

"Oh, and what is this in reference to?"

"We are looking for information on Henry Brooks," Chan interjected. "We know Crane and Campbell represented Mr. Brooks at his trial in 1964."

"Henry Brooks? Well, my, that was indeed years ago."

"Yes, Ma'am, is it possible we could speak with Mr. Crane or Mr. Campbell?" Tindal asked.

"I'm afraid not. Both Mr. Crane and Mr. Campbell passed away some time ago. This firm, what little is left, is represented by John Cruise, Mr. Crane's grandson. And I'm afraid he is away from the office today."

"Is there anyone else who could help us?" Tindal followed.

"We have two other lawyers, Mr. Strickland and Mr. Reynolds. But neither of them would have any knowledge about the case. They're both spring chickens." She laughed.

Chan furled his brow. He then smiled at the woman and mustered as much Southern charm as he could. "And what about you, Mrs. Darwin? Helen? Could you help us with the information?"

"Please," Tindal added.

Darwin grabbed the necklace hanging between her coat lapels and rubbed a few of the faux pearls as if they were rosary beads. "Well, I suppose I could let you look at the files. No harm there. They are just sitting in the basement collecting dust."

"That would be very nice. Thank you," Chan said.

4:22 PM

Under a naked light bulb, Tindal sat at a folding table in the basement of the old building, waiting. Chan, carrying a box of files, emerged from a back room. Mrs. Darwin followed.

"I think that's all there is," Darwin said.

"We appreciate your help," Tindal said.

"We certainly do," Chan followed as he gently placed the box on the table. "I'll put it all back when we finish."

"That will be fine," Darwin said. She turned to the stairs, hesitated and then turned back. "You know, I started working here in 1979, two years before Mr. Crane passed. We've always been successful as a firm—we've always had enough business— well, enough to keep the lights on. But that case..." She pointed to the box. "I can't help but think it's been a blight on our name for all these years. Some may even call it a curse."

"Henry Brooks has been a curse for many people, Mrs. Darwin. He's been a curse for our whole state," Chan said. "And its high time that curse was lifted."

Mrs. Darwin nodded. "Well, if you need anything else, I'll be upstairs at my desk." She turned and ascended the stairs.

Chan looked at Tindal and asked with a smile, "Shall we begin the exorcism?"

"Let's get to it," Tindal said as she reached deep inside the box and brought out a handful of files.

5:47 PM

The basement took on a quiet presence as they read through Henry Brooks' court files, police records and evaluation documents. Only the hum of the light bulb and the occasional turning of pages could be heard. For Chan, it felt like déjà vu, having already poured much of his life into reading and studying about the madman.

Tindal finally stopped, rubbed her eyes, and stretched in her chair. "What a piece of work, huh?"

"Not your typical pig farmer, that's for sure."

"It always amazes me how these serial killers can get away with it for so long."

"No one ever expects it to happen in their town," Chan said. "You build walls to keep the monsters out. You never think you're walling them inside with you."

"But he had no grand disguises. No real desire to hide his purpose. It seems someone would have known."

"We can't fathom the depth of that kind of madness. It's near impossible to detect. The same was true for Dahmer, Bundy, and Gacy. Rational people want to smile, shake your hand, be good neighbors. These guys want to cut your heart out and offer it up as sacrifice to the gods or have it themselves for breakfast. Brooks was the same way."

"Yeah, but listen to this," Tindal said. She pulled her hair back behind her ears, looked down at the file and read, "I know their souls. I can see it in their eyes. They blink and I can see their salvation. Or their damnation. I am the angel of light. I am the angel of darkness. I will decide their fate. I will seek them out. I will find them in the cribs of their babes, the beds of their whores, in the dark corners of their hiding places. I am everywhere." She looked up. "That kind of madness is hard to hide, right?"

"I guess by the time you knew that side of him, it was too late—you were his next victim." Chan leaned over the table to look. "What's that from anyway?"

Tindal turned the file so he could see. "It's from an interview the firm conducted with Brooks while he was in the state hospital." Chan picked up the file and flipped through it. "They were probably trying to ascertain how best to defend him in court."

Chan laughed as he continued flipping. "Yeah, good luck with that."

"An insanity plea must not have been enough."

"From what I was told, that was just another excuse to execute in those days."

"We've come a long way from those days…which is ultimately a good thing." Tindal stopped as she noticed Chan's stunned expression. "What is it?"

Chan looked to Tindal and then back to the file. He remained quiet; making sure his eyes weren't deceiving him. He then pushed away from the table and stood.

"Chan, what's the matter? What's wrong?" Chan moved to Tindal's side of the table and laid the file in front of her. "What?"

"The form. It's the state hospital permission form. The one the firm had to sign in order to have its meeting with Brooks."

Tindal glanced at the worn document copy. "Yes. What about it?"

"Look at the signature."

Tindal's eyes shot down to the bottom of the form. Her mouth gaped open. "My God…Sonny Watts."

JANUARY 3, 1964

3:27 PM

Sonny Watts sat on the wooden bench in the visitors waiting area of the maximum detention building on the campus of the South Carolina State Hospital. He had on a black coat and tie and black shoes. His brief case was at his feet. He rubbed his hands compulsively.

A buzzing noise sounded in the room. He watched as the red bulb above the door darkened and the green bulb came to life. He heard the heavy metal lock being turned, and then the door opened. A giant of a black man dressed in a white orderly's uniform emerged. He smiled at Watts.

"Are you with Crane and Campbell?"

"Yes," Watts said, straightening up. "I represent the firm."

"Have you been to see him before?"

"No. First time."

He smiled again. "You'll do fine. Come with me, please."

Watts stood, grabbed his brief case, and followed the orderly through the open heavy door. They walked a long corridor. There were no windows only unmarked and unopened doors. Watts became conscious of every step and every breath he took. The farther he progressed in the old building, the farther he felt like he was descending into hell.

They passed another locked door where an armed guard stood watch. Immediately after the guard, they passed a nurses' station. Three busy nurses hustled in and out of the cubicles and paid Watts no attention.

Four more corridors branched off from the nurses' station. Watts followed the orderly down the one marked "A." They reached a certain point and the big man held out his hand. "Wait here, please." The orderly disappeared behind a door.

Despite the cold winter day outside, Watts felt flush and began to sweat. He pushed his hair out of his eyes as he waited. The door opened again. A man in his late-fifties and wearing a lab coat over his shirt and tie emerged. He smiled to put Watts at ease and then shook his hand.

"I'm Cliffe Barron, the attending psychiatrist for this unit. Are you with the Crane group?"

"I am. I'm Sonny Watts."

"You look awful young to be a lawyer."

"I've just taken the bar, waiting on the results. I've clerked for the firm throughout my years in law school."

"And they sent you to conduct the interview with Henry Brooks?"

"Don't let my youth fool you, Doctor. I'm very perceptive. I can handle our client."

Barron smiled. "Of course. This way please."

He led Watts into another room, clear of any furniture save a small metal table with two folding chairs on either side. An iron ring was bolted to the floor's center.

"You will sit here," Barron said. "Your client will be brought in and will take the other seat. Your conversation will be private, yet I must warn you not to incite him in any manner." Barron pointed to the wall. "A panic button is there for emergencies."

Watts sat and nodded politely at the doctor. He opened his brief case and removed several documents and a leather-bound notebook. "I'm sure we'll be fine."

"Very well," Barron said. "Let us know if we can further assist you."

Barron left the room. Watts squirmed a bit in his seat in anticipation of Brooks' arrival. He had heard the whispers of the others at the firm. They said the man was truly repulsive. That it was hard to look at him much less speak with him. But when he did speak, his coldness, his savagery sent chills down one's spine. Watts was no dummy. He knew the old men at the law firm wanted nothing to do with this monster, but the press, the notoriety was worth taking the case. Watts was just the firm's sacrificial lamb.

A door at the back of the room opened. The black orderly who had escorted Watts earlier entered; he held Henry Brooks by the arm. Watts felt his breath escape him. He had never seen a man so frighteningly thin before. He could make out bone structure wherever the skin was exposed. He was particularly drawn to the man's head—a skull with pale blue eyes. Without the man even uttering a word, Watts felt he was in the presence of evil.

Brooks sat in the folding chair as the orderly took the loose chain around the detainee's waist and locked him to the floor ring. The black man tugged on the chain, and finding it secured, exited the room. Watts looked directly at Brooks. He could sense the man searching his soul.

Watts swallowed his anxiety. "Mr. Brooks, I'm...."

"I know who you are," Brooks said. "You are the deceiver—the giver and the taker. There is light and darkness here. I can see it in your eyes."

Watts tried to smile but couldn't. "Mr. Brooks, I represent...."

"War is coming. The end is nigh. No more pretending now. You shall be called. You must pick up the cause."

"Cause? And what cause is that, Mr. Brooks?"

Henry Brooks flashed his yellowed, crooked teeth. "You will burn, but you will rise from the ash. Your power is not to turn water into wine, but to turn the wine into poison. Betraying God is easy, deceiver, but when you betray the devil, there's hell to pay. My end is your beginning. It is your destiny."

JULY 4, 1976

6:22 AM

The Eastland Heights Trailer Park was located in a lot on the outskirts of the town of Macinaw. A scraggly pine forest stood to its left, and to the right, a high fence separated it from the yard of a salvage company. A low-lying fog covered the grounds making the trailers look like abandoned ships moored in some forgotten harbor.

Most of the inhabitants of Eastland were still asleep when five patrol cars rolled down the center dirt drive. Grubbs trailer was in the back of the lot—a shabby brown and white single-wide with loose underpinning. Grubbs' beat-up, red truck was there as were several motorcycles.

Crawford exited the lead patrol car, pulling the warrant from his pocket and making a fast approach. Local magistrate, Wilbur Shaw, one of Crawford's fishing buddies, came up with a drug search warrant based solely on the sheriff's late night say-so.

He banged on the trailer door. "Ryan Grubbs? This is Sheriff Crawford. We have a warrant to search the premises."

The silence inside was broken by startled movement. Crawford turned and winked at Deputy Haskit who was standing behind him. Haskit drew his weapon, reared back and kicked open the door.

At that same moment, a screen door swung open on the back of the trailer. Terrance Orton, the smaller man from the 7-11 incident, ran out barefoot and shirtless. He made it to the bottom of the back stoop when Deputy Evans stepped in and swung a two-by-four that clubbed him in the knee, sending him yelling and cursing to the ground. Orton rolled on his back and held his bruised knee.

"Well, what do you know?" Evans mused. "If it ain't the party-man himself."

With the entrance cleared, Crawford followed his deputy into the front room. Roland Wolfe, Orton's partner, sat on a couch in his boxers next to an overweight woman who was squeezed into an extra small tee-shirt. Wolfe had no expression but his eyes fired daggers at the lawmen.

"Where's Grubbs?" Crawford asked.

The back-bedroom door opened and Grubbs walked out—a naked woman partially draped in a bed sheet stood behind him. Grubbs was over six feet tall and well-built. Like the others, he had a beard and long hair that fell past his shoulders. He had had just enough time to slip on a pair of jeans.

"Well, well, the high sheriff himself. How's it hanging, Crawford?"

"I should ask you the same, Rhino. Long time no see."

"So, what are you and Macinaw's finest doing in my house so early in the morning?"

Crawford held up the warrant before returning it to his pocket. "Looking for drugs. We got wind that a pipeline may be running right through the center of your home."

Grubbs shook his head. "Not here, Sheriff. We're clean."

"Really? I hear meth comes through here by the truckload."

"I don't know who the hell told you that, but your info sucks."

Crawford moved closer to Grubbs. "C'mon, Rhino. You know if we search hard enough, we'll find what we're looking for."

Grubbs grinned at the not so subtle hint. "You boys always do." He then moved even closer to Crawford and lowered his voice. "What's this all about?"

Crawford grabbed him by the wrists and raised them to eye level. Grubbs had the same sigils of Abaddon and Michael tattooed on his forearms. "Do I really need to explain it to you, Rhino?"

Grubbs jerked loose from the sheriff. "They're just tattoos, man. Nothing illegal 'bout that."

"But murder is."

"Man, I didn't have nothing to do with killing them colored boys. I got witnesses."

"Who? These shit-bag rednecks?" Crawford indicated the couch. "You better come up with better witnesses than that."

Grubbs snorted like a mad bull. "What do you want, Crawford?"

"Information… for now. Report to the law complex this afternoon at one. And bring these *witnesses* with you."

Grubbs frowned. "Today? C'mon Crawford. It's the fourth of July."

"That's right. So be on time or we'll be back to put a firecracker up your ass."

11:00 AM

With the temperature already over ninety degrees, Macinaw was in for a blistering fourth of July holiday. Chan drew deeply on the offered cigarette and blew the exhaled smoke out the passenger side window. The breeze was hot but it felt so good to be out again. Norma had picked him up from the hospital in her ride, a '71 brown Pinto Runabout, and headed for the law enforcement complex to get his car.

"What's the latest?" Chan asked.

"Talked to William Anderson again. He still denies any knowledge of Henry Brooks."

"He's lying."

"I know, but what can you do? It's their dirty little secret and they're not telling anybody."

"Watts knew. He said it might be something major."

"But what could he have discovered between last week and yesterday?" Norma asked. "He claimed he knew nothing before."

"He said he hadn't seen the Macinaw Seven since the trial—unless one recently paid him a visit. Is that even possible?"

"I don't see how. Crawford has had the remaining three under constant surveillance."

"Right. So, barring some outside contact, Watts must have remembered something from six years ago," Chan said. "I'd like to read the transcript of the trial again."

Norma nodded. "There's something else."

"What?"

"There's growing sentiment in the black community that the police aren't going to be there to protect them. That we are on our own. Maybe even have to protect our own."

"Hmmm. That could be a problem."

"There's a meeting later at Anderson's church. Some high-profile organizers will be there."

"You going?"

Norma nodded. "Darby wants me to cover the parade today, but I plan to swing by there later."

"I'll do it. I mean, I'll cover the parade for you—take the photos, talk to the mayor, interview a few locals. You go take in the meeting."

"Feeling well enough to go?"

"Yeah. Besides, I plan on being at the fairgrounds tonight for the fireworks anyway so I might as well cover the whole thing." He hesitated and then added, "I've got a date." Norma looked over at her young friend and smiled at him until he laughed. "Is there some problem with me having a date?"

"No. Just wondering what kind of woman would go out with a man who had been shot at, dragged in the street and set on fire?"

"A very beautiful woman, thank you. Someone who doesn't mind a few scars."

"Oh, so she's blind then," Norma laughed.

Chan laughed too. "No, but if she is going out with me then perhaps her judgment is slightly off."

"Not at all. Seriously, that's great. Is it the cute nurse from the hospital?"

Chan nodded. "Jean Reid. She's a Macinaw local."

"I'm really happy for you, Chan. You're young. It's time you had some distraction from all this craziness."

"What about you?" Chan asked. "You've been dealing with this 'craziness' too. And for years, I might add."

Norma hesitated in her response, drumming her fingers on the steering wheel. "I try not to let it get to me, but it's there under my skin. Henry Brooks, the Macinaw Seven. They're stains that will never fully come clean." She looked over at him. "I've seen what those stories did to this town. And I can feel it happening again. You may have taken the physical brunt of the past few weeks, but I, like most every other citizen of Macinaw, live with the pain daily. There is no getting away from it."

1:47 PM

Special Agent Mike Dunn had been waiting in Crawford's chair, behind Crawford's desk when the door opened and the sheriff entered.

"Comfy?" Crawford asked.

"Not very, Sheriff. I must say that as a Southern gentleman, your hospitality instincts need some refining."

Crawford frowned. "I'm sorry, Agent Dunn. Did my deputies forget your coffee and donuts this morning?"

"This is no joke, Sheriff. I know all about your little raid with your questionable search warrant. And I know all about the group of tattooed long-hairs you brought in for questioning. What I don't know is why I wasn't informed of any part of it."

Crawford stood in front of his desk, leaned over, and pressed his fingertips down on the top. "Dunn, I told you from the beginning, I welcome your help. For God's sake, sir, I need your help… desperately. But this is *my play*. People in this town are dying. I can't sit around and wait for the big city super cop to come down here, comb through every file and badger prior witnesses while hot leads need to be hunted down and vetted."

"You're getting awfully close to being insubordinate, Sheriff, interfering with a federal investigation."

"Jesus, Dunn! That's exactly what I'm talking about! You want to be head-honcho so bad that you're overlooking what's truly important here. There are four unexplained murders about to boil over and you can't see beyond who should be saluting who. Hell, I have half a mind to give you my badge, go home to my wife, and let you deal with this whole damn thing yourself."

Dunn held up his hand to appeal for calm. He rose and walked to the front of the desk. He held up both hands, this time in a surrendering fashion. "You're right. I may have jumped the gun a bit. But I'm getting pressure on this one too—the federal government, civil rights groups, everyone. If some type of control is not implemented soon, your entire town could go under. It's the last thing anyone wants to see." He sighed and then said, "In that regard, tell me what I can do to help."

It wasn't exactly an apology, but Crawford took solace in Dunn at least recognizing a need for cooperation. "Grubbs and his crew are being fairly tight-lipped about the tattoos. Each one has the same emblems that Henry Brooks used to mark his victims. What does the Bureau know? Is there a gang connection to Henry Brooks?"

Dunn sat on the edge of the desk. "Not to my knowledge, but that doesn't mean there couldn't be. What does this Grubbs deal in?"

"Meth mainly. Although his few arrests have been for dealing marijuana."

Dunn nodded. "Many of our Southern rural OMG's deal in meth. It's easier for them to get as opposed to cocaine."

"OMG's?"

"Outlaw motorcycle gangs. It's a term the Justice Department likes to throw around. The Hell's Angels, the Bandidos, Warlocks, Pagans and the like. They have branch affiliations everywhere. And we have categorized over three hundred other OMG's in the United States. Often these gangs identify with a polarizing figure: Satan, Hitler, Charles Manson. They represent themselves with their mark or brand. I could definitely see how Henry Brooks might strike a chord with such a group."

"Would they murder in his name? Use his methods?"

"Deal, extort, kidnap, steal, rape. You name it and these guys have been known to do it. Murder? Yes, Sheriff, without any question."

4:22 PM

As he spied Jean walking from her house to his car, Chan felt a wave of anticipation that he had never experienced. Throughout his high school and college years, Chan had been out on numerous dates with different girls, but this one felt different. This one held a little more promise to it.

It also didn't help his nerves that Jean looked drop-dead gorgeous. Her outfit was a simple pair of blue jean shorts and a white tee-shirt with an American flag across the chest. But it was the way her hair fell about her shoulders, the way she walked, the way she gave him a little wave and smiled as she approached. Chan thought he might melt.

131

"Hi," she said as she opened the passenger door and slid in. "I hope I didn't make you wait too long."

"No, not at all. The parade doesn't start until five."

"Good. I didn't think my shift would ever end today."

"Tough day?"

"Well, just a long one. The floor was not too busy actually—especially since we sent our favorite repeat customer home today."

Chan laughed. He started the Torino and began to back up out of her drive. "I didn't realize how close we live to one another. My apartment is just three blocks over on Marshall."

"Oh, cool," Jean said. "Now you won't have any excuse not to come see me."

As they made their way through Macinaw, the conversation between them was free, easy and rapid fire.

"So, tell me about your home," Jean said. "What's life like in Villa Rica?"

Chan bumped his shoulder. "Small town. Easy living. Not much to tell really."

"What are the people like?"

"Like here, I imagine. Most are nice. But we have our share of problems."

"Like what?"

"Divisions. We have them too. Racial divides. Economic divides. The same as in Macinaw."

Jean scrunched up her nose as she thought about it. "But you don't seem to carry around any of those issues. Granted I've only known you for a little while, but you seem fairly level-headed when it comes to things like race."

"Well, contrary to popular opinion, not everyone down South is a racist, you know." He laughed but then became a bit more reflective. "It's how you're raised, really. If you're not taught to think along those lines, then they don't become a problem for you. When I was little, my mom worked for a local produce company in town. One day, while she was working in the stock room, a man entered from the back, held a knife to her throat and tried to force himself on her. Two of her co-workers, both black men, heard the noise and came to her rescue. Two months later one of those workers was fired for being five

132

LAWRENCE THACKSTON

minutes late to work—the first and only time that he had ever been late. It didn't equate for my mother so she complained to the management until it got her fired."

"That's terrible."

"Yeah, it was. It's probably why I went into journalism in the first place—to expose the hypocrisy, the unfairness—get the truth out there. People are just people as far as I'm concerned— no better, no worse." He looked over at Jean. "I have a feeling you were taught to believe the same way."

Jean smiled. "We were. Which didn't exactly make it easy on my sister and me when desegregation happened. But like you said—we moved on." She hesitated and then added, "I just wish everyone had."

As they made their way through town, they turned to more upbeat subjects, including their extended families, favorite hometown restaurants and their love for music.

They pulled into the lot behind *The Republic* and hustled over to the town square. The crowd, a mix of mostly happy, sweaty faces in red, white and blue, stood three rows deep, awaiting the parade's start.

Chan, with the paper's camera strapped around his neck, led Jean by the hand as they darted in and out the throng of people and searched for a place to get the best view. One of the square's park benches, that looked inward toward a Confederate memorial, was unattended, so they decided to perch themselves there.

"Can you see okay?" Chan asked.

"Best seat in the house." She gave his hand a quick squeeze.

The parade was led by the Macinaw High School marching band playing a series of patriotic tunes. Boy Scouts, the local Rotary club, a Minute Men re-enactment troop, festive floats and dignitaries in open convertibles were among those who soon followed. Chan took shots of it all.

An hour later and Chan was interviewing the Honorable Jeremiah Stone, mayor of Macinaw and the grand marshal of the parade. Stone was a likable man who had been Macinaw's mayor for the past twenty years. Slight of build and bespectacled, Stone's favorite saying was "It's a great day in Macinaw." In his interview with Chan, the mayor was concerned

133

about recent events, but he was delighted that much of the town had come out to celebrate the country's birthday. He hoped and prayed for better days ahead.

Afterwards, Chan found Jean waiting for him near the park bench. "Thanks for being patient," he said.

"No problem. What do you want to do now?"

"I need to get to the office and write this up. Shouldn't take too long. Then we can grab a bite before the fireworks at nine."

"Sounds like a plan," Jean said.

"Sorry I have to cram so much work in with our date."

"It's okay. Actually, I'm kind of excited to see how a real reporter writes up a story."

Chan shrugged. "Well, I wouldn't call the process all that exciting, and watching me type can at times be painful, but at least the building has air conditioning."

Jean laughed before blowing a fallen strand of her hair away from her face. "Then it will definitely be worth the visit."

6:13 PM

"Now is not the time for cowardice," boomed the deep voice of Reverend Daniel Howard of the Southern Christian Leadership Conference. "We must act decisively and just. We must show the people of South Carolina that we are stronger together than apart—that there are no cracks in our armor." The charismatic and statuesque African-American minister and head of the SCLC Action Committee moved from behind the altar with microphone in hand and addressed the swelling crowd inside the Northfork Chapel. "God is with us, lest we forget. God is with us."

Norma stood in the back and watched the proceedings. She noted that the three remaining members of the Macinaw Seven— Anderson, Johnson and Wells—sat together on the front row. Their heads were bowed down as if the attention was too much.

"Since the early days, we have had to protect our own," Howard continued. "When society cannot or will not protect its citizens, it is right, our duty, in the name of God, to take matters unto ourselves. We shall not be denied. The good people of Macinaw shall not be denied. On this, the two hundredth birthday of our country's independence, I look around and still see those yearning for that independence, still enslaved in a system that denies solace, denies fairness, denies justice."

As Howard continued to sermonize and endear himself to the enthusiastic crowd, Ja'Len Wells got up from the pew and walked discreetly to the church's side entrance. He came down the outside steps, loosening his tie. He sought out the shade of a large oak around which many cars were parked. He leaned against the tree and took a few deep breaths.

"Feeling the heat?"

Ja'len turned to look behind him. Norma was standing there. "I ain't got nothing to say to the press, Miss Norma."

"I know," Norma said. "But I thought you might need a friend."

"No, ma'am. I appreciate it. But just no...."

"Ja'Len, you must tell us what's going on. You must tell me." She moved closer and pointed back at the church. "You know what's happening inside. You know how badly this is spinning out of control."

Ja'Len shook his head. "I can't say nothing. I ain't saying nothing, do you hear?"

"Please, Ja'Len, there's so much at stake. Help me so I can help you."

"No, now, just leave me alone," Ja'Len said as he walked away. "Leave me alone."

Norma watched as he made his way across the parking area, slid into his grey Mercury and took off. Disappointed, she turned and headed back inside the church.

Down the road, Ja'Len pushed the limits of his old car. He was hot, angry, confused and still scared for his life. He tried to calm himself by reaffirming his actions. He hadn't told anyone what they saw that day. He had kept his promise for six long years. He had kept his mouth shut. He cannot be held responsible even if others had crossed the line. *He can't come after me. I have kept my word.*

He pulled to a stop at a crossroad in the swampy nowhere lands of Macinaw. The heat and his desperation were working on him. He looked to the right into the dark woods beyond and saw a flash of movement. He zeroed in on the area—beyond the river's run-off, the knotty cypress trees, and the moss-drenched oaks. He blinked and saw the movement again.

It was him—the skinny white man, the murderer, Henry Brooks. He was running from tree to tree, making his way through the swamps, coming through the tall river grass, coming after him—the boar knife in his hand—a wicked smile on his face.

Ja'Len leaned over, rested his head on the steering wheel and rubbed his tired eyes. *Get ahold of yourself, man. There's no one there. It's just your mind playing tricks.* Ja'Len straightened up and looked again into the swamp. There was only the wild green foliage and inky black water. He shook his head and even laughed at himself.

As Ja'Len drove on through the crossroad, confident he had his fears under control, a shadowy figure arose in the backseat of his car.

6:47 PM

Sheriff Crawford and Agent Dunn came into the holding room. Ryan Grubbs was pacing behind the table and chairs.

"Finally. What took so damn long? When the hell are you gonna let me outta here?"

"Shut up and sit down," Dunn ordered.

"This is bullshit, man. I want my lawyer."

"I said shut up and sit down, Grubbs," Dunn said.

"Do as he says, Rhino," Crawford said calmly. "You're not under arrest. You don't need a lawyer just yet."

Grubbs swung the chair around and sat in it with his chest against the back. "So why the hell am I here then? And who the hell is this guy?"

"This is Special Agent Dunn with the FBI."

"Oh, you brought in the FBI, big fucking deal."

"Listen, Grubbs. We need information," Dunn said also taking a seat. "And you're gonna provide it for us."

"Oh, I am, huh? You cops got some nerve keeping me and my posse locked up all day and the thinking I'm gonna give you any goddamn thing."

"We released your *posse* hours ago. We just want to talk to you."

Grubbs pulled his hair out of his face. "I already told Crawford. They're just tattoos." He held up his arms to show Dunn the Abaddon and Michael sigils. "I had nothing to do with killing them niggas. Not a damn thing."

Dunn dropped a folder down on the table. "Tell us then about the HBD's—the Henry Brooks Disciples."

Grubbs shook his head and sat up a bit. "Man... I don't know..." He waited and then, "All right, it's a club. You know—a motorcycle club. They're out of Savannah."

"And they run drugs?" Dunn asked.

"No, you dumb prick, they run toys for Santa when his sleigh is broke."

Dunn jumped up, reached over and slammed Grubbs' head on the table, blooding his nose. "Listen to me you son of a bitch, when I ask a question you give me a straight answer! You got me!?"

Crawford reached over and forced Dunn's hand away. Grubbs slid back into his chair, rubbing the back of his neck and wiping the blood from his nostrils. "Fuck you, man! I definitely want a lawyer now. I'm gonna sue the hell outta you pigs."

"Rhino," Crawford said, again with passivity. "Tell us the origin of the HBD's."

Grubbs took a minute to compose himself and then focused on Crawford, "Some guy from Savannah, Diamond Jack, they call him—a four-time loser in the Coastal State pen. Heard about Brooks. Liked his style. He started a market trail up and down I-95. I got recruited last year through some associates. The tats are just a sign of membership, that's all."

"What kind of numbers are we talking about here? How many are in the gang?" Dunn asked.

"I don't know. Thirty? Fifty? What do I look like? A freaking accountant?"

"Think hard now, Grubbs," Crawford jumped back in. "Has anyone come to you? Tried to recruit you or some of the other local HBD for something other than running drugs?"

Grubbs grinned and shook his head. "Look, Crawford, I know where you're going with this and my answer is still the same. I had nothing to do with knocking off them Macinaw Seven boys."

"No one has approached....?"

"No! How many times do I have to tell you? I had nothing to do with it."

Crawford paused as he looked over at Dunn and then, "Okay. If that's all you've got, then you're free to go."

Grubbs stood and kicked the chair out of his way. "That's it? You hold me in here all day, ask me two questions, nearly break my neck and then just turn me loose? What about a fucking apology?"

"Get the hell outta here, Grubbs, before we do charge you with something," Dunn said.

"Unbelievable." Grubbs walked out still rubbing the back of his neck. "Bunch of punk-ass pigs." The door slammed behind him.

"You believe him?" Dunn asked.

"Not as far as I can throw him," Crawford said. "We should probably keep a close eye on him and the other two."

"How are your rotations holding up?"

"We're thin. Even with Orangeburg and Colleton helping out."

"Need more men?"

Crawford stood and paced. "I'm worried about too big a presence. Things are already dicey between the whites and blacks, and the black community doesn't exactly have a lot of faith in the badge."

"So, what do you suggest, Sheriff?"

"We've got to catch this bastard and soon. Trap him, maybe.

"Live bait?"

Crawford nodded. "Live bait."

9:23 PM

John Philip Sousa's *The Stars and Stripes Forever* blasted from the fairgrounds' speakers as a series of blue, red, green, gold and silver pinwheels, comets and chrysanthemum bursts lit up the clear Macinaw sky. Chan and Jean sat atop the shaky wooden bleachers in the grounds stadium, a century old playing field that was used for special college football games prior to the 1950s and for horse shows and motor-cross events in more recent times. The Macinaw crowd applauded and cheered with each successive firework blast which grew in size and rapidity.

"Wow, that was a nice one," Jean said poking a subdued Chan in the side.

Chan drew down the corners of his mouth. "Yeah. Very impressive."

Jean laughed. "Well, you're not exactly enthusiastic about this, are you? I thought everybody loved fireworks."

"Oh, I do. It's just…"

"The story?" Jean asked. "You know you're allowed to forget about it for a little while."

"I know. I'm sorry, Jean. Don't get me wrong. I love this. I love being here with you. It's just it feels strange to be sitting here enjoying myself while others… aren't. Norma said something to me today. She said that Henry Brooks and the Dover murder are like stains that never come clean. I can feel that now too. It creeps into everything I do even while I'm trying to enjoy myself."

"We all feel it, Chan. Every one of us. But I've learned, like a lot of people, to put it aside, to suppress it when I must. It's necessary for sanity sake."

"I just feel so helpless. I wish there was more that I could do."

Jean reached out and gently angled his face towards her. "You will, Chan. I've got a good feeling about you. You're gonna be the one to break this story wide open. You're gonna solve this before it's too late." She smiled. "Don't ask me how I know, I just do."

In the night sky the fireworks raced to a mad dash finale popping fervently and stridently, showering colorful light everywhere as the music reached its thrilling crescendo. Below, oblivious to the several hundred cheering folks around them, Chan and Jean shared a kiss that lasted long after the final spark fell.

OCTOBER 3, 2016

9:15 PM

Chan and Tindal sat in silence as they raced down I-26 toward Macinaw. The discovery had been a revelation, but one that again led to more questions than answers. Sonny Watts had been granted access to Henry Brooks at the State Mental Hospital on more than one occasion and had lied about his knowledge of and time with the notorious murderer. Therefore, the number one question had to be: *Why?*

Immediately after seeing his name on the hospital permission form, Chan and Tindal had raced back upstairs and demanded to see the employment records of the firm. Sonny Watts had clerked for the Crane and Campbell during his years in law school but was never hired on once he passed the bar. There were no reasons given, he had simply become employed elsewhere. They did find an old picture of Watts in a file which allowed Chan to confirm that he was indeed the same man he met in 1976.

"So, what do we do with this?" Tindal asked as the headlights on the westbound lane flared across the windshield. "Do we go to the police?"

Chan rubbed at his forehead, a splitting headache on top of the news. "I don't know, Tindal. Eventually this is going to be your call. But I'd like to make a few inquiries first. Things that need to be verified anyway."

Tindal nodded, drove in silence for a few moments more, and then, "Chan, are you sure you saw Sonny Watts burn up in that house fire?"

Chan looked over at her. "I've been asking myself the same damn thing. It was dark, smoky, the house was falling apart and I was expecting him to be there, you know? There was a body but I... I couldn't swear to it one way or the other." He glanced out the window and then, "And there's something more, Tindal."

"What?"

"Watts employed several illegals to work around his place. He had them camp in the fields behind his home. There are no

140

records of these people so it would have been easy for him to lure one inside, knock him out or kill him, and then use the man's body as his double." Tindal clicked the roof of her mouth with her tongue at the mere thought. "On July fourth, the day I was let out of the hospital, and once I got my car back, I drove down to Watts' estate. I searched the fields behind the burned down house, but they were gone."

"Did you tell Crawford?"

"No, at the time I truly believed it was Watts who burned in the fire. And I was more worried that the immigrants would get into trouble for being in the country illegally. I understood their disappearing, and I didn't pursue it."

"He used you," Tindal said. "He called you and knew you would come to his house. You would witness his house burn. You would report that he died."

Chan bit down on his lip, a sudden rush of hatred and guilt overcoming him.

"But why?" Tindal continued. "Why fake his death? What did he have to gain by going through all that trouble? He couldn't be behind the Macinaw Seven killings, could he? He was their defense counsel for God's sake."

Chan pinched the bridge of his nose. "He sought them out quickly. He was the lawyer for the Seven before they even arrived at the jailhouse. He claimed to be a righteous defender, but what if Sonny had met with them urgently just to get inside their heads."

"What do you mean?"

"He brings them a warning. A warning not to say anything about what they saw in the Dover barn."

"And if they do talk, then somehow Henry Brooks would come after them. Hunt them down and kill them." Tindal grinned. "Holy shit, Chan, you may be on to something."

"We shouldn't get ahead of ourselves, but let's assume for a moment all that's true. Then the Seven must've threatened to reveal the truth—whatever that truth is—back in '76." Chan tapped his finger along the glass of the passenger window as he thought it through. "Perhaps the answer lies with Robert Dover. When we get back, I want us to go through Dover's murder trial again. There's something we're missing there."

141

"Agreed. And we should also take a closer look at the paper trail for Watts. Surely he had a will. Who benefitted from his death—who got his insurance money, bank accounts, et cetera?"

"Good idea," Chan said. He looked over to Tindal in the glow of the dashboard and smiled. He then indicated the speedometer. "Push it, girl. We've got work to do."

JULY 5, 1976

12:45 AM

Sheriff Crawford whipped his cruiser around the fire truck and the ambulance which were partially blocking oncoming traffic and pulled off on the bank of the dark road. Five sheriff deputies' patrol cars, two from Macinaw, two from Orangeburg and one from Colleton were also there. Crawford hopped out and trudged down the eight-foot embankment to meet with the others.

"What we got?" he asked Deputy Haskit.

"Ja'Len Wells' car, Sheriff. It's his Mercury."

"And Wells?"

"He's in there," Haskit said. "At the wheel. Dead. Puncture wounds to his throat. The Michael sigil carved into his chest."

"Jesus... how in God's name is that possible, Deputy? Didn't we have this man under surveillance?"

"Yes, sir, but he got away from our tail. He apparently left the Northfork Chapel where the black folks were having their meeting well before it was over. Our man looked for him for hours. It was just happenstance that he backtracked down this road and saw Wells' car down this embankment."

Crawford blew out another sigh. Per his usual lawman's habit, he then took a few moments to walk away from the direct scene and survey the area around him. River frogs and crickets were making their nightly racket and a swarm of fireflies were punctuating the swampy darkness with their own fireworks show. He sensed something beyond the fireflies, beyond the dark tree line—a presence—as if someone was out there—watching. Crawford shook his head, chalking up the paranoia to exhaustion and returned to his deputy. "Any prints leading away from the car?"

"Not that we can find. We'll dust the car too, but you know how careful this killer has been."

Crawford nodded. "Post up here 'til morning. Widen the grid once you get a little daylight. Check both sides of the road." He paused before adding softly, "Do all you can, Bobby."

143

"Sheriff Crawford?" The call came from the road above. Crawford turned, saw Agent Dunn at the top of the embankment and then climbed his way up to meet him.

Once at the top Crawford said, "Well, here we are again, Agent Dunn."

"Another one of the Seven?"

"Ja'Len Wells. He's been tagged with the Michael sigil."

"Time of death?"

"Coroner's on his way, but it looks like sometime late this afternoon."

"Might eliminate your boy, Grubbs."

"No, I'm not eliminating anyone at this point."

Dunn nodded. "Down to two of the seven now. You're running out of potential bait, Sheriff."

"Agreed. We need to set up our trap and soon."

"Any ideas?"

"A couple," Crawford said. "We can meet in my office later and discuss it."

"Okay, but you've got more problems than that. The blacks in Macinaw are staging a march and rally later today in your town. I had one of our agents sit in on the meeting and had him report back to me. There's a sentiment in the black community that if these victims were white more would have been done. They claim you're not moving fast enough to defend them."

Crawford took a quick glance back at Ja'Len's car and then back at the FBI man. "You know something, Agent Dunn? They're absolutely right."

6:35 AM

As soon as Chan entered *The Republic's* newsroom, he knew something was wrong. All the employees were standing around with despondent looks, including his boss. All the good feelings he had developed in his limited time last night with Jean, all the positive vibes, quickly evaporated.

"What's up?" Chan asked.

"It's Ja'Len Wells," Darby said. "The sheriff's department is reporting that he was murdered yesterday. They found him in his car with the angel marks on his chest."

"My God," Chan said. He leaned over a desk chair like he had been punched in the gut, but then quickly straightened. "You want me there?"

"I already sent Norma. She'll handle it." Darby pointed to his office. "But come with me please."

Chan followed him into his office and stood while Darby sat behind his desk. "Shut the door and have a seat." Chan did as he was told.

"What is it, sir?"

"Adams, I'm not sure how to ask you this." Chan smiled apprehensively. "Thing is, this situation with the Macinaw Seven has gotten very dangerous as of late. In a manner of speaking, it's out of control."

"You're not pulling me off the story, are you?"

Darby raised an eyebrow and shook his head. "No, no, to be honest I didn't think you'd stop even if I ordered you to."

"Damn right."

"Good. Because what I'm going to suggest may put you in more peril than before."

"I'm all ears, boss."

Darby rubbed his hands. "Pebo Clark, the information director at the sheriff's office, is my cousin—I didn't know if you knew that. He's been an especially good contact for us over the years as you might imagine." Chan nodded. "Anyway, Pebo told me last night that there's a new motorcycle gang that's using Henry Brooks as its primary symbol. They call themselves Henry Brooks' Disciples. They have the Abaddon and Michael sigils tattooed on their arms in some warped sense of allegiance to that dead bastard."

"Are they in Macinaw?"

"Yes. Ryan Grubbs, a local crystal meth dealer, is one of the members. And there are others involved."

"Do the police believe they are connected to the murders?"

"They have them under surveillance, so we have to assume so."

Chan leaned back in his chair. "But why? What would they have to gain by knocking off the Seven?"

"We don't know. Pebo seemed to think they may have been hired by someone to do the job. Killers for hire sort of thing."

Chan's thoughts went immediately to Ellis Dover, but he kept it to himself. "What do you want me to do?"

"I want you in there. I want you to pick up on any information from Grubbs and company. Find out if they had anything to do with this."

Chan thought for a second. "Despite what you may think, I'm not much of a crystal meth user."

Darby laughed. "You don't have to go that far, but you can hang out where they hang out. You can put your ear to the wall. They'll smell a cop within twenty feet, but they don't know you—they won't suspect you."

"Okay. Where do I start?"

"Grubbs lives in Eastland Heights. It's a trailer park outside of town. He hangs out a lot at Ricky's, a bar near Eastland, and at Dolly's Dollies, a strip club out near I-95."

Chan grinned. "Sounds like my kind of people."

"Don't take this or him lightly, Adams. Grubbs has a serious track record. And if things start to get ugly, I want you to get the hell outta there."

Chan stood. "Yes, sir, I'll do my best. I'll get started right away." He headed for the door but stopped. "And Mr. Darby, thank you for trusting me on this."

Darby looked him directly in the eyes. "You've earned that trust, Adams." He then soured the sentiment with, "Just don't screw it up."

10:36 AM

The offices at City Hall in Macinaw sat directly across the square from the County Courthouse and were adjacent to the First Baptist Church of Macinaw as well as the local post office. It was comparable to Charleston's intersection of Meeting and Broad streets which also comprised its four corners with local, state, federal and ecclesiastical law. But with *The Republic* offices only one door down, Macinaw citizens often bragged of having their square under the watchful eye of the press, thereby keeping their laws "honest."

The mayor's office was at the top of City Hall. A grand picture window behind the mayor's desk looked out over the square. Mayor Stone stood next to the window with his hands behind his back. He was getting an earful from Ellis Dover who had demanded an audience with his Honor.

"You let these outside colored folks have their march in our town and we'll be the laughing stock of the whole South. They'll make a mockery of justice," Dover said. He looked over to Police Chief Stodges who was sitting in front of the mayor's desk and was appearing more annoyed than anything else. "You'll have to bring in a wall of police. You'll have to keep the blacks from looting and raising hell. The fire department might have to blast the streets clean of them with their water cannons. Do you really want another Orangeburg uprising on your hands? This cannot happen."

"Take it easy, Ellis. They petitioned for the right to march. They've submitted the proper forms. What the hell was I supposed to do?" Stone asked.

"Deny them. Deny their requests. They denied me the life of my son, remember? Where was the outrage then? Where were the protests? It is only criminals being killed out there now—the same criminals who killed my son. Hell, we should be throwing a parade for the son of a bitch who's been knocking them off!"

"Ellis, please, you're being ridiculous," Stone said.

"Am I, Mr. Mayor? Am I? Well, we'll see who's being ridiculous after they march through your town, burning businesses, starting riots. And when they do, don't say I didn't warn you." He turned for the door, shaking his finger at the two men. "You need to be on your knees, gentlemen, praying to the good Lord, that you never know the tragedy that befell my family. That you never know that pain—the hell they put my son through." Dover exited and slammed the door behind him.

Mayor Stone lifted his glasses and wiped the stress from his face. He then looked to Stodges. "Contingencies, Chief?"

Stodges shrugged. "Well, I don't think we'll need a *wall* of police, but we will have plenty on hand. Highway patrol will help with traffic. Crawford's men will be on the ready if needed. We should be fine."

Stone glanced back out the window and then back to the chief. "I don't want to put any more emphasis on this than we have to. The less visible our forces are, the greater the chance this will go smoothly. I talked at length with the Reverend Howard. He's expecting a large but peaceful crowd."

"It's not the police you have to worry about, Mayor. And it's not the colored folk. It's Dover and his cronies. If they stay away, all will be fine. But mix the gas with the fire...."

"I hear you," Stone said. "Stay on top of it, Chief. Let me know if this office can further assist you."

Stodges nodded, hopped up from his seat and left the office. Stone turned back to the window and watched the traffic come and go. He shook his head in disbelief. "Henry Brooks, what the hell have you done to this town?"

4:32 PM

Still in her nurse's uniform, Jean Reid grabbed the bags of groceries from the back seat of her car and with her right foot slammed the car door. She made it half-way to her house when she saw Chan sitting on the front porch waving.

"Hey there," Jean said. "I wasn't expecting you here so soon."

Chan stood, put out his cigarette, and leaned against the porch railing. "Quick drop-by, I'm afraid. I'm gonna have to cancel tonight. I've gotta work."

Jean made a pouty face. "Aww. And I was going to make you my grandmother's world famous spaghetti tonight." She held up the bags in her hands.

Chan leaped the railing, went to her and grabbed one of the bags. "I'm sorry. I really hate missing it. Rain check?"

Jean smiled. "Sure. Come on in. You can help me put these away."

Chan followed her into the kitchen entrance of her small wood-framed home. She placed the bag on the kitchen counter and then flipped on the lights.

"Just put it there," she said indicating a spot on the counter. She started transferring groceries to the fridge.

Chan took a quick look around. "Love your place. Sure beats the heck outta my little apartment."

"It's a rental. The rooms are small, but it does have a nice backyard. My roommate Rachel and I have been here for two years now. She's a nurse too, did you know?" Chan shook his head that he did not. "She works on two-west with the mommas and the babies. I never see her though. We usually work opposite shifts."

"Y'all have done a fantastic job with it," Chan said. "Amazing how clean it is."

Jean laughed. "How about a coke?"

"Sure. I've got a few minutes."

Jean dug through the back of the refrigerator and found a can. "Here you go."

"Thanks."

"Have a seat," she said indicating the den area. "Give me a sec to change and I'll be right out." She reached behind her and having a little difficulty turned her back to him. "Sorry, but do you mind?" Chan felt for the zipper and pulled it half-way down. "Thanks," she said as she headed for her room.

Chan took a seat on the couch. He made a quick survey of the place noting the simple but elegant tastes of Jean and her roommate. In less than a minute, Jean returned. She was looking relaxed now out of the uniform, bare-footed and in a pair of blue running shorts with an orange Clemson University tee-shirt. She sat next to him and drew her leg up on the couch.

"So, work, huh? Does it involve the story?" Jean asked.

"Possibly. It's a different angle to it."

"I heard about Ja'Len. It doesn't have anything to do with him, does it?"

"No. Like I said there's something new on the horizon they want me to investigate."

"It's not dangerous though, is it? I don't want to have you as a patient again anytime soon." They both laughed.

"I hope not. But it may be very involving. It might be for a few days."

Jean leaned her head against a couch pillow and smiled. "How about next weekend? I'm off on Saturday."

"That could work," Chan said. "What do you have in mind?"

"Leave it to me," she said with a wink. "It'll be a surprise."

The way she said *surprise* made Chan momentarily weak in the knees. And the fact that she was so beautiful on top of it. In his mind this girl was perfect.

He leaned forward and put the soda can on the coffee table. "Sounds great. I can't wait. But unfortunately, I really do have to go now."

He rose and she stood with him. She grabbed him by the shoulders. "You be careful now, Chan."

"I will. I promise."

Jean leaned up on her toes, closed her eyes and lightly kissed him, a moment more and the kiss became much deeper. He felt it throughout his whole body; the fireworks from the night before had returned. He pressed against her; his arms wrapping around her waist.

He had only known her for a few short days, but he knew it now more than ever—this was the girl he was meant to be with—the one he would make his life with—Jean Reid was to be the one.

5:45 PM

Just the day before, the square in Macinaw had been the site of a joyous, flag-waving parade celebrating the freedoms that Americans share. Today the same locale was being used to exercise one of those freedoms: the right to assemble, but the tone of the event was a far different affair.

Reverend Howard had led the march down Main Street, two-hundred-plus African-Americans in tow. They locked arms and walked slowly, singing hymns, chanting together, seeking change, seeking justice. White Macinaw stood idly by, lining the sidewalks, arms crossed over their chests. There was no cheering as the day before. No happy faces.

Stodges had his men at crucial points along the route—eyes wide open, keeping in constant contact. The chief himself was stationed in the square with signals ready to defend, swarm or stand-down. He, like many other law officers in the state, had learned from the painful lessons of the Orangeburg Massacre: Bend, don't break. Defer but protect at all costs.

The marchers filled the grass inlay of the square, occupying nearly every inch. Norma was among them. She noticed that the remaining two of the Macinaw Seven, William Anderson and Deonte Johnson were nowhere around. She was told they were in their respective houses on lockdown, black armed security guards protecting them. She had talked with many of the marchers and found them all hesitant and scared for their future. There was such mistrust of law enforcement. History was not on their side and it skewed every reasonable tangent of conversation. Blacks and whites would never be able to see eye to eye on this or any subject, Norma reasoned. *Not in my lifetime.*

Reverend Howard broke from the front line and made his way onto the back of a flatbed truck that was to be used as the forum's stage. "Today was to be a day of reckoning," Howard began. "A day of healing and justice. But I fear I must report first of yet another tragic loss. Just last night we lost Mr. Ja'Len Wells to this madman who has already done the same to four of our brothers. Despised for who he was and murdered by that same hatred, Ja'Len has gone to a far better place. As such, I weep not for him, but for what he leaves behind: a world divided, bitter and inconsolable."

Ellis Dover, flanked by his three sons and family friend, Trey Richards, stood atop the stairs of the county courthouse and looked on as Howard continued. "Listen to him talk. What the hell does that darkie know about being inconsolable?" Dover asked. "He doesn't know a damn thing. I should sue the hell outta him for defaming the memory of my son."

"Let them have their day, Mr. Dover," Richards said, speaking like the lawyer he was. "Seems to me they're getting what they deserve anyway."

10:15 PM

Ricky's Pool Hall was housed in a singular, cinderblock structure that sat at the end of Plant Road next to Olsen Tools, which employed nearly three hundred Macinaw locals. Home to the labor-intensive nine-to-fivers, bikers and the Macinaw fringe element, Ricky's saw good weekday business and even better on the weekends. Calls to the police for drunk and disorderly patrons or outright bar fights were not uncommon.

Chan entered Ricky's with Thin Lizzy's *The Boys Are Back in Town* pumping from the corner jukebox. It was a typical, smoky bar, not unlike Allen's Bar and Grill, where he used to tend bar in Athens, Georgia. Small round tables fronted the place with an L-shaped bar on the back wall. A mirror behind the bar made the front room seem a little larger. Bathrooms and storage were to the immediate left, and on the right side, there was a room containing five regulation pool tables with rectangular Budweiser lights over the tables' green-clothed beds.

Chan took a seat at the bar with two regulars and plopped his smokes on the beer-sticky counter. The bartender, a thin, pony-tailed man of fifty with sunken brown eyes, approached. "Whataya have?"

"Budweiser," Chan said. "In a bottle."

"Well, you ain't gonna get it in a fucking soup bowl," he said which garnered a laugh from the two regulars. He opened the bar cooler and slid him the beer.

"Thanks," Chan said. He packed down his Marlboro Lights, drew one and then brought it to life with his lighter. He blew smoke to the ceiling and then nodded at the bar men who were eyeing him warily. "How's it going?" he finally asked.

The men seemed surprised he was talking to them. They nodded and muddled their response then turned back to their mugs.

"New in town?" the bartender asked.

"About three weeks now," Chan said. "I'm from Villa Rica, Georgia. Ever hear of it?"

"No, but I'm surprised whenever anybody moves here to Macinaw."

"Why's that?"

The bartender chuckled. "I'll give you three more weeks to figure it out."

Chan smiled and drank his beer. The bartender diverted his attention elsewhere leaving Chan to watch the TV at the end of the bar. ABC was telecasting Monday Night Baseball, a game between the Phillies and the Dodgers. The reception was poor, but Chan had little else to do.

Thirty minutes later and his luck changed. A pool player saddled in next to him and slipped a five dollar bill onto the bar. He rapped his knuckles on the top to garner the bartender's attention. "Need some quarters," the man said. As the exchange was being made, Chan noticed the pentagram on the man's left forearm. Chan glanced up at him quickly. He was of medium height, had an unkempt beard and long hair with a leather band around his head.

"Play for money?" Chan asked.

"Twenty a game," Terrance Orton said. "You want a shot?"

"I do."

"Well, come on then. I never get tired of taking other people's money."

Chan straightened, gathered up his pack of cigarettes and followed him to the pool room. He noticed the man was walking with a slight limp. A huge man with the same tattoos was sitting on a barstool near the open table. Chan felt Roland Wolfe's eyes intently on him like an intense watch dog. As Orton passed Wolfe, Chan heard him laugh about "fresh meat."

Orton pulled a twenty from his front pocket and put it on table and Chan did the same. "What's the game?" Chan asked.

"Eight ball," Orton said as he slipped a quarter into the table's slot. The balls released, crashed into the return tray and Chan racked them. "And since it's my quarter, I get to break."

11:53 PM

The table was clear, save the eight ball which was flush to the middle of the table's head rail in the area pool players call "the kitchen." Chan and Orton had split the two prior games and they decided to throw a hundred dollars on the rubber match. In addition to Wolfe, the game drew a few of the other late-nighters—most of whom were pulling for Orton and took every chance to let Chan know it.

During the second game, Chan managed to sneak in a question about the tattoos to Wolfe, but the big man just barely grunted a response. And a follow-up question was met with a terse "fuck off."

Chan was up. The cue ball was resting near the foot of the table and Chan leaned over to eye it. Orton stood directly behind him, bouncing his pool stick handle on the floor. It was at times like these that Chan was glad to have spent so much of his college days in the bar scene. "Corner pocket," Chan said, slapping his hand in the pocket opening next to his right. He drew back his pool stick and rammed it home. The cue ball shot out and smashed the eight ball which caromed off the rail and flew straight like a bat out of hell into the called pocket. The cue ball then followed, rolled an inch from the pocket on the opposite side and came to a dead stop. Chan held his position. He knew any kind of celebration might get the wrong reaction from the two Disciples. He slowly stood and tossed his pool stick on the table. He turned to face them.

"You some kinda hustler?" Orton asked.

Here it comes. "No way, man, just got lucky," Chan said.

"Yeah, well, I ain't paying no hundred bucks for luck, you got me?"

"Okay. Let's call it even then."

"No, what I was thinking was another game. You know, this time, winner take all." It was the way Orton said it, Chan knew he didn't really have much of a choice.

Before Chan could respond, another man walked into the room. He was physically impressive and he too sported the sigils. Chan figured this must be the ring-leader, Ryan Grubbs. Grubbs didn't say anything, but Orton and Wolfe knew that they were to follow.

"Some other time," Orton said, flashing Chan a grin from hell.

The throng of watchers broke apart as Orton and Wolfe headed out the front. Grubbs hung back taking a long look at Chan. He too then turned and disappeared out front.

Chan flipped another cigarette into his mouth and relaxed his shoulders. Round one was over, and at best, this one felt like a tie.

OCTOBER 4, 2016

Chan sat at the little table in his kitchen, bleary-eyed, his mind scrambled. He and Tindal had spent the entire night piecing the case together. Every square inch of countertop, kitchen cabinets, appliance surfaces as well as the breakfast table had some document, article or photograph taped on it. They had joked that when they finished wallpapering the kitchen they'd tackle the den next.

Chan was focused on a court document from the Dover trial when he heard Tindal return. She threw her handbag on the couch and came into the kitchen. "Any luck?"

Chan continued to read and grunted a no comment.

"Here," Tindal said as she dropped a white paper bag next to the document. "I found a little store that had some whole-wheat bagels."

"Thanks."

"Did you make the coffee yet?"

"Forgot."

Tindal smirked as she began the coffee maker. She then sat next to him at the table and dug into the bag. She tore a bagel in half and handed it to him. "Eat something before you fall over."

Chan looked up at her, ignoring the bagel. "Robert Dover's death was caused by hanging, yes?"

"Yes, the police report clearly states fatal neck injury from suspension."

"But look at the coroner's report," Chan said as he dug through the papers. He found it and then read: "Dover exhibited signs of hypoxia, a bluish complexion, pinpoint burst of blood vessels in the face and upper neck, and distended lungs."

"Right. All signs of a lack of oxygen. What's your point?"

"He used a rope." Chan scrambled to find the photo evidence and showed it to Tindal. "This rope."

"Okay, so…" she said with a mouthful of bagel.

"But go back to Payton Medlin's notes and testimony. Nowhere does he mention that the rope marks on the neck have that inflamed edge of vital reaction that happens in most hangings."

"What's vital reaction?"

"In a suicide or homicide by rope hanging, the ligature marks on the victim are usually raised to match the twists on the rope. They are 'vital' in that they happen because the victim is alive when the rope is put around his neck. Sometimes they're faint, and then later after the victim dies, they turn to a reddish, brown color."

"Rope burns."

"Essentially, post-mortem rope burns, but yeah. And one thing more." Tindal raised both eyebrows waiting for more. "Medlin states there were no rope fibers in Robert's hands or on his body. Strange, isn't it? How do you hang yourself without ever touching the rope?"

"So what you're saying is that Robert may have been killed prior and then the killer or killers used the rope to make it look like a hanging."

"Maybe." Chan said with a twinge of doubt. "After all he did show signs of asphyxia. But his hyoid bone was not broken and there were no other signs of strangulation." Chan put his own hands around his neck. "No bruises, hand prints, fingernail marks. Nothing to let you know that he had been strangled."

"So was this even murder?"

"Did you read all of the coroner's report?"

Tindal rubbed her eyes. "God, Chan, at this point, I don't remember." Chan went back to the file and flipped through the papers. He pulled one and slid it over so Tindal could see. "What's this?"

"The end of his report. From the complete autopsy of Dover's body. The one used in court."

Tindal scanned it with a confused look. "Do you want me to re-read all of the gory details."

"Just the second to last paragraph."

"I can't," Tindal said. "It's been black-lined. Redacted."

"Exactly my point. Out of the entire report on Robert Dover's autopsy, one small paragraph has been redacted. Remember, this is the official document used in the Macinaw Seven trial. My question is: Why?"

"Maybe they didn't want to bring it up in the court proceedings. Maybe it was embarrassing to Dover or to his family."

"I think you may be more correct than you know."

"But both sides, defense and prosecution, would have known what was redacted. It would have been agreed upon in the judge's chambers."

"Yes, that's true. So, if it was something that might have eliminated the belief that Robert had committed suicide or anything that didn't follow the official police report of him being strung up by the accused, the prosecution would have certainly wanted it out."

"But the defense wouldn't have, would they?" Tindal asked.

"Yes, they might, if Sonny Watts was the attorney and if he wanted to keep that information out of the courtroom too."

"Chan, what are you getting at?"

"The secret. The reason why Sonny Watts threatened the Macinaw Seven, his own clients. The reason why Henry Brooks made his appearance during that summer of '76. Don't you see, Tindal? This could be the key to everything."

"All of that revealed in a redacted paragraph of an autopsy?"

"I'll bet you anything that it is."

"But it's all a moot point anyway. We'll never know why Medlin's report was black-lined. That was so long ago." Tindal noticed the grin on Chan's face. "What?"

"He's alive. Payton Medlin is close to ninety years old, but he's still out there kicking."

"Around here?"

"In Palmetto Acres. About eight miles north, near the Orangeburg County line."

"Jesus, Chan, I don't know. I'm still not convinced about Watts, and now this? Talk about your wild goose chases."

"It's a thread, Tindal, I'll grant you that. But it's all we've got, and right now I'm hanging on to it for dear life."

11:09 AM

Showered, dressed and fully caffeinated, Tindal and Chan drove the eight miles to Palmetto Acres. It was a subdivision that was created during the housing boom of the early nineties.

Cookie cutter houses of brick, stucco and faux dormers lined the paved, symmetrical streets of the middle to upper class neighborhood. A few well-placed phone calls helped Chan snag the former coroner's address, and Tindal drove straight to it with no problem.

They stood together on the front porch as Chan rang the doorbell. A black woman in her early sixties answered the door. This was Medlin's caregiver, Annie Mae Mack.

"Yes, may I help you?" Mack asked with a doubtful look at the strangers.

"I'm Chan Adams and this is Tindal Huddleston," Chan said. "We're reporters doing a story on an old case, and we were wondering if Dr. Medlin wouldn't mind speaking to us for a few minutes."

Mack leaned back from the door and looked toward a side room and then back to the reporters. "Well, he is up now— sitting on the sun porch. But I don't know…"

"Please, Ma'am, we won't take up much of his time. This is very important and there are only certain questions he can answer."

Mack debated the reasonable request against her protective nature and eventually civility won out. "Okay, but only for a few minutes." She opened the door wider and led them in. "He's a former smoker, on oxygen now, so he wears down easily."

"I know how he feels," Chan said, rubbing his hand over his chest.

They entered the sun-porch, a room of deep windows and green plants. Medlin was in a wheelchair next to one of the windows. A nebulizer and oxygen tank were by his side. "Mistah Payton, you got two visitors," Mack announced. The thin, grey man with tubes running from under his nose turned in their direction. He furled his brow at their appearance.

Chan got on one knee in front of his chair like a knight before his king. "Dr. Medlin, I'm Chan Adams. I used to write for *The Republic*."

Medlin took only a few seconds. "The Macinaw Seven story," he said weakly.

Chan was taken aback by Medlin's clarity and smiled. "Yes, sir. Hard one to forget, isn't it?"

"Lord knows I've tried," Medlin said with his own smile. The smile faded and then, "What is it you all want?"

"They found Crawford's patrol car in the swamp. Back behind Henry Brooks' old place."

"I heard." Medlin pointed to a table loaded with newspapers. "I keep up with my friends. Dead or alive."

Chan indicated Tindal. "We are working the story. Some things have come up that may tie in to the Robert Dover murder in 1969." Medlin didn't respond but he maintained a look of interest. "I need to ask you some questions about your autopsy of Robert. Is that okay?" Medlin's look changed to one of discomfort but again he said nothing. "In your report, you stated that Robert showed signs of asphyxia, but there was no evidence that the rope allegedly used was the method of strangulation, correct?"

Medlin bobbed his head. "Yes, I found no other evidence that the rope submitted in court had been used to end Robert's life."

"But he was strangled with something, right?"

"Strangled, yes, I believe so. But I do not think he was hung with that rope. The surrounding tissues showed a lack of blood infiltration." He paused, took a deep breath and coughed. "There was no coagulated blood in the wounds."

"And there were no other surface marks, or bruises, correct? No fingernail marks. What, in your opinion, could have been used to strangle him?"

"I don't know. Nothing else was brought in as evidence if I recall."

"Could it have been cloth? A piece of clothing maybe?"

"Speculation, Adams. I don't deal in guesses. Never have."

"But could it have been a cloth material? To do that kind of damage and not leave any signature?"

The old man almost smiled. "Theoretically, it could have been almost anything."

Chan knew he was on the right track but let it go, he was just thankful the old man was still so coherent. "Dr. Medlin, one more thing. In your autopsy report, a paragraph had been taken out for the court proceedings. Do you know anything about that?" Chan turned to Tindal and signaled for the copy. She quickly pulled it from her handbag and showed it to the doctor.

"Right here, Dr. Medlin," Tindal said. "This paragraph has been redacted. We need to know why. Please, sir."

Medlin took the document in his frail hands and stared at it for a few moments. He looked back up. "Sensitive information of a delicate matter. They didn't want it to come out in court."

"Who didn't?" Tindal asked.

"The lawyers... and the Dover family."

Tindal caught Chan's eye before asking, "Can you tell us, sir? What was black-lined here?"

Medlin closed his eyes momentarily as if praying and then opened them and looked directly at Chan. "I'm an old man. I was sworn to secrecy those many years ago, but I don't wish to go to the grave with secrets hanging over me."

"Then tell us," Chan said, almost demanding it.

"When they brought Ellis Dover's boy to me, I did a thorough autopsy as I would in any situation like that. In addition to the effects of the obvious strangulation, Robert also suffered abrasions. Anal abrasions."

"He was sodomized?" Tindal asked.

"Yes, and done so vigorously, I may add."

JULY 10, 1976

Chan held the back of the canoe in his left hand and a small, white Styrofoam cooler in his right. He trailed Jean who was carrying the front of the canoe and leading them down an overgrown trail. They were both dressed in tank tops, shorts and flip-flops but their exposed skin was liberally lathered down in mosquito repellent.

"How much longer?" Chan hollered out.

"We're almost there. You can feel the temperature dropping quickly now."

Jean was right. The closer they got to the Edisto, the cooler the temperature became. The hundred degree Lowcountry heat could not reach them under the dark canopy of the river forest. And now away from the intense glare of the summer sun, Chan could see just how dense, green and richly varied the environment was into which they had stepped. It was truly like coming into another world. Giant oaks draped in Spanish moss stood watch over black willows, long-leaf pine, dogwood and oddly shaped maple trees. Under the trees, ferns and alligator grass mixed with fading wildflowers, and orange trumpet vine and wild kudzu, which seemingly sprung from everywhere, weaved it all into one natural tapestry.

The forest floor eventually opened a bit giving them greater visibility. They had to step over centuries' old fallen timbers and cypress knees as they neared the soft riverbank. They laid the canoe down so that only the bow touched the swirling black water.

Jean turned to face him. "Well?"

"Great so far," Chan said. "Are we going up river or down?"

"Let's go up and try for Watkins Bridge. That way when we burn out we can ride the current back down."

"Good thinking, Captain."

They were quickly underway with Jean again up front and Chan in the back. After a few missteps, they soon became synchronized in their paddling and were making lengthy strides up river.

They had only passed the first bend in the river, which was marked by a fallen gum tree, when Jean spotted their first snake. "Look there," she said, indicating with the tip of her paddle. The reptile slithered off the end of the gum and into the safety of the water.

"Moccasin?" Chan asked.

"Brown water snake. They're harmless."

"Hope you're right."

Jean laughed. "Now wait a minute, I know the man who stared down the barrel of a shotgun and ran through a burning house isn't afraid of a little snake."

"Let's just say I have a healthy respect for them and plan on keeping my distance."

"I think that's how the snakes feel about us as well, so we shouldn't have any trouble today."

Chan paddled a little more. "You seem very comfortable out here on the river."

Jean turned slightly, her blond hair resting on her brown shoulder. "My dad loved the Edisto. He used to take my sister and me out on it all the time. We'd fish or swim or sometimes just ride and look. I never tire of it."

"It is beautiful," Chan said, taking it in. "It beats work that's for sure."

Jean nodded her agreement. "Speaking of... how did work go this week? Any progress on Ja'Len's murder?"

"No. The police aren't giving details; they're making it hard to get a good read on things. But I get the feeling this thing is headed for a conclusion soon—one way or the other."

"What about the new angle you were working on? Any luck there?"

"No, but I've gotta keep trying." Chan couldn't go into the details with her, but nothing much had turned up on the Henry Brooks Disciples. Chan had spent a lot of the past week hanging out at Ricky's and monitoring Ryan Grubbs' trailer but to no avail. If they had something to do with knocking off the Macinaw Seven, he hadn't made that connection yet. "Hopefully we'll know more by next week."

"I hope so. For Macinaw's sake... and yours... and mine. For everyone's sake."

Chan could feel the weight of the story on them again and decided to change the subject. "So, what did you bring in the cooler?"

Jean turned again and smiled. "Open it and see."

Chan lifted the lid and pulled a can from the ice. "Old Milwaukee?"

"Tastes as great as its name," Jean said with a laugh. "Left over from our dinner you missed the other night."

Chan popped the top. "I'll help myself now if that's okay. You want one?"

Jean turned and crawled to the middle of the canoe and reached for hers. She sat on the middle bar and opened the beer. "What should we drink to?"

"How about to no more missed dinners?"

She squinted her eyes at him. "With you? Mr. busy reporter? Doubtful, but here's hoping."

They clicked cans, took a couple of quick sips and then just as quickly continued their way up river.

11:52 AM

The Reverend Daniel Howard sat in a chair next to Deonte Johnson in Crawford's office. The two black men were surrounded by sheriff's deputies, South Carolina Law Enforcement Division agents and FBI—all of whom were white. Crawford leaned forward in his chair with his forearms resting on his desk.

"Deonte, this could all be over in a matter of minutes," Crawford said. "You tell us what you know—who has really been behind all this—and I can guarantee you your safety." Deonte remained mute; his hands folded in his lap. Crawford waited and then, "Otherwise we can't do anything to help you. Five of your friends are dead. Now is the time to come clean."

Howard waited for Johnson, and when he did not respond, he leaned in. "I'm no lawyer, Sheriff Crawford, but I do know that these episodes have traumatized Mr. Johnson and Reverend Anderson beyond a reasonable measure. They have shut down, completely—to me, their wives, families, to everyone. I do not think, sir, that these gentlemen are in any position to help the authorities." He leaned back. "However, that does not negate your responsibility to protect these citizens in this matter. And I want your guarantee that they will be protected this time."

"You need not lecture me, Reverend Howard. We have gone to great lengths to protect these men."

"Pardon me, Sheriff, but all evidence stands to the contrary."

"We have a job to do here. And to do that, we must have cooperation from all involved."

"We have cooperated, Sheriff. And where has that gotten us? The majority of our people must live with your unjust and biased laws—civil rights, employment opportunities, potential for growth—all have been negated in this climate."

"I'm not talking about those realities. I leave all that pontificating to the poets and the politicians. I'm talking about catching a killer here."

"And you have failed on that count five times."

"Take a look around this room, Reverend. These men represent the finest in law enforcement from the county, the state and the nation. They are not here for their health. They are dedicated to the cause."

"And what cause is that, Sheriff? To watch young, black men in this town die? Isn't it enough that we must endure the injustices of a racist society? Must we also watch our people suffer like this?"

"I resent the implication, Reverend. We serve and protect everyone."

"Bull. Don't you think we know by now how it works? This isn't anything new." Howard stood and leaned on the desk. "We are the cannon fodder in this war. You shine your badges with big money from the deep-pocket folks and spit-polish it with the blood from the rest of us. It has been the way of this country for beyond two-hundred years, Sheriff. And some things never change." Howard turned to go. "Let's go, Deonte."

Johnson stood and the two men walked out. The door closed and everyone in the room looked to Crawford who leaned back in his chair. He paused, took a deep breath and said, "Well? How was my performance?"

Dunn moved from the wall and took the chair vacated by Howard. "It will have to do. The blacks and everyone else must believe that you're getting tired of the blame game."

"Believe me, I am. But do you think it will be enough?"

"We'll see," said Dunn. "We need them to believe that you're pissed enough to no longer care about protecting them. Hopefully when you start pulling the watchers from Johnson's and Anderson's houses, it will draw the killer in. And that's when we'll nab him." He looked over at Deputy Haskit. "What stands the presence there now?"

"Chief Stodges has two of his criminal investigators on the street and one in the home. And we have patrols going by there every thirty minutes," Haskit said.

Dunn turned back to Crawford. "We'll need to lose the parade. Eventually, we need to whittle it down to one undercover."

"What about Reverend Howard and his muscle?" Deputy Evans asked. "They're with him day and night also."

"Leave Howard to me," Dunn said. "I'll make a phone call and have him his crew out of South Carolina by tomorrow." Crawford could tell the rest of the team was impressed with Dunn's tough talk although the sheriff just saw it as more evidence of his arrogance.

Crawford then stood and looked at the group. "I think that will be all gentlemen. You'll have your orders soon." Everyone except for Dunn exited the office. The FBI man just sat there, folding his hands in a pensive manner. Crawford stared at him. "Did I forget something, Special Agent Dunn?"

Dunn went to his coat pocket and pulled out several photos. He tossed them on the desk. "Look at these, Sheriff. My men have spotted this man on several occasions outside Grubbs' trailer and at that bar he hangs out at. Do you recognize him?"

Crawford thumbed through the dark and grainy photographs. He nodded. "Name's Adams. He's a reporter for *The Macinaw Republic*. He's probably staking out Grubbs too." Crawford tossed the photographs back. "He's harmless."

"Point is, Sheriff, he knows about Grubbs. He knows there's a possible connection. How does a small-time reporter know about such an important suspect?"

Crawford frowned and shook his head. "Don't know. Word must have got out."

"And that's what bothers me, Sheriff. Do you trust everyone on your team?"

"Come again?"

"Do you trust them? Our plan to catch this guy will only work if everyone's on board."

"Yes, of course I trust them. Most have been with me for years."

"We can't have a slip up with this or it could be a disaster. We can't have our plan, as you put it, getting out."

"We're a small town, Agent Dunn. Word travels fast. Hell, half the old women in this town have police scanners just to keep up with the latest gossip. But with this… count on it being airtight. There'll be no slip ups."

1:23 PM

Shirtless, buzzed and more than just a little tired, Chan laid out on the sandbar like an old river gator after a big meal. He and Jean had finished the six pack of beer and devoured the pimento cheese sandwiches and apple slices she had tucked away in the cooler. After circling under Watkins Bridge with arms raised in victory, they coasted back to the sandbar—only a short float away—for a well-deserved lunch and rest.

"This feels great," Chan said. "I may never want to leave."

"I hear you," Jean said, who was lying beside him. "I can't think of a time when I was more relaxed."

Chan threw his arm over his eyes to block the rays that had managed to slip through the umbrella of trees. He could feel beads of sweat inching down his chest. "It's still hot though. Wish we had brought our bathing suits."

Jean sat up. "You really are a river rookie, aren't you?"

"What do you mean?"

Jean stood and grabbed his hand. "Stand up." He slowly and begrudgingly got to his feet, dusting the sand from his back. "Now, turn around," she instructed. Chan turned toward the canoe, which was beached right next to him.

"What now?" Chan asked. He jumped a little when Jean's tank top flew past his shoulder and into the bow of the canoe.

But then a big smile drew across his face. Her jean shorts were next, followed quickly by her bra and underwear. Her splash into the river was his cue to turn back around.

Jean surfaced and slicked back her hair. "Okay, Georgia boy, your turn."

"And your time to turn around," he said with a laugh. Jean pretended to be put out as she turned to the far bank of the river.

Chan faced the canoe, unbuttoned his shorts, slid them past his ankles and then did the same with his boxers. A loud wolf-whistle followed. Chan jumped in and surfaced. "Hey, no fair peeking like that."

"Aw, c'mon, when you were in the hospital I peeked lots of times," Jean said with a smile.

Chan laughed and swam toward her. "How are you maintaining your position like that? The current is so strong here."

"Come closer. There's a fallen tree about four feet under that stretches to the sandbar. You can grab hold and hang on."

He made it to the submerged tree and put his feet down. Jean reached out and grabbed his hand to steady him. Being naked with the cold river water rushing over his body was exhilarating enough, but being so close to her now was almost too much for Chan to handle. He inched closer until they were face to face. With her hair slicked back, her eyes seemed even bluer than before. She was so beautiful.

There were no words as they embraced. His hands moved up and down every inch of her body—smooth, silky—finding their way. They kissed more deeply than ever before. He felt her legs wrap around him and he pulled her in tighter.

The current finally whisked them away from the sunken tree and Chan had to kick a few strokes to make it back to the sandbar. He picked her up out of the water and gently laid her down in the sand. She reached out and grabbed the back of his neck, pulling him closer.

On this little strip of isle, in the middle of this black water river, time stood still for Chan and Jean. There was no past, no future, no stress, no worry. Only the present. Only the moment. Only them.

3:48 PM

Ellis Dover drove his black Cadillac Eldorado convertible through the back entrance and down a small privacy drive of Macinaw Memorial, the town's oldest cemetery. He was alone, but he had his handgun in the glove box. He motored through the old, shabby, colored section which was filled with unmarked graves of former slaves, sons of slaves and their forgotten descendants.

He passed through a cut-road which climbed a small hill and which led to the white burial section. He passed the giant oak at the top of the hill and then branched off to the right where the hilltop not only provided a scenic view of the nearby winding Edisto but was also a parcel of prime real estate where only the most aristocratic of Macinaw's citizens were laid to rest. He pulled off under another oak and parked. He sat there and debated his next move. Caution won out—he grabbed the gun from the glove box, stuck it in his waistband, and exited the car.

As he had done hundreds of times before, he made his way near to the river's edge where his family marker, a large handsome granite slab stood. The massive and ornate memorial ironically had a sword waving statue of the Archangel Michael rising from its center. All the Dovers, beginning with Ellis Dover's great grandfather, were buried in the plot. His was a family of farmers, planners, town makers, and history creators—important people in both life and death. Ellis Dover held all who were buried here in the highest regard including his beloved wife, but his attention was always drawn to Robert's small bronze marker.

Dover went to his knees in front of Robert's grave. He closed his eyes and hung his head.

"Can he hear you?" a voice called from behind.

Dover turned and then rose to his feet. He stared down Ryan Grubbs. "Yes, I believe that he can."

"Can you hear him?"

Dover furled his brow. "What do you mean?"

"Ain't he in there saying 'Daddy, daddy, get me out. I can't breathe down here,'" Grubbs said laughing.

"That's not funny, you sick son-of-a-bitch," Dover shot back.

Grubbs held up his hands. "Take it easy, big daddy. Just trying to lighten the mood—out here in a damn graveyard of all places.'"

"This place is sacred to me, so no more jokes, understand?"

"Fine. It's your dime. You invited me here. What does the richest man in Macinaw want from a guy like me?"

Dover straightened, trying to calm himself. "I just wanted to let you know that I got word the police are backing away. They're gonna be pulling back from the other two."

"The other two?"

"The two remaining of the Macinaw Seven. Crawford and the cops are gonna be pulling back their forces. Those colored boys will be vulnerable again."

"What's that to me, old man?"

Dover took a step forward. "So that you can strike. So that you can get rid of them. Finish them off."

"What makes you think I give a damn about that?"

Dover drew a heavy hand across his forehead. "You're a Henry Brooks Disciple for Christ's sake. The other five have had the angel sigils carved into them. Surely you and your gang are behind this."

"Hate to disappoint you, Dover. But like I've told the police: I ain't had nothing to do with it."

"Then who?" Dover asked.

Grubbs shoved his hands in his front pockets and shrugged. "I ain't got no idea." He motioned to the grave beyond. "You're good at talking to ghosts apparently. Maybe you should be thanking Henry Brooks himself."

8:22 PM

Chan entered the kitchen door of Jean's house and dumped the cooler's ice in the sink. He heard Jean call out to him from the back of the house, "Chan?"

"Yeah, I put the canoe back behind the pump house like you asked."

Jean came into the kitchen carrying bandages and a bottle of iodine. "Okay, thanks. Have a seat there and let me take a look at the cut."

Chan sat at the kitchen table and held up his injured right hand showing the laceration to his palm. "It's not too bad. The bleeding has stopped."

"Well, let me see," Jean said as she sat next to him. "I can't believe you're so injury prone."

"I'm not really. I just wanted to see you in action as a nurse again," he joked.

"And on my day off too," she said, doctoring the wound. "Next time we're on the river, no more diving from the sandbar for you, Mister."

"I was just trying to keep up with you. Who knew another underwater branch would be right there waiting on me?"

"You're not a professional river rat yet, remember? Maybe you can move up the ranks one day," Jean said with a smile. She completed the wrap. "Done. How does that feel?"

Chan flexed his fingers in and out. "Better than ever, thanks."

"So, what now?" Jean asked.

Chan hesitated and then looked to the phone on the kitchen counter. "Maybe I should call Norma. See what's happened today."

"Can't let it go, can you?"

"No," he drew a cigarette from the pack, lit it and leaned back in the chair. "I'm sorry."

"It's okay. Your need to know mirrors Macinaw's need. And it's gotta be in your hands first before it's in ours."

Chan paused as he blew smoke. "What do you remember about Henry Brooks?"

Jean shook her head as she thought about it. "Not much. I was twelve at the time of his trial. Daddy probably kept most of the horrifying news from us. I do remember stories he told me later about how on pins and needles every parent was during that time. They talked about it in hushed tones and made doubly sure the children were always safe." She drummed her fingers on the table. "I do remember the day when they caught him. Dad came in the house all relieved, told us it was over. He was shocked too—that it was Brooks. Dad had done some work for him out at his house years before. Thought he was a nice enough fellow."

"What kind of work?"

"Shelves, I think. Or cabinets. I told you dad did carpentry work on the side."

Chan nodded. "When was this?"

"Before all the madness began. '61 or '62."

"He didn't notice anything strange about the man?"

"Just that he was super skinny—a bean pole, my dad called him. But he was pleasant and he paid him right there on the spot."

Chan flicked his ash in a plastic cup. "I wonder what made Brooks snap."

"Lord knows, but it was quite the turn to evil, wasn't it?"

"Deputy Haskit told me the other day that the Macinaw Seven believe that it really is Henry Brooks coming after them—that his body may be dead but his evil presence lives on, hunting them down. You don't believe that, do you?"

"Maybe not in physical form, but I do think strong emotions can transcend time and place. And hate is very powerful."

"So how do you stop it?"

Jean smiled. "With love of course. There's nothing that evil fears more than love."

Chan smiled back. He extinguished his smoke, reached over and locked his fingers within hers. They became quiet—their eyes connecting.

"Stay with me tonight," she whispered.

Chan leaned over the table, kissed her cheek and then said in his own whisper, "I thought you'd never ask."

OCTOBER 4, 2016

Tindal glanced over at Chan who was still lost in thought staring out the passenger side window. She didn't want to disrupt his thought processes but her questions couldn't wait.

"You knew, didn't you? You knew that the sodomy of Robert Dover was what was redacted from the coroner's report."

Chan nodded, but continued to look out the window. "I had a feeling."

"So why didn't the prosecution use it in court? It could have been more fuel for the fire if they believed the Macinaw Seven had also raped the boy."

Chan turned to face her. "That wasn't the evidence. Remember there were no other marks or bruises on Dover's body. He hadn't been beaten up, nothing broken; his clothes had not been torn. If he had been raped by the Seven there would have been more evidence of that."

"He was a willing participant in the sodomy?"

"Yes. And those seven black kids had nothing to do with it. I don't know why they were there at that barn exactly, probably had some harmful intent, but they didn't carry it out because of what they witnessed."

"And what did they witness?"

"Do you know what a gasper is?"

Tindal nodded. "Someone who is engaged in erotic asphyxiation—I actually did a report on it for Reuters several months ago. They intentionally restrict oxygen to their brain for sexual arousal. Are you saying that was what Dover was doing?"

"It makes sense forensically, doesn't it? He is strangled to death while someone is sodomizing him from behind. Probably used a shirt or even his underwear to bind around his neck. They say that when the brain is deprived of oxygen and combined with orgasm, the rush is more powerful than any drug."

Tindal nodded and tapped the top of the steering wheel with her hands. "That's true. Back in the day during public hangings male victims often developed erections that lasted even after death."

"Right. Some even ejaculated after death," Chan said. He then smiled and added, "What a way to go though, huh?"

Tindal rolled her eyes. "So accidental death. And then Dover's partner freaks out and tries to make it look like a suicide."

"Which might have worked except you had seven witnesses caught running from the barn. Seven black kids who saw the whole thing."

"Which changes the cover-up from suicide to blaming the Macinaw Seven."

"Yes, except the evidence for that scenario did not add up and the Seven are set free."

"But they are forewarned by Sonny Watts not to say anything or else."

"Exactly."

"So who was Dover's partner? Watts?" Tindal asked.

Chan shook his head. "Watts was meeting with clients in Macinaw. They say he got a call that day and then rushed down to the jailhouse."

They both went quiet for a moment. Tindal finally spoke up, "Do you have a suspect in mind?"

"No, not really. Someone connected to Watts obviously. Someone with the power to make it happen. The Dovers were allied with some very powerful people—the list could be endless." He paused and then, "How many times did Watts meet with Henry Brooks?"

"Five documented times. Who knows outside of that? Hopefully we'll get some more info once we get to his old office."

"Right." Chan turned again to the window and looked at a scarecrow in a passing cornfield. "We're coming after you, Henry Brooks. And this time we're gonna nail your ass."

MARCH 15, 1966

10:52 PM

Father Andrew Carroll sat in the waiting room at the Columbia Correctional Institute where the families of death row inmates would gather before being led into the observation room of the "death house" to watch the execution. It would have been the priest's job during this hour to comfort the grieving family before the horrendous deed was to take place. Tonight, however, he held his Bible and looked sadly at the other chairs—all empty—there would be no family members, no loved ones, coming to witness the death of Mr. Henry Brooks.

Carroll had done this unfortunate calling twice before—two black men who had pleaded with him in their final hours, begging for forgiveness, seeking mercy of the highest order. It had been gut-wrenching to listen to the men relive their crimes, desperate for forgiveness and redemption. He did not know if he had the stomach to go through it again. He was a last-minute substitute for this execution and had not yet met Henry Brooks. But he knew all men in the fore moment of death seek some form of absolution and there was always a critical need for a man of God to be present.

He anxiously rose from his chair and went to the oblong-shaped, grate-covered window. A powerful spring storm stirred outside the old building. *God's wrath*, thought Carroll. *The Supreme Being would have nothing to do with man's killing of his fellow man.*

Chick Haynes, a correctional officer, stuck his head into the waiting room. "Time, Padre."

Carroll followed Haynes through a series of heavy doors, out into the rainy prison yard and then back inside the institute's death house. A dark hallway led to the cells where the condemned awaited their fate. The cells were small, foul-smelling and frighteningly old. They reminded Carroll of the catacombs in Edgar Allan Poe's gothic tale, *Cask of Amontillado*, which he had read as a boy. He was at least comforted that most of these dreary cells were empty.

174

A second guard met up with Haynes and then led them all to cell number six where Henry Brooks sat in a folding chair facing the cell door. Brooks had been completely shaved and looked sickly thin, his prison garb falling off his shoulders. He was hunched over but sat up a little as the door was opened. Carroll walked in and stood in front of Brooks. Chick Haynes closed the cell door but stayed at attention behind it with the other correctional officer.

"Mr. Brooks, I'm Father Carroll. I've come to talk with you. See if you'd like the comfort of the good book. Maybe you have a favorite verse I can read to you? Or perhaps you'd care to repent at this hour."

Henry Brooks stared the man down with his vulture eyes, cleared his throat and said, "*Isaiah* 13 *verse* 9: Behold, the day of the Lord cometh, cruel both with wrath and fierce anger, to lay the land desolate: and he shall destroy the sinners thereof out of it." The convicted murderer then laughed and said, "Repent? Nosah, I have nothing to repent. I have been a vessel for my God. I have carried out His wishes here on this earth and I shall be richly rewarded." He hesitated and squinted at the priest. "You, however, have much to repent, don't you? I can see it in your eyes. Yessah, you do. Why does Abaddon call you to the fire?"

Carroll shook his head. "Abaddon? Sir, I have nothing…"

"Oh, you do, Father. What is your vice? Little girls? Little boys?" Brooks moved around his seat like a stirred cobra in a basket, moving his head to different angles. "That's it, isn't it? You like the little ones."

Carroll scrunched his brow. "Sir?"

"You will lead dark forces in Armageddon's final wave. Until then you shall burn for your unforgivable sins."

"This is absurd, Mr. Brooks. I'm here for your comfort."

Brooks flashed his crooked teeth. "But you'd rather be back at your church screwing them little fat-bottomed choir boys, ain't cha?" He snapped his teeth down like he was biting him.

"The hell…?" Carroll backed away.

The priest turned to Haynes who just shook his head. "All right, Brooks. That's enough." He unlocked the door again. Carroll quickly stepped out, shaken and confused. The guards entered, cuffed Brooks, forced him to stand, and walked him out of the cell.

Brooks turned to look behind him and laughed at the holy man. "They gonna fry me now, Father, but your time is comin'. Yessah, your time is comin'."

Carroll followed them as they made their way through the labyrinth of the old building—rain falling through the leaky ceiling. He tried to read a verse of scripture he had prepared but stumbled through the words. Once they reached the execution room, Carroll went gratefully into the viewing area and stood with his head down behind the others.

The guards were met by Warden Perry Haldwell and Doctor Nate Carlson who would call Henry Brooks' death. They strapped Brooks to the chair with belts that crossed his chest, groin, arms and legs. They moistened a sponge with brine and attached it and a metal skullcap with an electrode to his head. Haynes lifted Brooks' pants leg and attached an additional electrode to his shaved calf. They rolled up his shirt sleeves to tighten the straps holding his bony arms to the chair. On his right forearm was the Michael sigil, and on the left was Abaddon's— they were not tattoos but carvings done by his own hand. As a last measure, Chick Haynes blindfolded Brooks.

With Brooks strapped to the chair and everything prepared, the four men joined the others who had come to watch the proceedings. In addition to the priest, Macinaw County solicitor Tommie Frierson, Macinaw Sheriff Justin Crawford, *The Macinaw Republic* reporter Norma Wiles, WIS TV reporter Frank Beacham, and defense attorney Matt Campbell stood in the observation room watching through the glass windows. Also there, but standing away from the others was Sonny Watts.

Although Watts now worked for another law firm, he had asked his former bosses at Crane and Campbell for permission to attend. Though bewildered by the request, they granted him access and Watts' guarded appearance in the observation room went largely unnoticed by the others.

Warden Haldwell pressed the call button. "Any last words, Mr. Brooks?"

"You think it's done? Nosah, it's just beginning. Remember what I told you. Good and evil—souls are but one or the other.

The true power lies in who decides which is which!" He laughed heartily again.

Haldwell released the call button and all went silent in the observation room. He checked the wall clock, turned to Haynes and nodded. Haynes signaled the executioner who pulled the switch and sent 2,000 volts into Henry Brooks. Brooks jumped and shook as the electricity ran through him zapping his life away. His pale skin reddened and those rabbit eyes of his finally popped out of their sockets, blood seeping into the blindfold. Only Crawford and the correctional crew didn't turn away from the horror.

After a final series of jolts, it was done. Henry Brooks, killer of thirty-eight people, lay slumped over in the electric chair. After taking a few moments to gather himself, Dr. Nate Carlson entered the execution room to check the body. He pulled a stethoscope from his bag, first holding the diaphragm to the killer's chest and then the bell. He listened for over a minute.

Haldwell became anxious and pressed the call button. "Well?"

Carlson turned and nodded. "He's dead. It's over."

There was a sense of relief from all who had gathered, their shoulders relaxed, they breathed easier, and nodded their satisfaction.

All except for Watts who remained standing alone in the back. He stared at the dead body of Henry Brooks and then whispered to himself, "No, it's not over. There will be a time for such unqualified madness again."

JULY 16, 1976

1:23 AM

Dixie Love stepped out through the curtain of beads, under the glare of the multi-colored spotlights and into the gaze of ten lonely truckers who sat around the stage waiting for Dixie to do her thing. She wore white cowboy boots and little else—a red, white and blue G-string with tiny silver stars over the ends of her ample breasts. Her makeup was caked on and covered an aging face—once pretty but beaten down after dancing in too many smoky dives like this one. Her body, however, was still firm yet lissome. And she knew how to work it, much to the delight of the patrons. She had become the star attraction at Dolly's Dollies as most of the other dancers had neither her looks nor charisma. She gave them a glimpse and a smile every night even when it took all she had just to get out there. Like many of those who survived in this business, Dixie had learned to cover the scars and bruises of her life well.

Chan watched her from the bar area. He had been to the strip joint the week before, but it had been a slow night and he could find no one from whom to solicit information on Ryan Grubbs or the Henry Brooks Disciples. But he had been impressed with Dixie that night and he didn't exactly mind that he had to take in her performance again. He did feel a bit sleazy being in place like this, especially since Jean had now become such a big part of his life, but he rationalized it was his job and the story demanded his presence.

The strange techno music coming from the jukebox that accompanied her routine came to an end, and she delighted in the calls, whistles and dollar bills that were thrown her way. As the next dancer appeared on stage, Dixie slid the bills into her G-string and headed for the bar. Once there, she motioned to the bartender. "Jim, get me a gin and tonic."

Chan, leaning against the bar, raised his beer bottle to her and smiled. "Nice job out there."

Her eyes were on him for only a second. "Money talks, sweetheart, bullshit walks."

Chan threw a twenty on the bar. "How much talking will that give me?"

Dixie leaned over and grabbed the twenty before answering. "Another twenty and we can have us a private dance." She then turned up the femininity in her voice, looked his way and smiled. "You think you'd like that, big man?"

Chan nodded and threw another twenty on the bar. "Lead the way."

Dixie grabbed the money, her drink and Chan's hand in one swoop motion. She led him across the room, in front of the stage and to a little private room beyond the juke box. Once inside, she closed the door, sat Chan down in a cushioned chair and pushed play on an eight-track tape deck which was built into a side wall. Jimi Hendrix's *Purple Haze* came through the private speakers and Dixie went immediately into her moves.

Chan watched for a moment and then stood. He pressed the pause button on the player.

"What the hell you doing, cowboy?" Dixie asked.

Chan grabbed Dixie by the wrists and gently sat her down in the chair. "My forty bucks, my dance," he said.

Dixie's puzzled look turned to concern, and she shook her head. "No, no, we aren't allowed to do that in this place. The manager will...."

"Relax. I just want to talk with you."

"Talk?"

"Yeah. I figure I bought about five minutes of your time and I want to use it the best way I see fit."

Dixie leaned back in the chair, snapped her G-string against her hip and looked blankly at the stranger. "Okay. So, what do you want to talk about?"

"Dixie Love," he said. "Nice name. Is that your real name?"

"Are you kidding me? If we're gonna talk names, then I'm outta here."

"Okay, okay," he said. "To be honest, I'm looking... to score some meth, and I hear a train runs through here every now and then."

"Who told you that?"

"People."

She eyed him cautiously. "What's that got to do with me?"

Chan kind of shrugged. "Thought maybe you might help a fellow out."

"Listen, sweetheart, I ain't getting involved in this." She stood up but Chan blocked her from leaving.

"Well, then tell me somebody who *can* help me with this," Chan demanded.

"I'm sorry, I don't know nobody."

"What about Grubbs?"

Dixie furled her brow. "Grubbs? How do you know Grubbs?"

He gave her another shrug. "People."

"Same people, huh? Damn this is getting weird." She tried to get passed him but again he stopped her by grabbing her arm.

"A friend of mind. He's a Disciple. You know, a Henry Brooks Disciple."

Dixie's look of concern morphed into fear, and she shook loose from his hold. "Man, you don't know who you're fucking with." Dixie bolted past him and left the private dancing room.

Chan eased out the room as well. There was another stripper on the stage and everyone's attention seemed to be on her. Chan went back to the bar and stayed for another forty-five minutes, but for the rest of the night, there was no more sign of Dixie Love.

8:33 AM

Justin Crawford sat at his desk and rubbed the sleep from his eyes, ignoring the paperwork in front of him. Deputy Haskit was across from him in a guest chair reading *The Macinaw Republic*. The deputy eased the paper down on his boss's desk and looked up.

"Norma quotes the state head of the NAACP as saying you've turned your back on the blacks in this county."

Crawford shrugged. "I know. I read it earlier. After we catch this bastard, I've got a lot of fence mending to do."

Haskit scratched his chin. "What about hiring a black deputy? You know ol' Red Tie, Sheriff Seigler, did it down in Colleton recently. Maybe that would be a good move for us."

Crawford laughed. "Can you imagine? Ellis Dover would have my head in a vice if I did that." He paused and lost the smile. "But maybe the world is going that way. The South is sure different from when we were kids."

"No doubt," Haskit said. "In ten years, we'll probably have us a black sheriff too."

Crawford raised his hand in a stopping gesture. "Bite your tongue, Deputy." They both laughed at that.

The phone rang and Crawford picked up. "Sheriff's Office. Crawford speaking."

It was Agent Dunn on the line. "Sheriff, Grubbs is on the move. He's in his truck and headed out of Eastland."

Crawford covered the receiver and snapped his fingers at his deputy, "Who's on watch now?"

"Deputy Evans is covering Johnson and Chief Stodges has one of his investigators on Anderson," Haskit said.

Crawford nodded and went back to the phone. "Which way is he going?"

"He's on Medway—heading east towards town."

"You on him now?" Crawford asked.

"We're four cars back, but yeah we got him marked."

"Sheriff," another deputy urgently called from the office's open door.

Crawford looked up. "What is it?"

"Fire downtown. Looks like it could be a big one," the deputy said.

"Shit. Where?"

"The Piggly Wiggly. The fire chief says he may need some help."

"All right. Tell him I'm on the way." Crawford held the phone—anguish spreading throughout his face.

Haskit jumped to his feet but waited on the sheriff to make his move.

Crawford put the phone to his ear again as he stood. "Dunn, we've got a fire I've got to get to. Stay on Grubbs and let me know through radio." He didn't wait for Dunn's reply and slammed down the receiver.

"Of all the rotten luck..." Crawford said as he made his way toward the door.

"When it rains, it pours," Haskit added as he followed Crawford out.

9:23 AM

Chief Archie Howe directed his two ladder teams as they brought the blaze under control at the popular grocery store. Hoses ran everywhere and the parking lot was covered in an inch of water. EMT's moved in and out of the fire zone making sure all emergency personnel were safe. The city police and sheriff's deputies had the area cordoned off and helped with traffic and crowd control.

Crawford sat in his patrol car with the door opened—his left foot on the lot's pavement as Haskit walked up to him. "Looks fairly well contained. Chief Howe said they may be able to enter the building in a few minutes."

Crawford blew out a breath. "That's good. Thank God no one was hurt."

"Any word on our boy, Grubbs?"

"Dunn reported that he pulled into a red dot and has been inside for the past thirty minutes."

Haskit checked his watch. "Fairly early to be getting your drunk on, but we are talking about Rhino here."

Before Crawford could add anything else, the radio crackled with Dunn's voice. "Target on the move. He's back heading east on Medway. Past the Shell station now and taking Highway 54."

"He's gonna cross the tracks into the colored section of town," Haskit offered.

Crawford nodded and waited for Dunn's next report.

Within a few minutes, it came: "He's picking up speed. Taking a right onto Montgomery now."

"Montgomery?" Crawford asked rhetorically.

"That's the Nance Subdivision," Haskit confirmed. "He's headed for Anderson's house."

"Come on," Crawford yelled as he cranked his patrol car. Haskit slid in on the passenger's side and they peeled out of the parking lot—the wheels grinding and the engine humming.

Crawford reached for the radio mike. "Dunn, he's headed for Anderson's. Time to call in the cavalry."

"They're on the way," Dunn shot back.

9:32 AM

Ryan Grubbs pulled over on the corner of Montgomery and Whitman Street. He hesitated for a moment, checking all the mirrors on his truck to be sure. He reached across the seat, grabbed a brown bag and then exited the vehicle.

He walked slowly—like a predator—his eyes scanning in every direction. He cut across Whitman Street and then made his way down the sidewalk. A few more steps and he would be there.

He turned and leaned against the fence of the small brown house—the house of William Anderson. It was dark and there was no activity, but Grubbs knew Anderson was inside. *Probably on his knees praying.* He played it cool and waited knowing this would be his big moment.

"Freeze right there, asshole!" a voice came from behind him.

Grubbs did as he was told. He froze like a statue. Anderson's watcher, Lieutenant Lucas Webster of the Macinaw Police, kept his .38 trained on the back of Grubbs' head.

Within seconds, Whitman Street was filled with blaring sirens and unmarked cop cars sliding to a stop. Agent Dunn came hustling out of one, passed the lieutenant and stuck his pistol in Grubbs' back. "Easy does it now. Hand over the bag."

Grubbs handed him the bag without a word. As Dunn backed away, Webster patted Grubbs down.

Dunn opened the bag. He remained motionless for a moment and then reached inside and pulled out a bottle. "What the hell is this?"

Grubbs finally turned and faced Dunn. "It's a bottle of scotch. Good stuff, so I hear."

Dunn ignored him and shot a look at Lt. Webster. The cop shook his head. "He's clean, sir. He's got nothing on him."

Sheriff Crawford and Deputy Haskit arrived and ran up as the interrogation continued.

"What are you doing here, Grubbs?" Dunn asked, pissed as hell.

"Making a delivery. Every so often, I deliver for Pete's Red Dot on Medway. Pick up some extra cash."

"Reverend Anderson ordered a bottle of scotch?" Crawford asked.

183

Grubbs grinned. "Nope. A Mr. Ron Harrington did." He pointed in the direction with a tip of his head. "I believe his house is three more doors down."

"Son of a bitch!" Dunn yelled, much to Grubb's amusement.

Crawford was shaking his head when it dawned on him. "Wait a minute," he said with urgency. "The fire this morning and now all this..." He trailed off as he grabbed his walkie-talkie from his belt. "Deputy Evans, come in please. This is Sheriff Crawford—over." He waited and then, "Deputy Evans, do you copy?" The return silence on the radio was deafening. Crawford started backing up towards his patrol car. He pointed at Lt. Webster. "Take him to the law complex for questioning and hold him there."

"Hey, man, I didn't do nothing," Grubbs said.

Crawford ignored Grubbs as he and Haskit jumped back into their patrol car and took off.

Dunn took a quick glance at Grubbs and said through gritted teeth, "For your sake, you better hope that Johnson is still alive." Dunn and his men then drove away as well.

Two uniformed policeman joined Webster and ushered Grubbs to a waiting police car. The Disciple put up no resistance and even smiled as they forced him into the backseat. *Brilliant move, Henry Brooks. Absolutely brilliant.*

9:55 AM

With weapons drawn, Crawford and Haskit bounded through Deonte Johnson's front door. "Deonte?!" Crawford yelled. They continued down the hallway. "Deonte?!"

Haskit signaled Crawford to stop and be quiet, and when he did, the sheriff heard it too. Crying was coming from a room down the hall. The two lawmen crept down the rest of the way to the room, Deonte's bedroom. Crawford could feel it in his gut even before he entered.

Deonte's wife, Sophia was on her knees next to Deonte's body at the foot of the bed. The Michael sigil had been savagely cut into the man's chest. Sophia turned and looked up at Crawford with a blank expression. "I just went out for a moment. Had to go to the laundry mat." She sucked back tears. "He said he'd be fine—promised to keep all the doors locked."

Crawford's shoulders sank like a deflated balloon. He holstered his gun, moved to Sophia and dropped to his knees beside her. He put a hand on her back. "I'm so sorry, Sophia."

She looked at him through watery eyes. "You said you wouldn't let this happen. You said you'd stop this killer. You promised, Sheriff. You promised."

Crawford could say nothing—she was right.

"Sheriff," Haskit said to get his attention. "I'll go check on Jimmy."

Crawford only nodded, knowing what Haskit would probably find.

11:22 AM

"They found a gas can in a dumpster behind the Pig," Chan told his editor. "Chief Howe is 99 percent sure it was arson."

Darby sat on the edge of his desk listening to Chan's report. "Did you get any art for us?"

Chan nodded. "I took a couple of shots. The best one is from the side. You can see the char of the burn run the entire brick wall."

"Okay, get them to the processing lab and get started on your draft. We'll lead with the fire in tomorrow's edition."

"Yes, sir," Chan said as he stood. He turned for the door but froze when Norma appeared. She seemed drugged—drained of emotion.

"Norma? Are you all right?" Darby asked.

Chan grabbed her by the hand and led her to the office chair. "What is it, Norma?"

Norma slowly sat. "Deonte Johnson is dead."

"What?" both men asked.

"He was murdered this morning. While the fire was happening downtown."

"How can that be?" Darby followed. "Did the police pull back entirely?"

Norma looked at her boss and then to Chan. "Deputy Evans was on watch. They found him in his car across the street. He had a stab wound to his throat. He's dead too."

"Jesus Christ," Darby said. "Do they have anyone in custody?"

185

Norma shook her head. "It's like all the others. No leads. No witnesses. Nothing."

Darby put his hands on his hips as he thought it through. "Okay, okay. Chan, I want you down at the law complex, pronto. See what else you can find out."

Chan nodded but still stood by Norma holding her hand.

"Norma, are you good to go on this? Or should I get someone else…"

"No," she said. "I'm good. It's just…" She looked at Chan. "He's not going to stop, is he? Not until the last one is dead."

"They'll stop him, Norma, somehow," Chan said giving her hand a squeeze.

"I pray that they will." She squeezed his hand back. "But I have a bad feeling they won't."

OCTOBER 4, 2016

3:46 PM

The Davis, Davis and Milton Law Firm was headquartered behind the Macinaw Courthouse on Beasley Street. The beautiful brick building once housed Fenster's, a five and dime store that saw its heyday back in the '40s and '50s. The onslaught of superstores eventually killed the family-run business and the three-story building sat unused for nearly six years.

Louis Gaines Davis, a Macinaw native, purchased the address along with law partner, Alex Milton in 1967. Refurbished through the years with hardwood floors, multiple conference rooms, a chandeliered reception hall, a well-equipped exercise room and plenty of office space overlooking the courthouse, the landmark building became the desired workplace of every lawyer in town. The firm became quite successful covering all types of law from civil disputes to divorce cases to real estate. And in 1968 they brought in a young attorney named Sonny Watts.

Chan and Tindal sat in the office of Louis Davis Jr. who, through sheer nepotism, advanced quickly to partner after joining the firm in 1988. He was a large, doughy man who wore ill-fitting clothes and had a penchant for leering at his female guests as Tindal was now uncomfortably aware.

"My secretary tells me you are interested in the employment record of one of our former associates. Is that correct?" Davis asked, followed by a floppy smile.

"Sonny Watts," Tindal replied. "He was an associate here from '68 until his death in '76."

"Yes, of course. And what exactly is it that you're hoping to find?"

"We think certain information about him may help us link together clues to the Macinaw Seven murders. Perhaps even solve the mystery behind the disappearance of Sheriff Crawford."

Davis rocked back and forth in his chair and raised his eyebrows. "Well, now, you have piqued my interest, Ms.

Huddleston. But I still fail to see how there could be a connection with all that and Mr. Watt's employment record."

"If you'll let us look at the records," Chan interjected, "we have other research that might make that connection clear."

For the first time, Davis shifted his eyes to Chan. "I just realized who you are Mr. Adams. You're that reporter from *The Macinaw Republic*. You're the one who did that exposé on the Macinaw Seven all those years ago."

"That's correct."

"You wrote a book about it, didn't you? Something about Henry Brooks' spirit or something?"

"*Chasing Henry Brooks' Ghost*," Chan corrected. He pointed. "It's right there on the shelf behind you."

Davis did a slow swivel, looked at his book collection and turned back again. "So it is. How about that?" He waited and then, "Still chasing ghosts, are we?"

"Perhaps. Listen, Mr. Davis, are you going to help us here or not?"

Davis sat back in his chair. "Well, what exactly do you need from his employment record?"

Tindal jumped back in. "Social security confirmation, former employers, records of his cases even. Afterwards, we plan on going next door to probate court to look at his will."

"His will?" Davis rubbed the arm rests of his chair. "Well, I guess we can come up with something for you two. You know, despite the acclaim he won for daddy's firm with the Macinaw Seven trial, I only met the man a few times in the years he worked here."

"What do you remember about him?" Tindal asked.

Davis thought about it and then smiled. "His hair. Kind of fell into his face like a sheep dog." He laughed at the comparison.

"What else?"

"Other than that, all I remember was how nice a man he was."

8:17 PM

Chan sat on one side of the booth at Shoney's restaurant reading through a yellow legal pad containing their notes on the afternoon discovery of Sonny Watts. Not only did Davis provide the desired employment information, but Watts' most recent will before his death had also been prepared by the firm and their copy saved them time and a trip to the probate office.

Tindal slid into the booth on the opposite side with her plate from the salad bar—dark green lettuce, chick peas, broccoli and pasta. She also had her *iPhone* out and was in the process of sending a text message.

Neither spoke for a few minutes until Chan looked up. "Savannah, Georgia."

Tindal nodded. "He was there for four years—from '64 to '68. An associate at Bingham and Dodd. There was no mention of his time at Crane and Campbell in his résumé."

Chan tapped his pen on the notepad. "The HBD's originated out of Savannah. What do you want to bet there's a connection there?"

"I've already made a few calls to some reporters I know in Savannah. They'll check on all that for us. But the real news is the will."

"What did you find?"

"Besides the burnt, worthless, uninsured house that he left to his ex-wife—*thanks for nothing, sweetheart*; his holdings, life insurance, stocks and other accounts—everything else—went to his cousin, Dale Watts, in Miami."

"Lucky cousin," Chan said.

"Yeah, except there is no cousin."

"What?"

"I checked for every version of the name, looked into Watts' family records, ran the social security numbers given on the executor's instructions, et cetera, et cetera. He doesn't exist. Never did."

"So what happened to Watts' money?"

"The Davis law firm wired it to a bank in Miami—in holding for whom they believed to be this mysterious cousin. It had a transfer time limit in the bank, specifically instructed in the executor of the estate's list of duties. It sat there for two months and then it was sent to an offshore account in Andorra—all two million."

"So, Watts fakes his death, pulls his Henry Brooks stunt and then later recoups all of his old assets from this offshore account."

Tindal nodded. "Yes. But get this: From what I could find out, the account is still active even today. They won't hand out any specific information to me obviously, but I did find out that the account has passed to three private bankers in the Banca Privada d'Andorra over the past forty years."

"Maybe he's drawing from the account living in Europe somewhere. To think that bastard might be out there in the world now, living it up, having the last laugh—makes me sick to the core."

Tindal nodded taking a bite of her salad. "And don't forget, he was no doubt paid handsomely for arranging the return of Henry Brooks."

"You're right. He had a good life here in Macinaw as a lawyer. He must have been paid a pretty penny to go through all that—burning his house, killing one of his migrant workers, having his hand in the deaths of the Macinaw Seven and Lord knows what else.

They suspended the conversation momentarily as the Shoney's waitress brought Chan his cheeseburger and fries. He chewed on a fry as Tindal continued to probe: "How long was it between the time Watts was supposedly killed in that fire and when Sheriff Crawford disappeared."

"Nearly six weeks. Why?"

"Where did Watts go—what did he do? He fakes his death but to what end? Did he slip out of the country then? Was he involved in the actual murders of the Macinaw Seven or was he just manipulating things, pulling the strings? There are still a lot of unanswered questions."

Chan bit into his burger. "He was in court the day Luther Jennings was killed—so that rules him out of that one. And they believe that Cheeseboro and Grimes were killed in late afternoon which would have been hard to place him at that motel at that time without someone knowing. I'll have to double check his whereabouts, but my guess is he was the manipulator. The HBD's or another hired killer may have done the dirty work."

190

"But even as manipulator wouldn't he have stuck around Macinaw after he faked his death? Just to make sure everything went according to his plan."

"What are you getting at Tindal?"

"The man is supposed to be dead. His house is gone. If he was directly involved in the murders of the Seven or not, he still would have hung around—to manipulate things like you said. So the question is where did he hide out? Where did he live for those six weeks?"

Chan smiled at his quick-thinking partner. "Where no one would have ever bothered to look for him. The home of Henry Brooks."

"Yes."

"That's why Crawford was out there. He found out somehow. He was looking for Watts. Damn it, that's gotta be it."

"It would make sense," she confirmed.

Chan shook a fry at Tindal like a teacher with a ruler. "We've got to get in there. We've got to search that old house."

"You heard Sheriff Monroe. The FBI won't allow it."

Chan flipped the fry into the air and caught it in his mouth. "What the FBI doesn't know won't hurt them."

JULY 28, 1976

"Where the hell is he?" Agent Dunn asked for the third time.

Crawford moved from behind his desk and shut the door to his office. He indicated for Dunn to sit and then the sheriff returned to his own seat. "He's safe, Agent Dunn. That's all anyone needs to know at the moment."

"That is not all I need to know, Sheriff," Dunn said adamantly. "This investigation is under my watch. I am responsible for Reverend Anderson. We had an agreement, remember? You must tell me where he is."

Crawford put an unlit cigar into his mouth and chewed on its end as he debated what to tell the FBI man. "He's in a safe place, sir. My chief deputy has a cabin not far from here. We thought it best to move him without notifying the FBI, SLED, ATF, DOJ... the whole alphabet of law enforcement. If the deaths of Deonte Johnson and Deputy Evans told me one thing, it's that we had too many people in the know."

Dunn quieted and nodded his head. "I can assure you that the leak, if there is one, did not come from our end. But I'll take your reasoning on that for now." He paused and then asked, "Who else knows of the location?"

"Just me and Chief Deputy Haskit."

Dunn ran his fingers across the desktop. "How long will you protect him? How long will you keep him there?"

Crawford shook his head. "I don't know. We haven't gotten that far in our thinking. Took me forever to convince him it was in his best interest."

Dunn leaned back, taking a deep breath. "Well, we've still got eyes on Grubbs and his crew if they try to make a move. Too bad there wasn't anything we could pin on that son of a bitch to keep him locked up."

"Grubbs is dirty, a real pain in the ass, but I don't think he's the main threat here. Someone from the outside is running the show."

"We've managed to infiltrate the HBD's in Savannah. But so far we don't have anything. What about Ellis Dover?"

"He's got a pile of gold and a reason to hate, but I don't think he has it in him to orchestrate a mass killing. He's just an old blowhard with an axe to grind."

"Which leaves us where?"

Crawford nodded. "Back where we started, I'm afraid—with Henry Brooks. Whoever is behind this has played every angle in a highly imaginative way—from getting inside the heads of the Macinaw Seven to the ruse at the Piggly Wiggly."

Dunn agreed as he stood to leave. "Yes, but in my experiences as a lawman as I'm sure it is with yours, when someone is up to no good and they complicate things too much, they always mess up eventually." He made a move toward the door. "By the way, how's Anderson holding up?"

"He's almost catatonic. Won't say a word to anybody."

"Easy to kill a man who's already dead."

Crawford nodded. "But apparently damn near impossible to catch one."

10:16 AM

Chan sat at his desk in the newsroom pecking away on an article about a recent proposal to build a new high school in town. Macinaw High had not had an upgrade since desegregation and there was an urgent need for classroom expansion to accommodate the growing population. Like most issues in public education, however, the question came down to funding—an always contentious subject in the rural county. Of course, the article held little interest for Chan. Although things were far from over with Henry Brooks and the Macinaw Seven, life continued to move on and *The Republic* had to keep up with it— mundane as it might be. But Chan's interest was still on the larger story. He wondered once everything was over, if he would be satisfied with the usual small town stuff like this proposition debate. He already had thoughts about moving to a bigger town: Columbia, Charleston or maybe Charlotte and work for a paper with a larger circulation. Jean was a registered nurse and could find work in any city—and he hoped she would be a part of any new move he would make.

With Jean on his mind, he grabbed the desk phone and made the call. "Three West," he told the hospital operator. And then, "Jean Reid, please."

"This is Nurse Reid," she said after making it to the phone.

"Hey. It's me. How about we go out for dinner tonight?" Chan asked.

"Did you not like the home-cooked meals we've had the past three nights?" she teased.

"You know I did. I thought you might want to do something a little special."

"Of course, I'd love that. Where do you want to go?"

"Norma was telling me about this little seafood restaurant near Mt. Pleasant."

"The Trawler? It's wonderful. I've been there several times. But it's Wednesday. You sure you want to drive all that way tonight? I don't get off work until seven and then I'd have to go home and change."

"I could swing by your place and get some clothes for you— pick you up at the hospital."

There was a brief pause and then, "Sure. Sounds great. I'll see you then."

After saying goodbye, Chan hung up the phone and stared off into empty space. His thoughts flew in all directions as he tried to make sense of recent events in his life. It had been such a rollercoaster the past few weeks with the move, new job and then these terrible murders and his injuries. But through it all, he had found Jean, and he discovered feelings that were beyond anything he had ever felt before. He couldn't really put it into words, but she completed him—made him happy like no other. He questioned it: *Is this love?* He had seen his parents' marriage fall apart and knew nothing was guaranteed, but he failed to see how he could do anything else in his life without her at his side. *Perhaps it's time to up the ante a little bit.*

"Adams," Darby bellowed from his office. "Get in here."

Chan made the quick jaunt to his office and slid into the guest chair. "Sir?"

"How's the article coming?" Darby grunted.

Chan shrugged a shoulder. "It'll be ready for you by four."

Darby nodded quickly as that was not the point of his calling him to the office. "And what about the other thing?" He lowered his voice, "Any progress on Grubbs or the Disciples?"

"Grubbs is back on the street. The police had nothing to hold him on after Deonte was killed. But he's been low-key ever since."

Darby fanned out his mustache. "Anyone willing to give up info on him?"

"Not really. They're a close-knit group. Although one of the dancers at Dolly's seemed a bit frightened when I mentioned the Disciples to her."

"You follow up with her?"

"She disappeared that night, and I haven't had a chance to revisit."

"Do it. Get to her. Any insight may prove invaluable at this point."

"Yes, sir."

Darby leaned onto his desk and encouraged Chan to do the same. He went back to a low tone. "With only one of the Seven left, something has to break soon. Either this Henry Brooks ghost gets to Anderson or the cops get their man, and we need to be there when it happens. Capiche?"

Chan nodded and then leaned back in his chair. "You want him worse than the cops, don't you?"

"He's fucked with our town long enough. Time for him to go down."

1:37 PM

Norma huddled down in the seat of her Pinto with an eye on Reverend Anderson's place. The house on Whitman Street was quiet. Norma would have sworn that no one was there, but with recent events, she figured it might just be Anderson's way of staying out of sight. She tried calling and even knocked on the door several times but to no avail. She decided to sit tight and wait him out.

She was drained by this point, numb to the killings and its fallout. She never thought that her journalistic career would be bookended with such heinous crimes so devastating to her community—especially connected as they seemingly were. But here she was again, staking out the last member of the Macinaw Seven, waiting to see if Henry Brooks would appear.

Norma sat up in her seat as someone made an approach to the house. But it wasn't Henry Brooks. It was another young black man, and he wore a ball cap and jacket—highly unusual in the height of this Macinaw heat. He stood at Anderson's fence and looked all around him before entering the gate. Norma watched as the man climbed the stairs and then knocked on the front door. He waited, peered through windows and knocked again.

Norma quietly got out of her car and slowly approached the man. She got to the gate when he swung around and saw her. He looked anxiously to the left and right but had nowhere to go. Norma stopped at the bottom of the steps.

"Antwan?"

Luther Jennings little brother froze upon hearing his name. He then nonchalantly put his hands in his pockets acting as if being caught here was not a big deal. "Hey," he said. "I'm looking for William Anderson."

"Me too. I'm Norma Wiles with the paper."

"I know who you are, Miss Norma. You were the one who found my brother on his kitchen floor."

Norma nodded. "What are you doing here, Antwan?"

Antwan turned to look at the door and then back at her. "Just checking on Willie. Make sure he's okay. It's been a rough couple of weeks, you know."

"Yes, of course. I didn't realize you were that close to him."

"Oh, yes ma'am. I knew all them boys. We grew up together."

Norma could see the shame and guilt on his face and she went for it: "Antwan, do you know anything about these murders? Do you know why Henry Brooks came after your brother and his friends?"

Antwan opened his mouth but the words caught in his throat.

"Please, Antwan, if you know something…."

"I don't. I don't know nothing. I'm sorry." He then ran down the stairs, passed her and went quickly out of the gate.

Norma watched as he disappeared down the street. Another closed-mouth response—another runner. *But what could the kid truly know anyway?*

Norma sat down dejectedly on the last step of the house. She felt even emptier now, more powerless. Henry Brooks' cold, dead hand was still holding a grip on her people. And it was tightening.

4:39 PM

Dixie Love grabbed her bag out of the back of her Chevy Malibu and headed toward the back entrance of Dolly's Dollies. The house lights were on as she entered; the old building's wear and tear showed under the scrutiny—cracks in the concrete walls, chipped tables and chairs, and cheap red carpet stained with beer and cigarette ash.

She cut across in front of the stage and entered the dressing room. She always liked to get there early as to take her time in putting on her make-up and to give the pills in her little bottle time to work their magic. But as she made her way to the dressing mirror, she found out she wasn't alone.

"How'd you get in here?" she demanded.

Chan turned in the little stool in front of the mirror and stood—a cigarette hanging from his mouth. "Walked right in the back door. Apparently, security is not on par with everything else in this fine establishment."

She pointed behind her. "Yeah, well, you better get the hell outta here, or I'll start screaming."

Chan laughed. "They're probably used to screams coming from in here."

"What the hell does that mean?"

Chan held up his hands. "Look, give me two seconds and I'll leave on my own."

"What do you want?"

"I told you the other night. I want to meet with Grubbs. I want you to set it up for me."

Dixie's eyes narrowed. "Who are you?"

"Just someone who wants to get on the train, that's all. Tell me what you know about Grubbs. Or his connection to the Henry Brooks Disciples. I want in."

Dixie shutdown completely. She reached into her bag, pulled out a .45 revolver and stuck it in Chan's face. "Get outta here now."

"Look, I just want...."

She pulled back the hammer until it clicked. "I said now."

"All right, all right. I'm going," he said, heading towards the door. This was getting him nowhere and he knew it. Darby would be disappointed, but this story angle had reached a definite impasse. Chan left the building through the same back door he had entered, jumped into his Torino and took off.

From the back exit, Dixie watched him drive away. She then walked over to the bar area in the main room. She reached under the lip of the bar counter and pulled out the house phone. She sat it on the bar and dialed up a number. She waited and then, "Yeah, it's me. We've got a problem."

6:22 PM

Every time William Anderson walked across the cabin floorboards they creaked like an old sailing ship being tossed at sea. This posed a bit of a nuisance as he had been given to fitful pacing ever since Sheriff Crawford hand delivered him to Deputy Haskit's cabin the night before.

From what Anderson discovered, the cabin was a nice enough place—simple in design and accouterments—a one bedroom, one bath, and kitchenette log cabin. It had a stone fireplace centered living area that Anderson admitted would have been a nice addition during the winter months. As it was the end of a very hot July, it was still the best area to sit and read as the room received the most sunlight.

The cabin was far out in the country of Macinaw County, on hunting land, Anderson supposed. There were trees in every direction and the only visible road was the dirt one that led to the cabin door. Anderson assumed a pond was nearby as the walls were covered in mounted fish and duck trophies. It was isolated, that much was certain, which for Anderson was both a blessing and a curse. He hated to leave his family behind but Crawford convinced him they would be safer without him around and he would be safer being away from his known hangouts. But being alone was incredibly painful for Anderson. Not only did he feel vulnerable, but he worried his mind would get the best of him.

He sat on the overstuffed chair in front of the fireplace and thought the scenario through as he had done thousands of times now since Tyrell James was killed. He was the last of the Macinaw Seven. He was the only one to know the truth. Of course, Crawford and Haskit tried to pry the information from him, but he had made that blood pact six years ago, and he knew one wrong word would bring Henry Brooks. And that's what bothered him so. Did all his friends go back on their word? Did they all betray the devil? The Watts man told them if they did there would be hell to pay. Anderson closed his eyes for a moment and breathed deeply. He had not said a word about what he saw. He knew he would be okay.

He grabbed his well-read Bible and flipped to familiar verses trying to take comfort in the good word. But as he read, the holy passages bled together and his mind formed those images from six years before. Running to that white man's barn, spray cans in hand, they were going to make a statement for the entire world to see. They would not let the deaths of their Orangeburg brothers-in-arms go unforgotten. A jury had found the troopers not guilty. Once again, society had turned a blind eye to justice. But to William Anderson and his friends, the deaths of Smith, Hammond and Middleton, the three students shot dead that day in the Orangeburg Massacre, would not be in vain. They were to paint their names on the side of Dover's barn, the most visible symbol of privileged society in Macinaw. It was a small gesture, perhaps limited, maybe even foolish, but their anger and their desire to express that anger needed to happen. It superseded all rational thought.

They stealthily approached the barn and heard noises coming from inside. They crept closer and together watched from a crack between the old barn doors. Both men were naked—the one behind the other—a gold and blue tie tight around Robert's neck—his face turning scarlet red. At first the young blacks were amused to see such a sight, barely containing juvenile laughter. But then Robert collapsed, panic set in and the cover-up hastily followed. They continued to watch as Robert's body was quickly redressed. A rope was found and a noose went around the dead man's neck. His body was then lifted from the barn's hay loft, as the other man pulled the rope through the barn rafters. It was at that instant when the stunned watchers crowding against the barn doors caused one of the old doors to swing inward. They all turned and ran—Luther and Tyrell yelling at the rest to follow.

Anderson ran as fast as his short legs would allow. His heart pounded in his chest and his lungs burned as he sucked down air. He flew past the barn, Mrs. Glazer's house, down the back side of the hill and continued to the two waiting cars. He threw up in the grass before being pushed into the backseat of the second car.

They took off, speeding away, riding in frightened silence. It was the longest ride of their young lives—made all the longer when the flashing blue lights appeared behind them. They were beaten, cuffed and hauled away. And then thinking it could get no worse, they were herded into that room in the jailhouse, summoned by the Devil himself.

Anderson looked up from his Bible as he forced the thoughts of the rest of that terrible day away. He stood with the Bible in hand and walked to the window, gazing out at the deep forest. He was meditating, clearing his mind when he heard the noise— the creaking sound of the cabin's floorboards. He held his position and scanned all around him. But the noise wasn't coming from inside the cabin. Someone or something was on the porch outside. Crawford and Haskit told him they would not be back for two days. That they had left him enough supplies for at least that long.

He strained to listen for a few moments more and heard nothing. Anderson was close to dismissing the noise as happenstance when it came again—the same creaking as before. It was outside on the porch, nearer to the door now. He placed the Bible down on the windowsill and lightly moved near the fireplace mantle. Haskit had also left his Beretta 12-gauge shotgun there for him with plenty of shells—two were already in the chamber. Anderson grabbed it off the mantle and continued his slow walk to the door. Despite his light-footed approach the cabin floorboards gave him away as well. Sweat formed on his forehead as he inched closer.

Anderson made it to the door, a solid oak piece with two locks. He carefully took the safety off the shotgun and raised it to chest height. With his left hand, he turned both locks on the door. His heart was pounding as fast as it did six years prior. He felt he may even throw up again. He grabbed the handle and then in one quick motion he yanked the door open and leveled the shotgun—his finger heavy on the trigger.

He brought the barrel down to the floor in a flash, relaxed his shoulders and blew out his held breath. "That was too close. I thought you were Henry Brooks." He put the gun by his side and stepped back. He then curled his sweaty brow. "What are you doing here anyway?"

7:39 PM

Chan looked over at Jean and smiled. She was next to him in the Torino, the windows were down and the wind was playing with her hair. As gorgeous as she looked in the little blue dress he had brought for her to wear, he had to admit he was more anxious to see what she looked like out of it. He had it bad for her now and he believed she felt the same for him. He didn't know what tomorrow would bring, but the night, this night, had a certain magic in the air. And he was going to make sure the magic continued.

"Music?" he asked as he pointed to the tape deck.

"Sure."

"What do you want to hear?" He pointed again, this time to his eight-track carrying case at her feet. She picked it up and dug through the selections. She found *Wings at the Speed of Sound* and popped it in. *Silly Love Songs* started playing and they both laughed with embarrassment, recognizing exactly how on the nose the song was.

As the music continued, Jean turned to Chan. "So why the special trip tonight?"

Chan shrugged. "Like I said on the phone, I thought you could use it. I know I could. Just couldn't wait for the weekend."

She agreed as she pulled back stands of her hair. "Any word on the story? What's the latest?"

Chan frowned a bit. "It's weird. William Anderson has all but disappeared. Norma can't find him anywhere. And with the police pulled back in dark corners, Macinaw is almost like a ghost town now. I'm running into dead ends myself."

"Such a nightmare," she said with a sigh. "I don't know if the town will ever be the same."

"Probably not, Jean, too much has happened. But I have noticed something about your town... the Lowcountry... the whole state for that matter—the people are resilient. Blacks, whites, everyone. You've dealt with a lot of tragedy and heartache, but you've met the challenges and you'll be a stronger people for it."

Jean smiled at that. "I hope you're right."

"I am." He paused before adding lightly, "I'm always right."

She laughed but then noted the sudden change in his expression. "What is it? What's wrong?"

Chan indicated the rearview mirror. "Those guys behind us. They're coming up fast."

Jean turned and saw two motorcycles eating up the distance between them. They got very close to the back of the Torino, riding the bumper. Chan put both hands on the wheel and kept glancing in the mirror.

"Take it easy," Jean said softly. "They'll pull around us in a sec."

But they didn't. They pushed them for several more minutes. When Chan slowed down, so did the bikes. When he gave it the gas, they stayed with him.

"What do they want?" Jean finally asked—her voice a little shaky.

Chan kept quiet although he knew. He knew all too well. Unfortunately, this part of the Lowcountry Highway was a swampy stretch with no turn-offs and nowhere to pull over. The drop-offs to the swamp on either side were rather steep.

One of the choppers finally broke around and raced up to be even with Chan's window. It was Orton, the guy he had beaten in pool. Orton looked directly at Chan and then flipped him off.

"Do you know these jerks?" Jean asked.

"Yeah. They're part of the investigation I was telling you about," Chan admitted. "Definitely not the friendly types."

Orton sped up some more and got in front of the Torino. They had them blocked in now.

"Jesus, what are they going to do, Chan?"

"I don't know, but if he tries to stop us, I'll run right over his ass."

A semi came barreling down the road from the opposite direction. Chan saw his chance and tried flashing his lights and honking the horn. The trucker just honked back and waved as he passed.

Orton slowed again and began fishtailing in front, covering both lanes of the highway. He then reached into his leather vest and pulled out a pistol of some sort. He waved it back towards them. Chan glanced over at Jean—her eyes big with worry.

"Jean, grab hold of the arm rail and the dashboard."

"Why? What are you going to do?"

"Just do it. Brace yourself."

Chan jammed on the brakes and whipped the wheel hard to the left. He timed it perfectly—the Torino skidded into the far lane and did a complete 180 turn. The other chopper rider, whom Chan believed was Wolfe, flew past them in the right lane and nearly slammed into Orton. Chan gunned the accelerator and headed back toward Macinaw.

Their escape however was short-lived. As Chan made it up a small rise in the road, he saw Grubb's red truck bearing down on him. "Shit!"

Chan pulled the same maneuver as before—he whipped the car around and headed back the other way. He figured he had a better chance with a head to head against the two bikes. And those two were obliged to bring it—Orton was heading towards him in the right lane and Wolfe was in the left.

"Y'all might be crazy as hell, but so am I," Chan said. Jean pressed herself as far as she could into her seat—every muscle in her body tight as a drum. Chan gripped the wheel and stayed in the right lane—he wanted Orton bad. He maxed out the speed to over one hundred miles per hour. The Torino was now but a few yards from a head-on collision with the chopper. At the very last moment, Orton veered to his left. The Torino clipped his tire sending the Henry Brooks Disciple spinning off the road and tumbling ass over handlebars down the embankment. Chan flattened the brakes and smoke screamed from the singed tires.

The Torino spun again and skidded to a stop on the left side edge of the embankment.

The car vibrated for a moment and then everything became completely still. Chan gathered himself and looked to Jean. "You all right?"

Before she could respond, Grubb's truck came out of nowhere and slammed into the driver's side of the Torino. The car was lifted several feet into the air, and when it came down, the edge of the embankment could no longer hold it. Chan's car rolled three times down the twenty-five-foot drop. Glass and metal erupted all around them. There were sickening sounds of crunching and popping that followed the car all the way to the bottom. The Torino came to a sudden rest in an upright position in the watery ditch.

At first Chan thought his body was covered in blood, but it was only the water that had entered the car from the river's swollen run-off. Besides the seat belt that ripped a permanent scar across his hips and pelvis, and the glass cuts to his forehead, he was not seriously injured. He took a few more deep breaths to overcome the shock and then, "Jean? Are you okay?"

He looked to his right. Jean was still in her seat—the seatbelt holding her upright. Her head was hanging forward and her eyes were open but there was no spark in them. "Jean?"

Chan unbuckled his seatbelt. He reached over and touched her face. "Jean? Can you hear me? Jean? Jean!!"

Chan got on his knees in his seat and unbuckled her. She slumped over in his arms. "No, no, no! Jean, please, no!" He looked around frantically as if there was something he could do. He started panic breathing—his chest heaving at an accelerated rate. He grabbed her face in his hands. "Jean!! Goddamnit no!!! No!!!"

He pulled her to his chest and held her there—tears streaming down his face. "No Jean, please don't do this, please don't...."

OCTOBER 4, 2016

10:42 PM

"Chan? Did you hear what I said? Chan?"

Chan turned from the passenger side window. "What? Yeah, sorry. You were saying...?"

"How much further down the Brooks' road should we go?" Tindal pointed ahead at the meandering dirt road.

"Pull off anywhere around here. We can travel through the fields to the house from this point. I don't think Monroe would send patrols down this far anyway."

She pulled her rental car off the road and into the cover of the weed-infested field. She shut off the engine and they exited the car. They were both dressed in black for their covert action and they easily disappeared into the night.

"You know, I'm surprised no neighboring farmer has thought to buy this property," Chan whispered as he picked his way forward. "If for nothing else but the land."

"When I researched the property, I found that several locals had made offers over the years, but Searson-Thompson, the real estate management group, refused them all," Tindal said.

For the remainder of their journey, they kept silent, watching their feet for snakes and listening out for police patrols. Within twenty minutes they made it to the edge of Henry Brooks' yard. They could make out the outline of the house against the night sky. They crouched down in the brush and surveyed the area.

"See anyone?" Chan asked.

Tindal shook her head. "I think they are more concerned with protecting the patrol car site than the house. Let's go for it."

They approached the dilapidated porch of the old house. Yellow crime-scene tape encircled the entire worn structure. Tindal eyed the front. Besides the underbrush that had grown through the porch and blocked the way, the old door also appeared to have a police padlock around the handle. "I don't think we're getting in that way."

"Come on," Chan said. He led her around to the side of the house. Next to the chimney a broken window about seven feet off the ground was partially open. He found a half board and used it to inch the window open even more. He then went to one knee and cupped his hands together. "Go ahead. I'll boost you up."

Tindal grinned. "Chan, I was a level ten gymnast in high school." She leaped up, grabbed the edge of the windowsill and pulled herself up and through with no problem.

After dusting herself off, Tindal pulled a small flashlight from her pocket and scanned the interior. It was as expected: a fifty-year-old time capsule. Nothing much had been touched since the day Henry Brooks was arrested in 1963. Of course, time had whittled the house down to a shell of its former self. There were cobwebs everywhere, the ceiling had fallen in at certain points, the floors were sunken if not completely rotted away and a few of the walls were fragmented. But all his furniture and possessions were basically where Brooks left it. *Or maybe as Sonny Watts left it.* She saw a table, a gas stove and an ice box and figured she was in the kitchen area.

She was stepping into another room when she heard Chan attempting to get in the window. She returned to find him with his head and one of his shoulders partially in. He looked up at her, struggling. "I was *not* a level ten gymnast."

She smiled and grabbed the back of his shirt and helped pull him the rest of the way in. He got to his feet and then he too pulled a flashlight out to look around. They donned latex gloves and spread out—determined to find a link to Watts.

They dug through everything: drawers, cabinets, closets, mattresses, chairs, couches and rugs. A singular patrol from the sheriff's office passed through the yard at one point and streamed his flashlight through the house, but Chan and Tindal laid low and easily evaded detection.

As it neared midnight, in an old desk in a back bedroom, Tindal found several newspaper clippings that covered the years of Brooks' first wave of murders, but nothing to tie in to Watts. Frustration and exhaustion were starting to set in when she heard Chan call from up front. "Tindal, come here."

Tindal made her way to the parlor room, a small sitting area with a couch and two chairs. Chan was standing in front of a cabinet. "See this?" he asked.

"Yeah, I checked it earlier. I didn't see anything. Pictures and little knick-knacks."

Chan grabbed the cabinet and tried to shake it. "It's the only piece of furniture in the house that's bolted to the wall."

Tindal scanned it with her flashlight. "It's a nice piece—probably the nicest piece in the house. Looks handmade."

Chan nodded and smiled as he remembered Jean's story about her father's work in the house. "I wonder…" He opened the cabinet doors and felt around the lining of the shelves. "Put your light under here," he directed.

Tindal leaned into the cabinet and shone the light under the first shelf. She noted Chan's reaction. "What is it?"

"A latch of some kind." He slid the latch and the faux back panel of the cabinet fell forward. Chan pulled the panel out and sat it on the floor. Tindal then focused the light into the recessed area of the wall.

"Oh, my God," Tindal said. "There—in the back."

Chan reached in and with the deliberate care of a surgeon removed an eight-inch boar knife. He held the knife up in Tindal's light and marveled at it as if it were a priceless piece of art. "It's the knife. Henry Brooks' knife."

Tindal became anxious. "What else? What else is in there?"

Chan blinked his eyes in rapidity like he was waking up from a dream. He handed the knife to Tindal and dug back in the compartment. He felt around until he pulled out a small metal case. Tindal showed her light on it as Chan placed the case on the cabinet lip and opened it. He pulled out a funny-looking cigarette, sniffed it and held it to the light. "It's a Kretek. Christ, the son of a bitch was here."

"A what?"

"A Kretek—a clove cigarette from Indonesia. It was Watts' favorite type. The Devil's smoke."

Tindal said nothing at first—her eyes wide with excitement. She swallowed her incredulity and said, "I can't believe this. That's it then. We were right about Watts. We can go to the police now. We've got the connecting evidence. They'll be able to test for his prints or even his DNA on the case or the cigarette."

Chan nodded but then found and pulled a folded piece of paper from within the back of the case. "Wait a minute. Jesus, look at this."

"What is it?"

"A letter, handwritten."

"What does it say?"

Chan scanned it at first and then read it aloud, "*I remember what you did. I was there. I saw what you did to that man. You want to keep it quiet. I want money. I want fifty thousand dollars or I will tell everyone what you did.*" Chan looked to Tindal. "This is it. The motivation—the reason why Henry Brooks returned to Macinaw that summer—a blackmail letter."

Tindal moved closer to see it as well. "What else does the letter say?"

Chan looked back to the letter and read: "*Put cash in a bag and put it under the dead soldier's foot. I'll be watching. You have three days or everyone is going to know.*" Chan looked up and flipped the letter to the back and then the front again. "That's the end of it. Not addressed. No signature. Nothing else."

"Dead soldier's foot?" Tindal asked.

"The Confederate memorial in the square downtown. There's a statue of a soldier on top. His foot is raised like he's marching off to war."

"So, one of the Macinaw Seven was blackmailing Robert Dover's killer."

"But that doesn't make sense." Chan stepped away for a moment as he thought it through. "If you're one of the Seven, you've been forewarned by Sonny Watts not to speak a word about what you saw. And then six years later, you suddenly do this? You send a threatening letter when you know it will bring the wrath of Henry Brooks or worse? What am I missing here?"

"Could one of the seven have leaked the word and someone else blackmailed Dover's killer?"

"Not likely. Telling someone what happened would have been just as taboo as blackmailing him yourself."

"Well then... perhaps you were either so desperate as not to care or you didn't believe in Watts' ability to raise the dead." She paused and then, "*Or* maybe you weren't given the warning like the rest of the seven were."

Chan slowly nodded. "Right. Maybe you saw what happened to Robert Dover, but Sonny Watts didn't get the chance to warn you." Chan hesitated again and then snapped his fingers. "The trial. In the Macinaw Seven trial, the prosecutor's prime witness claimed she saw *eight* young black males running away from the barn. It was a piece of testimony that Watts used to help acquit the Seven."

"Eight instead of seven. So, if that's true, one got away. But who?"

Chan hesitated and then, "I'm not positive, but I've got a pretty damn good idea."

JULY 29, 1976

3:22 AM

Chan sat on a bench in the emergency room's waiting area at Macinaw General—alone. He rode with the ambulance to the hospital but refused to be checked himself until after the doctors had finished with Jean. He knew she was dead. He knew there was nothing they could do, but he was already deep into a state of denial and he wouldn't let it go. He just sat there, an unlit cigarette in his mouth, red-eyed, wishing it were him instead of her.

The emergency room doors opened and Norma came running through. She ran to the check-in desk, but saw Chan sitting there before she spoke to anyone else. She took a seat next to him.

"Chan? Are you okay?"

Chan simply shook his head that he was not.

"Chan, I am so sorry."

"I can't... I can't stop shaking," Chan said.

Norma held out her arms as to embrace him. She hesitated for a moment and then leaned in and put her arms around him. The cigarette fell from his lips; tears resurfaced and streaked down his cheeks.

"This wasn't supposed to happen, Norma. She wasn't supposed to die."

"I know, honey. I am so, so sorry."

Chan suffered through the anger, bitterness and torment as Norma held on to him. She pulled him close, allowing him his moment, protecting his dignity, sheltering him from this cruelest of realities.

11:22 AM

Deputy Haskit rode shotgun to give directions to Agent Dunn, who was driving his Crown Victoria—the standard auto of the FBI. Sheriff Crawford rode in the back. They had turned off the main highway and were heading down the dirt road to Haskit's cabin.

"So, you have the Disciples rounded up at this point?" Agent Dunn asked.

"Orton is in the hospital with multiple fractures," Crawford said. "And Wolfe turned himself in last night. We still don't know the whereabouts of Grubbs, but we've got everybody out looking for him."

"And who was this young girl that was killed?"

"Friend of Adams, the reporter. She was a nurse at Macinaw General, right Deputy?"

Haskit nodded. "Yes, sir. Pretty little blonde. Remember Dan Reid with Reid's Construction? It was his little girl."

"Well, at least that should take care of the Disciples for a while," Dunn said. "You've got 'em on manslaughter if not a whole lot more."

Crawford agreed but then added, "Certainly sounds like they planned it as an attack, but why go after Adams?"

"Maybe he discovered something on them—something that connects to the Macinaw Seven," Dunn said. "We'll need to have another talk with the reporter."

They continued down the dirt road. The forest became thick in all directions and grabbed Dunn's attention. "Good hunting grounds out here, Deputy?" Dunn asked.

"Yes, sir. Some of the state's best deer hunting is right here in Macinaw. You'll have to come back one day and give it a shot."

Dunn grinned. "Sounds good to me. I think once we relocate Anderson to a sanctioned safe house and get this killer behind bars, I'm going to take a little time off—maybe do some hunting or fishing."

As they arrived at the cabin, all three men immediately noticed the open front door. "What the hell?" Dunn asked as he pulled the car to a stop.

"I told him to keep that door shut and locked at all times," Haskit said as he emerged from the car.

With the cabin's security breached, the lawmen drew their weapons and eased their way onto the porch. They crossed to the entrance—the floorboards creaking away. The cabin was dark and there was no noise coming from inside. Crawford took position on the left side of the door, Haskit on the right and Dunn stood back, covering both.

The sheriff took a quick look inside. His lowered weapon and slumping shoulders said it all. Haskit and Dunn followed him into the cabin. On the floor in a puddle of blood was Reverend William Anderson—his shirt was cut down the middle and the pentagram sigil of Abaddon was carved into his chest.

"It can't be..." Haskit said, turning to the others. "There's no fucking way!"

Dunn gnashed his teeth. "Damn it! Not again!" Dunn made a quick turn and went for the radio in his car.

Haskit looked to Crawford. "How can this be, Sheriff? Nobody knew he was here. Nobody."

Crawford took a hard look at his deputy and then back to Anderson. "I don't know, Bobby. This killer has a way of always being three steps ahead of us. And Lord only knows what direction he'll be stepping now."

OCTOBER 5, 2016

10:43 AM

Chan and Tindal marched up the first flight of stairs at the Hilldebrand-Dunwoody Apartments, a government housing project in the black section of Macinaw. It was three separate apartment buildings—three floor levels each—with a central community rec-room and row after row of clothesline substituting as the project's backyard. Although constructed in the 1990s, the apartments had been neglected by the owners and government management alike, and the living conditions were sub-par at best—over the years many of the units had become home to filth, roaches, drug deals and desperation.

"You never did tell me what happened to Norma through all this," Tindal said as she rounded the paint-chipped metal stairs.

"She eventually burned out and retired from the newspaper game in 1980—took a teaching position in Orangeburg. I saw her once or twice after, but she eventually moved on with her life. In 1998 I got a call from her daughter Rene that Norma had cancer. I saw her for the final time that September—six months later she was gone," Chan said blankly.

"I'm sorry. I know she was your friend. That must have been difficult."

Chan nodded. "It was. She taught me everything about being a reporter and especially about being a reporter in a small town like this. More importantly, she taught me how to be a better human being. If you're lucky, Tindal, you'll run across special people like that in your life. Get to know them—it's well worth your time." He paused as he thought about it. "I think her greatest regret was that we failed to stop the Macinaw Seven killer. She was so sure we would figure it out."

Tindal attempted a smile. "I'm sure she's proud of what you've figured out these past few days."

"I hope that she and many others can rest easy very soon."

They made it to the third level and came to apartment 301B. Tindal knocked on the door. A black woman in her mid-twenties holding a three-year-old on her hip answered. "Yes?"

"Is Antwan Jennings here?" Tindal asked.

"Who wants to know?"

"We're reporters. We need to ask Mr. Jennings a few questions."

"What about?" she asked abruptly.

Tindal and Chan shared a tired look. A man's voice came from the back of the apartment. "Who is it, Asia?"

The woman, Asia, turned from the door and yelled, "Reporters, Daddy, they want to talk to you."

There was some noise from the back and finally Antwan appeared behind his daughter. He was over sixty like Chan and also sported a grey-peppered beard. "What y'all want with me?" he asked.

"Antwan Jennings?" Tindal asked for confirmation. "We'd like to ask you a few questions about Robert Dover."

Antwan stared at Chan and Tindal like they were creatures from another planet. He looked at his daughter and then back to the reporters. "Hold on just a minute." He then closed the door on them.

After a little while, the door re-opened and Antwan signaled for them to follow him. They silently went back down the stairs, behind the apartment building and stood between two bed sheets hanging on the clotheslines. He gathered the reporters in with his eyes and then said, "Don't come around my place saying that name. Not in front of my family like that. Now what is it you two want?"

"You were there, weren't you, Antwan?" Chan started. "You went to the Dover barn with your brother and his friends."

"You saw what happened," Tindal added. "You saw who killed Robert Dover, didn't you?"

"What the hell are you talking about?" Antwan fired back.

"You were there, Antwan," Chan said. "You saw the whole thing. But you missed out on the warning the other seven received. Six years later you sent Dover's killer a letter asking for money."

"Man, you're crazy. I don't know nothing about no letter."

"We do," Tindal said. "We saw the letter. It was handwritten, Mr. Jennings. The FBI will soon see it as well—

they have experts who will be able to tell it's written in your hand."

Antwan rubbed his forehead and cast his eyes on the ground between them.

"Norma Wiles saw you coming from William Anderson's house on the day he was killed," Chan continued. "She told me so herself. You came to Anderson because you knew that the letter you had sent the killer was causing all those deaths that summer—your brother and the rest of the Macinaw Seven. You went to warn him about what you had done, but he wasn't there."

"No...." he said with anger.

"You asked for fifty thousand dollars. To be placed under the soldier's foot at the Confederate memorial," Chan said. "In the summer of '76, Antwan, you bused tables at the Palm Leaf Café. You would have been able to keep an eye out for the money drop from there." Chan took a step closer and forced eye contact again. "You were a kid, Antwan. And you saw an opportunity for easy money. But the truth is you had no idea that that action would raise Henry Brooks from the dead. You had no idea that would unleash the killer who took the life of your brother and his friends."

"Jesus Christ...no!" Antwan blurted out. He slowly went to his knees overcome with grief, holding back tears. He held his silence for over a minute and then spoke—his voice shaky. "I didn't... I didn't mean for it to happen...."

Chan went to his knee as well. "I know, Antwan. It wasn't your fault. You didn't kill your brother. You didn't kill the Macinaw Seven. You are not responsible."

Tindal crouched down as well. "Mr. Jennings, it's time to come clean. We are here for you to set the record straight. Tell us what happened that day. Tell us what you saw."

Antwan rocked back on his haunches and covered his face with his hands. After a few moments, he put his hands on his knees and looked at them directly. "I was sixteen-years-old at the time. We got word that the white patrolmen were not gonna be held responsible for the deaths of Smith, Hammond and Middleton. We went crazy—blew up—we were ready to set the goddamn town on fire. Tyrell came up with the idea of spray painting their names on the Dover barn—it sounds foolish now, but at the time we felt it was the best way to express how we felt. The seven met at my momma's house and planned it all out. I insisted they take me with them. Luther told me no, but I convinced the others I could hang. I rode in Ja'Len Wells' car. We parked at the bottom of the Dover hill. Luther told me to stay back—you know, to watch the cars, be on guard. But I didn't want to miss the action. I waited a few minutes and then followed up the hill. They were all crowded around the barn door, watching. I found a loose board on the side of the barn and watched from there."

"What did you see?" Tindal asked.

Antwan shrugged a bit. "I saw *them*. They were going at it. The Dover boy had a tie around his neck." He hesitated for a moment as if the embarrassing details might be too much for Tindal. Her look back to him demanded he continue. "They were trying to get-off at the same time, but it got too rough... Dover suffocated and... died."

"Did you run then?" Chan asked.

"No. I wasn't sure what had happened. I thought he had just passed out. The other boys didn't run, so I hung around too. We saw the cover-up—the fake suicide—the fake hanging. It was after that when one of the barn doors got pushed open—must have been opened by accident. That's when we ran. And we ran like hell. All the way back down the hill."

"Why didn't you get back in the cars with the others?" Chan followed.

"Luther grabbed me and told me to hide. Said he would come back for me later. He was worried the cops would catch up with them." Antwan blew out a breath. "And he was right. He was just trying to protect me."

"Where did you hide?" Tindal asked.

"Bottom of the hill. There were woods next to the curve where we parked. I ended up staying there all night."

Chan jumped back in. "And Luther never told you what happened at the station? Nothing about what Sonny Watts told them?"

"No. I still don't know. Luther told me to never mention what we saw—we could never speak, write, or even breathe a word of it ever again. And we didn't. After the trial and the

Seven were freed, we went about our lives. Luther never told me anything, never indicated there was any secret, and we definitely never said anything about what happened in that barn again."

Chan and Tindal shared a quick glance before Tindal said, "So six years later you decide to blackmail Dover's lover for fifty thousand dollars. Why?"

Antwan shook his head. "Like y'all said earlier, I was working for peanuts at the time. The man was moving up in the world. I saw a chance."

"Moving up?" Tindal asked.

Antwan cut his eyes between the reporters. "My God... you two don't know, do you? You don't know who it was."

"It was obviously someone powerful enough to have Sonny Watts perform his Henry Brooks trick," Chan said. "And someone whom you felt you couldn't cross once you learned how your letter backfired."

"More powerful than you know. More powerful than a couple of white reporters. And a helluva lot more powerful than some poor black man from Macinaw."

"Give us his name now," Tindal said. "And we'll take him down together."

FEBRUARY 8, 1969

6:01 PM

The Macinaw Seven sat around an oblong table in an office conference room of the Macinaw Jail. They were bloodied and beaten, nursing their wounds, scared to death. They all were quiet until William Anderson spoke up, "Hey, man, what are we gonna do?"

"Just keep quiet," Luther Jennings said. "We ain't done nothing. They can't hold us for doing nothing."

"Yeah they will," Brandon Grimes protested. "They gonna say we killed that boy. They gonna say we hung him. And all y'all damn well know it."

"We didn't kill anybody," Tyrell James said. "And we know who did. We'll be outta here before too long."

"Man, you're crazy," Grimes continued. "Jake's Grocery got robbed last week and the cops came and got my cousin and his friend just because they were standing on the same street corner as Jake's. They gonna nail us for this shit I swear."

"Shut up, Brandon." James said. "All of you listen to me. All we gotta do is tell the truth. Tell the truth and we'll be fine."

The door to the conference room opened and a man in a dark suit with a black brief case entered. The Macinaw Seven became quiet and attentive. He went to the middle of the table, placed the case flat and angled it so that when opened the contents would be visible only to him. He brushed back his hair and caught the eye of each member of the Seven to make sure he had their attention. "Gentlemen, my name is Sonny Watts, and I am a lawyer. Before we proceed any further, I need to know if any of you have informed the police about what you witnessed today. Anyone?"

The Seven remained silent—a few weakly shook their heads that they had not. Watts smile was thin and cutting. "I say again, before I can offer my services to you as litigator, I need to know if any of you have mentioned what you saw today to Sheriff Crawford or his deputies or anyone else in law enforcement?"

"Hey, man, we didn't kill that boy," Grimes said.

"I didn't ask you that, did I?" Watts snapped. "Now my patience is running thin, gentlemen. Did any of you talk to the police?"

"We haven't said anything to anybody," James said. He looked around and pointed at his friends. "None of us."

This time Watts' smile grew wider. "Good," he said. "And you never will."

"Never will? What do you mean?" Anderson asked.

"Just like I said—you never will mention what you saw today to anyone—ever. Not to the police, your families, not even to each other. What you saw today did not happen."

"But how are we supposed to defend ourselves?" Anderson asked.

"Leave that to me. You will face charges of murder, no doubt, and you may even go to trial, but you will not be found guilty. You will walk away as free men."

"Murder?" Jennings asked. "We didn't kill anybody. We shouldn't have to face murder charges."

"Even if you protest, claim your innocence in this matter, what do you think will happen? Let's be honest here. Seven black males are caught running from the Dover barn—Ellis Dover's youngest child is dead—what do you think the police will do?"

"I done told them," Grimes said. "They gonna lock our black asses up and throw away the key."

"This man is correct," Watts said, pointing at Grimes. He leaned forward on the table, lowered his voice and spoke in a menacing tone, "Claim to the police what you saw today in that barn, mention a certain person's name to anybody, and I can assure you that jail time will be the least of your worries. Do you gentlemen understand me?"

"But you said we would go free. How?" James asked.

"By doing and saying exactly as I tell you."

"I can't lie," Anderson said. "I won't put my hand on the holy book and betray my oath."

"God will forgive your indiscretion, young man. But betray the Devil, and there will be hell to pay."

"What do you mean—the Devil?" James asked.

Watts unlocked the snaps on his brief case and opened it up. He withdrew the eight-inch boar knife and held it up to the light. There was nervous bravado from the Macinaw Seven.

"What?" Jennings asked with a quick laugh. "You gonna stab us all if we tell?"

Watts did not answer as he marveled at the weapon under the light. He then drew the sharpened point across the palm of his left hand—blood poured from the cut and rained down into the open brief case. James and Grimes, who were sitting closest to Watts, moved their chairs away.

"Jesus, man, what the hell are you doing?" Jennings asked.

Watts held his bloody palm up to show the Seven. "Just a small cut, gentlemen. Nothing to be nervous about." He then wiped some of the blood along the blade. "I have shed my blood for you and now you shall do the same for me."

"Man, you're fucking crazy," Ja'Len Wells said.

Watts stared Wells down. "Don't you know whose knife this is? Don't you know who I represent?" He then turned to the others with his sadistic smile. "Today I offer you a one-time deal. You will swear to me on your life that you will never mention what you saw today to anyone ever again and I will grant you that life as free men. But betray that trust, cross that line—today or at any time in the future—and you shall be put to death by the cold hand of Henry Brooks."

Anderson frowned and then shared what everyone was thinking, "Henry Brooks? That crazy bastard has been dead for over three years now."

"No. He lives—of that I can assure you. You cannot kill someone that powerful. He was chosen by God to determine good and evil, to determine your fate. Shall we find out what fate lies ahead for you today?"

Jennings slammed his hand down on the table. "Man, this is bullshit! That son-of-a-bitch is dead and this cracker is playing us for fools! Get the cops in here now! I want to tell them what I saw!" Jennings jumped up from his chair.

Watts gave the Seven another passive-aggressive grin, placed the boar knife in the case, locked it and headed for the door.

"Wait!" James said. Watts stood motionless facing the door. Tyrell James turned to Jennings and the others. "What do we have to lose? If we tell the cops what we saw they'll bury us anyway. I think maybe we should do this."

"But you just said we should tell the truth," Wells said.

"I was wrong. Brandon was right. They ain't gonna believe us. Think about what happened in Orangeburg. Three blacks were killed by white cops and only a black man went to jail for it. It will be the same thing here." He turned back to Watts. "What guarantee do we have that if we agree to your terms we'll go free?"

Watts turned around slowly. "It is one hundred percent guaranteed if all stipulations are met. We will win this case. You will walk away as free men." He put the brief case back on the table and opened it up again. "Of course, a guarantee from Henry Brooks requires a bit of a down payment from each one of you."

Watts held up Henry Brooks' knife in his right hand and flashed them his left palm—slashed and covered in coagulated blood. He smiled. "So... which one of you is first?"

AUGUST 5, 1976

Chan sat across from Sheriff Crawford's desk with his head hung low, wishing the world would just somehow open up and swallow him whole. He reached for another cigarette, but like him, the pack was empty. He crumbled it up and threw it in a wastebasket.

The door swung open and Sheriff Crawford and Deputy Haskit entered. Crawford took his seat and Haskit stood behind Chan. "Mr. Adams, I sure am sorry about all you've had to go through," Crawford said. "We, Deputy Haskit and myself—the whole department really—would like to express our condolences over your recent loss. Jean was a pretty girl and a helluva nurse from what I've been told. She'll be sorely missed."

Chan nodded and mumbled something that sounded like "Thanks."

"I wanted you come here today so that I can tell you a few things and also find out a few things from you, you understand me?"

Again, Chan nodded.

"Well, for one thing, we finally caught up with Ryan Grubbs. The FBI tracked him down in Florida late last night. He was held up in some flea-bag apartment in South Dade County. The feds moved in to make the arrest. Unfortunately, he did not go quietly. There was a shootout and Grubbs was killed. Special Agent Mike Dunn took a shot to his shoulder, but thankfully it looks like he will be making a full recovery."

"That's good," Chan said quietly.

"Yes, but Grubbs' death does leave holes in our case here. We will probably never know now the extent of his involvement in the deaths of the Macinaw Seven. And, at the present time, Orton and Wolfe are not telling us anything either. That's where you come in. We need information from you to help figure out the part he and the Henry Brooks Disciples played in this mess. Do you think you're up for that?"

Chan nodded again. "Yes."

222

Haskit joined in, pulling up a chair next to Chan. "You followed Ryan Grubbs the past few weeks, didn't you? For your newspaper coverage?"

"That's right."

"You kept an eye on his place there in Eastland, and some of his hangouts. We'd like to know what you may have discovered during your surveillance of the man."

Chan sighed and rolled his shoulders. "There's not much to tell, really. He's a small-time hood as you know. He has a cover job at a local liquor store but deals in meth and pot. He hangs out at Ricky's at times and the strip club out near the interstate."

"We know all that," Crawford said. "Is there anything you may have come across, anything you might have seen or anybody you might have talked to that would warrant the attack they delivered on you and Miss Reid?"

"I beat Orton in pool one night. It pissed him off, but I would hardly say that was cause for what they did."

"How deep did you get with the Henry Brooks Disciples?"

"Surface level only," Chan said. "The gang has a high secrecy factor—it would be hard to get any information on them. And those that may know a little something about them are generally too scared to talk."

"Like who?" Crawford asked.

"Like this stripper—she goes by the name Dixie Love—out at Dolly's Dollies. When I asked about Grubbs or the HBD's, she became very frightened. She even threatened my life the last time I brought it up."

Haskit caught the sheriff's eye and then asked, "And when was the last time you talked with Dixie Love?"

"Last week. The day Jean was killed. I saw her at Dolly's."

"She threatened your life?" Crawford asked.

"Well, she did pull a gun on me, but I didn't take the threat seriously—she just wanted me to leave—get out of her face—so I did."

Crawford and Haskit grew quiet for a moment. Crawford then leaned forward in his chair with a hint of a smile. "Chan, now I'm gonna ask you something that sounds like its straight outta left field, but it needs to be asked."

"Okay."

"Do you think there was ever anything… supernatural in the deaths of the Macinaw Seven?"

"I don't believe in the supernatural. I don't believe in ghosts. But fear can be manipulated by human hands and I think that was definitely the case here. Someone has expertly used the murderous rage of Henry Brooks—making it seem like some necromantic communication—to cause all this death and destruction for his own gain. Someone smarter than us with infinite resources. Someone who may have gotten away with it and sadly will probably never be revealed to us."

12:48 PM

Norma got up from her desk and stretched a bit. She then grabbed her empty coffee cup and headed for the bullpen. Dennis Darby was the only other person in there. He was reading copy and drinking his fourth cup. He moved over slightly so that she could get to the coffee pot. He then spoke to her without looking up. "How are you today, Norma?"

"The same. Confused, mad, depressed." She added sarcastically, "Thanks for asking."

Darby pulled out the chair beside him and indicated for her to sit. She did staring at the steam rising from her cup. Darby waited and then said, "We've been through a lot, you and me, personally and professionally. We've covered a lot together. But this…? Well, let's just say our little town of Macinaw has gone through some tough times of late."

"Tough times? More like the town has gone through hell, Dennis."

He nodded. "You're right. This one has shaken us to the very core. I sincerely hope we can recover from it." He looked over at her. "I pray you're not thinking of leaving us any time soon."

"I'm tired. I'm tired of the madness and the lack of answers. I'm tired of our town divided on every issue. I'm tired that we see everything as either black or white." She paused. "Did you know I saw Ellis Dover walking about town yesterday? He had the biggest shit-eating-grin on his face that you've ever seen. I know he lost his son and I know he thinks the Seven were responsible, but it's like he won the goddamn sweepstakes or something. And he's supposed to be the pillar of this community? Something's wrong with that, Dennis. Something is seriously wrong with that."

Darby could only nod. He sat in silence for a moment more before asking, "Have you talked with Adams lately?"

"Not since last week. He's not going to quit, is he?"

Darby shrugged. "I heard that rumor, but I hope not. I think... I think the kid's got potential."

Norma smiled. "You really do, don't you?" She laughed. "I knew you were an old softy at heart."

"The hell I am," Darby said with a slight smile. "I just don't want to lose a good reporter, that's all."

"When is he due back?"

"I gave him two weeks off. He'll be back next week, but I'm afraid it may be too late by then. He's really going through it."

"Yeah, I know. You want me to talk to him?"

Darby patted Norma's hand. "You're better at it than I am. Besides, if you help me get the kid back in the game that means you're back in as well."

"You're nobody's fool, are you, Dennis Darby?"

He bumped Norma's coffee mug with his and said, "I'll drink to that."

7:22 PM

Chan opened the door to his small apartment and let Norma in. A thunderstorm had developed in the early evening and the rain was pouring down. Norma shook the droplets from about her as she stood, looking around.

"How are you, Chan?" she asked with a mix of sympathy and curt directness.

"Lost," he said simply. Chan moved to the kitchenette table and invited her to sit as well. "I went to see Crawford today. He said the FBI killed Ryan Grubbs last night."

Norma slid her raincoat around the back of the chair and sat. "I heard. One less nuisance in the world."

Chan nodded as he pulled two Marlboro Lights and slid one to Norma. He leaned over and lit it for her. "Still... it leaves the puzzle wide open."

She blew smoke. "Think he could have killed them?"

Chan shook his head that he did not. "The seven were killed by a pro—someone who knew how to kill in the exact manner as Henry Brooks. I think Grubbs was in on some of the plans, but I don't think he had the skills to do the actual killing."

"I agree. So who do we look for?"

"Not we, Norma—you. I'm done."

"Done? C'mon, Chan. You can't give up now. We owe it to the town, to the Seven. Even to Jean…"

"No." Chan shook his head. "And that's the thing, Norma. See, I didn't mind so much when it was just me—when death was staring me in the face on this story. I can accept that risk, but I can't be responsible for someone else's death."

"You're not. Ryan Grubbs killed Jean."

"Only because she was with me," he turned slightly as his eyes became wet again. "She was my responsibility."

"Chan…."

Chan fished his cigarette around in the ash tray. "No, Norma, I can't." He looked directly into her eyes. "I'll never put another person I care about at risk like that again. I just can't." He made a fist and pounded the table. "I won't."

Norma allowed his anger to settle and then said, "It comes with the territory, my friend. These types of stories happen rarely, but they do happen. And you'll have to accept all that goes with it." She took another drag. "Chan, you're a bright, young man—smart and intuitive. A couple of old dinosaurs like Darby and I won't be able hang around long enough to see this through—you will."

Chan was about to protest again, but Norma stopped him. "Trust me, Chan Adams, I know what I'm talking about. You will recover. You'll bounce back and when you do, you'll figure this whole thing out. I've seen how you've worked this story. You know when to be sympathetic, when to be cautious and when to kick ass—you've got great instincts for this kind of work. I'd hate to see you throw it all away now." She paused to let her words sink in. "Give yourself a few more days. Just don't rush to make your decision, okay?"

Chan sat motionless, the cig hanging from his lips. He then looked at her and briefly nodded.

"Good," Norma said as she sat back in her chair. She took another drag and smiled. "And Chan, when you eventually do figure out who is behind this, give it to the son-of-a-bitch with both barrels."

OCTOBER 6, 2016

11:22 AM

Chan walked up the steps of the Cannon House Office Building in Washington, D.C. It was a cloudless day in the nation's capital and the bright sun and autumn air emboldened his every step. At the top, he paused and shook off any last-second doubt or fear.

He entered the large center doors not helping but to note the grand Beaux Arts style of architecture of the century old building. He bypassed a crowd of people and was soon in the massive rotunda surrounded by eighteen Corinthian columns, supporting its detailed, coffered dome. Chan took only a moment to look around. Although he had been to Washington many times before he had never been in this building. But his purpose there was too overriding for sightseeing, and he continued his march to the elevator doors.

His prior arrangements through the offices of Representatives Jim Clyburn and Joe Wilson of neighboring South Carolina congressional districts enabled his passing of security, and he was directed to the special elevators which took guests to the fifth floor. The elevator doors opened, and Chan walked calmly and directly through the nose bleed section of Cannon House. He came to room 527, office of South Carolina's eighth district representative, Treywick Boland Richards.

Richards' political career had been a highly successful one beginning with his election to the state's senate in 1976. He had served judiciously in that position for three terms before setting his sights on Congress in 1988, where he had been re-elected every two years since. The still vibrant seventy-three-year-old Richards had become a popular mainstay in Washington introducing lasting legislation, serving on several committees and even chairing the Ethics Committee in recent years. He was pegged as a hard-working family man, who had built solid friendships on both sides of the aisle. There was even talk that, despite his age, he may be up for a cabinet position after the upcoming presidential election. Ellis Dover would have been very proud to see his prodigy become so successful.

A secretary's desk was immediately to Chan's right upon his entering the larger office of 527. He was greeted by an older woman with a pleasant face.

"Yes, sir. May I help you?"

"I'm here to see Congressman Richards," Chan said coldly.

"Do you have an appointment," she said as she pulled reading glasses to her eyes and scanned the day's agenda.

"No. But what I have to say he needs to hear."

The woman frowned. "Well, as it turns out, he is here in the office today." She paused and then asked, "Is this of a personal nature?"

Chan nodded. "Oh, yes."

She picked up the phone. "And what is your name, sir?"

"Tell him… Henry Brooks is here."

The woman frowned again and relayed the message in a hushed tone. Almost immediately the door to Richards' private office opened. An assistant and two interns hustled out.

Trey Richards then appeared at the door. He looked very distinguished, almost regal—a young man's face under a grey head of hair and a fit body in a flattering grey suit. He stood motionless for a moment eyeing Chan. After the recollection, he smiled. "Chan Adams," he said. "I was expecting one ghost and found another." He tapped his door with his hand. "Come in, please."

Chan followed him inside, pulling the door closed. Richards walked behind his grand desk and sat in his leather back chair. Beyond the desk, a picture window, wrapped in golden drapes, provided a beautiful view of the bustling city below.

"Would you care to sit?" Richards offered.

Chan shook his head.

Richards eyed him strangely. "Well, let's see now, Adams. The last time I saw you I had just been elected to Congress for the first time. Am I right?"

"That's right."

"Still in Macinaw?"

Chan nodded.

Richards leaned back in his chair and put his hands behind his head—relaxed, confident. "So, tell me, what have you've been up to?"

"It's a long story," Chan said with no emotion.

"Okay. Then tell me why you're here. What can I do for you?"

Chan felt it bubbling up inside him and he couldn't suppress it any longer. "Well, for one, you can go straight to hell."

Richards attempted a smile and turned his ear as if he misunderstood. "Pardon?"

"I said, you can go to hell, you spineless son of a bitch."

Richards sat up in his chair and cleared his throat. "Perhaps this wasn't a good idea. Maybe you should come another…"

"I know all about it, Richards. I know it was you in the Dover barn that day."

"Excuse me?"

"It was you. You were having sex with Robert Dover. You had your tie around his neck—as some sort of erotic asphyxiation—you choked him to death."

Richards picked up his phone. "I think you need to leave now."

"There were eight of them, Richards. Eight witnesses to your crime, not seven. It was the eighth one that sent you the blackmail letter."

Richards put down his phone and feigned confusion. "Blackmail letter? Adams what the hell are you talking about? God, man, I know the Macinaw Seven story affected you. I heard that you began living from bottle to bottle, but this…."

"You were part of the Davis and Milton law firm back in 1969. After you killed Robert and your fake suicide went to shit, you called Sonny Watts to save your ass. Only problem is you set the devil on the seven arrested but you didn't get to the eighth witness. And in 1976 after you won your party's nomination for the South Carolina senate, that witness sent you a letter demanding fifty thousand dollars. You were loaded so I'm sure you didn't give a damn about the money. But you couldn't risk the embarrassment or lose the chance at your growing power, could you? Not with all those black boys still out there running around that knew the truth. So you got your old buddy Watts to bring Henry Brooks back from the grave to murder the Seven. I wonder how much that cost you."

"Now, Adams, these are serious and slanderous accusations, and I will hold you personally responsible for spreading these lies."

Chan's laugh dripped in sarcasm. He then leaned on the desk—hatred in his eyes. "Fuck you, Richards! You're going down for all of this. For the Macinaw Seven, for Crawford, Haskit, Evans..." His voice broke slightly. "...for Jean. You're going down for all of them."

Richards rose from behind his desk and held out his hand. "Now, hold on, Adams." He paused, thinking—his hand still out like a traffic cop. "This is all speculation. You can't prove any of this."

"Yes, yes I can. I have evidence of Sonny Watts' ties to Henry Brooks and the HBD's, including Henry Brooks' knife. I have Peyton Medlin's amended autopsy of Robert Dover. I have the blackmail letter. And most importantly, I have the eighth witness who will swear as to what you did in the barn that day."

Richards drew his hand across his face and held it against his mouth. He then looked directly at Chan and said, "Mistakes may have been made, Adams. But we can be reasonable about this. What is it that you want?" He went back to his desk and fumbled for his checkbook. "How much do you want? How much to make this go away?"

Chan shook his head sadly. "You don't get it, do you, Richards? Sometimes you just can't make things go away."

Richards began to breathe heavily; his face looking much older than a few minutes ago. He slammed the checkbook down on his desk. Somehow in a matter of seconds his life had all fallen apart—his entire, well-crafted plan had imploded. In desperation, he reached in a drawer and pulled out a handgun, .38 caliber. He pointed it at Chan's heart. "Oh, yes, Mr. Adams. I can make things go away. One way or another."

"You're going to shoot me here? In your office?"

"You attacked me. Came in shouting crazy things. I have a right to defend myself. My staff will back me. And the world will believe me over some drunk, has-been reporter."

231

Chan undid the buttons on his shirt and showed Richards the wires and listening device taped to his chest. "I haven't had anything to drink yet, Congressman."

AUGUST 6, 1976

Sheriff Crawford sat in a rocking chair beside his wife's bed. Now in the final stages of ALS, she had been confined to her bed like this for months. With his two sons grown and out of the house, the sheriff had to hire sitters for her for much of the time he was away. Whenever he was home, her care became his second job. It had become a painful way for both to live. He looked at the frail woman's face as he rocked away, trying to remember the beautiful woman he once knew. He checked his watch. *Less than four hours to go*, he thought.

He heard a knock on the front door and went to answer it. Chief Deputy Haskit rushed inside. "Sorry to barge in on you, Sheriff, but I think I may have something."

"What about?" Crawford asked, standing firmly in the doorway.

Haskit continued into the living room unabated and Crawford reluctantly followed. They stood together in the dimly lit room. "I got to thinking about what Adams told us yesterday. You know, about how that stripper, Dixie Love, started acting antsy whenever he mentioned the Henry Brooks' Disciples. And then how she threatened him."

"It was probably nothing."

"I don't think so, Sheriff—cause I did some digging around about this woman and found out a few things."

"Like what?"

"Well, for one thing, she's got a record—a two-time repeat offender. Her real name is Audrey Sawyer—from Savannah."

"Savannah?"

"Yeah. Just like the HBD's. My buddy, Walt, over in probation and parole, knew the agent in Georgia who had her as one of his cases. Said she was a complete nut."

"But that doesn't…"

"And get this," Haskit said excitedly. "She did five years at the Women's Transitional Center for gigging her ex-boyfriend."

"Gigging?"

233

"That's right, Sheriff. She gigged him with a knife. Cut him up pretty bad from what I was told."

"C'mon, Bobby, what are you saying here? You think because she has a record and used a knife once that she had something to do with all this?"

"Think about it, Sheriff. She knew Ryan Grubbs—she at least had knowledge of the Disciples. Somebody like that could have gone unnoticed. Everybody's been looking for a Henry Brooks type—she could be the female version."

"No…"

"I think it's worth looking into," Haskit pleaded.

"Bobby, how could a woman like that take on seven young black males? Deputy Evans too?"

"Cause she's the one with the knife. She gets close to them. They wouldn't expect it coming from her. There are plenty of women in the lockup who have taken men down. And I think Jimmy might have gotten careless. It's not impossible."

"You're grasping at straws now."

"I disagree. No one thought it could have been Henry Brooks either, remember? I believe it's worth checking out." He paused. "Really, Sheriff, we've got nothing to lose."

Crawford sighed and cut his eyes back towards Judy's bedroom. He checked his watch again and was about to say something when Haskit continued, "I called the strip joint— she's not working tonight. But I got her address and want to go over there. No harm in checking her out."

Crawford nodded reluctantly. "Okay. But I'm going with you. Let me call my neighbor Mrs. Townsend and see if she'll sit with Judy until I get back." He then smiled at his deputy as he went for the phone. "Who knows? Maybe we will get lucky."

9:48 PM

Far-off lightning streaked the night sky as Haskit drove his squad car down an unmarked dirt road in Southwestern Macinaw County. Sitting on the passenger's side, Crawford took in the flashes in the distance with concern.

"We better get there before too long," Crawford said. "Looks like a storm is heading our way."

"Shouldn't be far now if I read the directions correctly," Haskit said. "I think I see porch lights up ahead."

Within a minute, Haskit pulled his squad car into the front yard of the small house, littered with strewn trash and junk car parts. The two lawmen approached the front door—a slight wind and electricity in the night air.

"Better let me handle this," Crawford said as he knocked on the door.

Bearing a joyous smile and dressed in shorts and a halter top, Dixie Love answered. Her smile faded almost immediately. "What's this?"

"Miss Love, my name is Sheriff Crawford. Deputy Haskit and I would like to ask you a few questions if you don't mind."

She squinted her eyes at Crawford. "What about?"

"The murders of the Macinaw Seven, Miss Love. We have reason to believe there may be a connection between the murders which only you can help us with. It will take just a few minutes."

Love gave the sheriff a long, hard look and then shrugged her shoulders. "I don't know if I can help, but come on in."

They entered the small front room which was as disheveled and unkempt as the yard. Haskit scanned the room quickly and indicated the two packed bags by the couch. "Going somewhere, Miss Love?"

"Gonna see my mom in Texas," she said as she sat on the couch and crossed her bare legs. "Is that a crime?"

"No, ma'am. Just seemed a weird time to be traveling," Haskit said.

"Don't care for the heat, Deputy. I always travel at night." She looked up at Crawford. "Now what's this all about?"

Crawford stood in front of Love with his deputy behind him. "Henry Brooks."

"What about Henry Brooks?"

"The hour is late, Miss Love. Do you know anything about him?" Crawford asked.

Love glanced quickly at Haskit and then back to the sheriff. "Yes," she said simply. "I know all about him. In fact, I can take y'all to him if you want."

"Wait. What? You can take us to him?" Haskit asked with a laugh. "The man's been dead for ten years."

Dixie grinned at him with child-like exuberance. "Oh, he ain't dead, Deputy. Not by a long shot."

Haskit leaned into the sheriff's shoulder and whispered. "What the hell?"

Crawford turned to him and said under his breath, "Just play along. See where this takes us."

"So you're gonna take us to him? Henry Brooks?" Haskit asked incredulously.

Dixie Love stood and smiled. "I will. Actually, I'm dying for you to meet him."

11:27 PM

A hard rain fell as they drove back through Macinaw and headed across the Edisto River toward Henry Brooks' farm. Crawford told Haskit that he would drive the squad car so that the deputy could sit on the passenger side and keep a close eye on their guest in the backseat. Haskit had unsnapped the sheath from his sidearm as they rode.

The lightning continued to pop all around them coloring the old farm and the surrounding swampland in a wicked blackish blue.

"Keep to the right," Love said as they passed the farmhouse. "Stay on the farm road until you reach the curve by the river."

"I sure hope you know where you're taking us," Haskit said.

"Don't worry. It won't be long now, Deputy," Love replied.

After the road curved, Crawford pulled off in a thick, weedy patch. There was an incline to their left which ran down into a group of trees and the swamp beyond. "Is this it?" Crawford asked.

"I think so," Love said.

"Is this what?" Haskit asked.

"The drop off point," Crawford said.

The deputy looked at his boss with a lost expression. "Drop off for what?"

"I'm sorry, Bobby. I didn't want you out here. I didn't want you to come. But you insisted."

"What do you mean? What are you talking about?"

"I hate that it has to end this way, Bobby, but you went snooping around, looking for information on Dixie and you wouldn't let it go. Knowing you, you would have figured it out sooner or later."

"Sheriff, I don't understand. Figured out what?"

Crawford pulled his weapon from his left-sided holster and aimed it at Haskit's chest.

Haskit stared at the sheriff's gun hand and then it dawned on him. "You're left-handed," Haskit mumbled. But his moment of clarity came too late.

"I'm sorry, Bobby..." The sheriff pulled the trigger—the gun shot exploded inside the patrol car. Haskit's body was thrown against the passenger door. A trickle of blood appeared on the window.

Crawford held his position for a moment—smoke rising from the barrel. He then holstered his weapon and turned to the backseat. Dixie Love was holding her hands over her ears. "It's over," Crawford said. "He's gone."

She leaned up in her seat and kissed Crawford on the cheek. "I'm sorry, Justin. I know you didn't want to have to do that."

"All a part of this madness, Dixie. I didn't want to have to do any of this shit to be honest. But three quarters of a million dollars will make a man do almost anything."

She smiled and ran her red fingernails through his hair. "We'll start over. Find some little tropical island somewhere. Live out our lives together."

Crawford nodded. "We will. After the devil pays us his due."

"Here he comes now." She pointed through the windshield at the figure approaching. Crawford rolled down the car window part of the way—the rain finding its way inside.

He was wearing a black trench coat and hat and carrying a bag. He leaned over and peered inside the open window and saw Haskit's body. He blew strands of wet hair from his face. "Last minute business, Justin?" Watts asked with a laugh. "I knew from the moment I saw your reaction to Henry Brooks' execution, you were cold-blooded enough to get things done."

"Never mind that. Show it to us."

Watts smiled. He opened the case and revealed stacks of hundred dollar bills. "Seven hundred thousand. One hundred thousand for each kill. Just like we promised." He closed it quickly. "My client wishes to thank you both. And I wish to thank you for honoring Henry Brooks so precisely—your right hand, Miss Love, and your left hand, Sheriff. Abaddon and Michael thank you." He laughed again and then quoted *Hamlet*, "Angels and ministers of grace defend us."

Crawford hurried him on. "The deed's been done. And I returned the knife to the hiding place in the house yesterday. So, what's the plan now?"

Watts produced two plane tickets and identification papers and handed them to Crawford. "After we get rid of this patrol car, you and Miss Love will fly out of Charleston at 3:00 a.m.— destination Bogota, Columbia—then you're on your own. I will be heading in another direction. We shall never speak again. Is that clear?"

"Fine by us," Crawford said. He reached back and grabbed Dixie Love's hand.

Watts tilted his head slightly. "Aww. Isn't that sweet? The couple that slays together, stays together." He looked back at Dixie. "Now aren't you glad I found you in that awful jail cell in Savannah? You must admit we've had so much fun together."

"Watts, it's getting late. Give us the money and let's get on with this." Crawford said.

"Oh, yes, of course. But there is one more thing…" Watts said as he dropped the bag and reached inside his coat again. He pulled out a .45 with a Blackslide silencer and instantly popped Crawford in the temple. The sheriff's head slammed against the seat. Dixie Love screamed but there was no escaping her fate. Watts fired again splitting open her throat. Blood splattered all over the back windshield. He watched her squirm until she became completely motionless.

With the rain falling all about him, Watts felt in his coat pocket again for his cigarette case. "Damn…" He picked up the bag then turned and headed back toward the house. He would gather his things and then return to dispose of the squad car and the dead bodies. Everything was going to work out perfectly.

Henry would be so proud.

OCTOBER 6, 2016

4:15 PM

Tindal brought two shots of Johnny Drum to the table in the Jack Rose Dinning Saloon, Washington D.C.'s premier whiskey bar. Chan was seated across from her—his eyes scanning the thousands of bottles that lined the saloon walls. She sat down and slid his shot towards his open hand. They quickly toasted the moment.

"Here's to you, Chan."

"To both of us," Chan corrected. He took a drink and then raised the glass again. "To the end of a very long story."

Tindal drank and then put her glass on the table shaking her head. "Unbelievable. I just can't freaking believe it. Congressman Trey Richards." She smiled broadly. "Who would have ever thought Richards was behind all this?"

"I know. It's all so surreal. But in a way, I should have known. He was always so close to the family. Always hanging around with them. And then there he was in Sonny Watts' same firm—just a phone call away. It all seems so easy to piece together now."

"Nothing easy about it, Chan. Quite frankly, it was brilliant journalism on your part."

Chan shook his head. "No, there was some hard work and long nights but a lot of lucky guesses, too. And, of course, there was that huge push from a certain reporter—Reuters' next Pulitzer Prize winner." He winked at her.

Tindal smiled. "The piece is extraordinary. My bosses love it. They can barely contain themselves." She paused for another sip and then, "And what about Crawford? He was also involved?"

"Apparently so. I'm not sure of everything, but when the FBI put the cuffs on Richards, he started ranting about how he didn't kill anyone. How it was all Watts' plan and how Crawford and Dixie Love had been hired as the assassins to kill the Seven." He shook his head. "If any of that turns out to be true, it will shake Macinaw to its foundation. Crawford was a legend there. I just can't believe he would have had anything to do with it."

"Seems to be an unfortunate truism, Chan, but even the good guys can be corrupted if the price is right."

"Must have been a helluva price."

"Yeah, which takes us back to Watts. He may have assassinated his assassins and taken their share too."

Chan nodded his agreement. "Made it an even bigger payday for himself."

"Why do you think he went through the trouble of pretending to die in that fire?"

"Again, just my theory, but he probably thought the Macinaw Seven would start coming after him, pressuring him with what they knew. Or he may have thought that if the press had continued looking into his life, we would have eventually discovered his connection to Henry Brooks. And he couldn't have that."

Tindal nodded. "My friend at the Savannah Morning News made Watts' connection to the Henry Brooks Disciples. She said while at Bingham and Dodd he represented Jack Neufeld."

"Diamond Jack?"

"Yes. The same man who started the Disciples. And she also told me Watts represented another Savannah jailbird: Audrey Sawyer. You know her better as Dixie Love."

Chan grinned and shook his head at the mind-boggling connections. "Damn...."

Tindal's phone lit up and she read the text. "It's Sheriff Monroe. He's outside now. I'll go get him." Tindal was quickly out of her seat and headed for the front of the saloon.

Chan sat in contemplation, running his finger along his empty shot glass, still shaking his head. Within seconds, Tindal returned with the Macinaw sheriff in tow. Monroe was dressed in his Sunday best—looking huge in his blue sport coat. Chan stood and shook his hand.

"How was your flight?" Chan asked. He then signaled the bartender for three more shots.

"Pretty good," Monroe said as they all sat back down at the table. "But, hey, with the news you guys broke, I think I could have grown wings to fly up here if I had to." They all laughed.

"What's the plan now?" Chan followed.

"We're gonna take Richards back to South Carolina. Charge him with seven counts of first degree murder—murder for hire, plus a whole lot more. He's gonna pay dearly for all the pain he caused."

"He's one of many that caused that pain," Tindal said. "I don't think we'll ever find him, but I wish we could get our hands on Sonny Watts too. He manipulated the whole thing."

Monroe sighed and tilted his head a little. "Yeah, well, about that...."

"What?" Chan asked.

Monroe reached into his jacket and pulled out a folded manila envelope.

"What's that?" Tindal asked.

"It's a copy of the FBI's DNA analysis of the three bodies found in the squad car." He threw the envelope on the bar table. "It's a game changer."

OCTOBER 7, 2016

7:56 AM

"That's a fascinating story, Mr. Adams. But I'm still wondering why you had to bother to come all the way up here to tell me this," Andrew Searson said. The CEO of the Searson-Thompson real estate firm was standing at the door of his incredible estate on the outskirts of Hartford, Connecticut. He wore a black silk robe over his tall, rotund form. His pudgy face was a mixture of pleasantry and concern.

"Well, it was on that property your company bought thirty years ago, sir. We thought maybe you'd just want to know." Chan was standing tall on the immense front porch. Tindal had remained in the driver's seat of the rental car in the estate's driveway, waiting.

Searson held his position, rocking on the heels of his bare-feet, his hands jammed in the pockets of his robes. "Okay," he said, measuring his words. "But I thought you said this Watts person died in that fire at his house. How could he have been the one to sponsor all those crimes if he was dead?" His words had a bit of undeserved anger behind them.

"We don't know everything for sure, but our theory is that he set the fire himself. We think he invited one of the migrant workers to his house that night. He was always hiring them to do menial chores around his place. The workers were there in South Carolina illegally so there would have been no record if one went missing. And they would have thought nothing of going to his place. Watts probably killed him and placed him in his den. I saw the body myself during the fire—thought it was him the whole time."

"But I still don't get it. How do you know it was Watts who organized all this in the first place, Mr. Adams? You say you found a couple of his type of cigarettes in the Brooks' house, but really those could have belonged to anyone."

Chan smiled. "That's the interesting part, Mr. Searson. You see, the FBI's DNA evidence report came back yesterday from the tests performed on the remains found in the squad car." Chan

242

reached into his coat pocket and pulled out Sheriff Monroe's copy of the document.

"And?" Searson asked timidly.

"And... they confirmed the bodies of Dixie Love and Sheriff Crawford. But not that of Deputy Haskit. You see, the body that everyone believed was Haskit, even wearing Haskit's tattered old uniform, was really that of Sonny Watts."

Searson felt a pain in the pit of his stomach; he lifted his now trembling chin. "I don't..." He swallowed hard. "I don't understand."

"Actually, I think maybe you do. You see, I believe Haskit might have been wounded during the exchange of gun fire, perhaps even severely, but it did not kill him. The police found a bullet from Crawford's weapon lodged in the passenger side of the squad car where Haskit was probably sitting. Those two must have gotten into an argument—perhaps Haskit found out Crawford's true intentions. And later, when Watts terminated the sheriff, he wasn't counting on Haskit still being alive." Chan leaned forward and looked Searson directly in the eyes. "I figure the deputy somehow managed to open his door after Watts walked away. He pulled his own weapon and fired. The FBI confirmed that the person in Haskit's decayed uniform was shot in the back... with Haskit's weapon."

Searson's face darkened; he took a deep breath. He grabbed the door jamb to steady himself.

"With Watts dead, and the assassin's money now lying there, Haskit saw his chance, a golden opportunity if you will. He switched clothes with Watts, threw him in the passenger seat and then put the squad car in neutral until it rolled down the embankment and came to rest in that thicket of kudzu down there near the Edisto on what is now your property—where it remained hidden until recently."

Searson began to look ill; he closed his eyes briefly as it all came flooding back to him. He then opened his eyes and cast them heavenward as if cursing that one moment of fate.

Chan continued, "With the money, Haskit was probably able to make a new life for himself. New identity. Plastic surgery. The works. With plenty left over to start a new business." He looked beyond Searson and into the interior of his palatial home. "Live the good life."

Searson cleared his throat and asked weakly, "Do you think they'll go after this man, this Haskit? Now that they know."

Chan paused for a long moment and stared at the man before him. "I imagine. He killed that bastard Watts, but he also took all the money. I imagine the FBI will have a lot of questions for him. But I don't think they'll know where to look for the deputy, Mr. Searson. It happened such a long time ago."

Searson nodded and whispered, "Yes. A long time ago." He looked directly at Chan. "And what about you, Mr. Adams? Will you be pursuing this matter any further?"

Chan pulled down the corners of his mouth as he thought about it. "Deputy Haskit saved my life way back then; I reckon I owe him for that. Besides I'm retired now. I don't have any interest in chasing ghosts anymore."

Searson wiped tears from his cheeks and nodded.

"Well, I thought you would want to know, Mr. Searson. Know the whole story."

Searson looked at Chan and forced a little smile. "Very kind of you to tell me."

Chan turned to go but swung back around. "Oh, one more thing, Mr. Searson. You might want to think of selling that property down there in Macinaw—the old Brooks farm. Nothing but swampland down there."

"Thank you, Mr. Adams. I'll take that into consideration." Searson made a final head dip of gratitude then backed into his mansion and shut the door.

Chan turned and bound down the steps toward the rental car. Tindal fired up the engine as he slid in on the passenger's side.

"Well...?" she asked. "Were you right? Was it him?"

Chan looked out at the mansion as they pulled down the estate's drive. "I don't think so." He turned to her and grinned. "Maybe. Who knows?"

Tindal returned the smile. "Well, I got all I wanted out of this story. Maybe we should just let sleeping dogs lie."

"A very Southern thing to say, Ms. Huddleston. And I happen to agree completely."

11:22 AM

Chan and Tindal stood together near the United Airlines ticket desk at the Bradley International Airport. Tindal held her flight ticket home in her hand. "I got lucky," she said. "I leave in ten minutes."

Chan smirked. "Another four hours for me to wait."

She smiled. "Sorry. I could change flights if you want me to."

"No, no, no. You go ahead. Maybe I'll grab a book and read a little bit."

"Maybe you should grab some paper and start writing your next book, *Kicking Henry Brooks' Ass.*"

They both laughed.

"No, I think I'm done with all that."

"Really, Chan, I've got plenty of friends in the publishing business. It would be a bestseller for sure."

"You write it. Maybe I could do the forward or something."

She smiled. "It's a deal." She paused, looking long into his sad eyes. She recognized his need for long-awaited closure and whispered in his ear, "She would have been proud of you, you know."

Chan nodded and then leaned over and kissed her on the cheek. "Thanks for everything, Tindal. Have a safe trip home."

Tindal smiled, turned and headed toward her gate. Chan watched until she disappeared into the swelling crowd.

OCTOBER 8, 2016

10:10 AM

Chan leaned against the rail on the far-left edge of Watkins Bridge watching the Edisto twist and turn its way underneath. The sunrays caught portions of the river as it flowed southward casting a reddish tinge on its unsettled waters. Chan held still for a moment listening to the river as it went past, carrying away fallen leaves, sand and debris.

He knew he was but a few hundred yards from that sandbar where he and Jean had fallen in love those many years ago. The sun felt the same on his skin now as it had that day. He dug into his front pocket and produced a small box. He hesitated and then opened it. It was an engagement ring, Jean's engagement ring. He had planned on giving it to her that night after they had dined in Mt. Pleasant. He was going to drive out to the Isle of Palms and take her for a walk along the beach. He would have gotten on one knee, told her that he was in love and wanted to be with her the rest of his life. *You would have said yes, wouldn't you?*

Chan held the diamond in the morning sun allowing it to glisten in its light. He then brought it close and kissed the top of the ring. "I miss you, Jean, and I'll never forget you," he said as a solitary tear fell. "But it's time to move on—time to let you go." He then dropped the ring over the side. A simple splash and it was gone forever.

The Edisto welcomed the ring into it depths as it does with all things destined to be forgotten. Her waters swept past the bridge and continued as they have for centuries—past the tall oaks, the Spanish moss, the kudzu, the cotton fields, the small towns, the dirt roads—washing the banks clean of blood and tears, easing the hurt and cruelty of times gone by, ever moving forward, picking up steam, heading for the coast.

ACKNOWLEDGMENTS

Like my first two novels, *Carolina Cruel*, has taken an unorthodox path to publication. It has been a long road of false hopes, heartache and delays, but I believe the end of that journey has led me to some place wonderful. I am proud to now be associated with Rivers Turn Press, and I look forward to shepherding new and engaging Southern fiction for many years to come.

I'd also like to sincerely thank all the experts upon whom I relied to help steer *Carolina Cruel* into the novel that it has become. The contributors are far too numerous to name; however, I must give a huge thank you to Phil Webster, Joseph Sutcliff, Gregg Frierson, Fred Jeffers, Alexis Bates, Turner Perrow, Holly Holladay, and Jeanna and Billy Reynolds for their invaluable input, creative eye and sage advice. And please note: any errors in content and storytelling fall strictly on my shoulders.

I wish to thank my colleagues, former and present students, friends and family for their continued support. Writing can be at times a bit of lonely business, but these people are my biggest supporters and help me maintain a balanced life, and for that, I am forever grateful.

The fifty-year scope of *Carolina Cruel* required a large cast of characters to make up the numerous reporters, lawyers, police, FBI, doctors, town folk, victims, and villains. I'm often asked how I come up with character names in my novels. Sometimes I use names of people I know, but for many, I simply pull the names out of thin air. Their physical descriptions might be based on actors or people I have seen in the news. Most are a hodge-podge of various sources. For example, Chan Adams, the main protagonist, is a name combination of a childhood friend, Chandler Deery, and Hemingway's short story hero, Nick Adams. Chan's life experiences are based loosely on those of my friend and fellow author, Ken Burger. Reporting partner, Tindal Huddleston, is based on an enthusiastic young reader I met at a book signing in Florence, SC years ago as well as several strong women I have known throughout my life. And three of the characters were named for contest winners. I hope you enjoyed your characters: Jean Reid and Ryan Grubbs. (The third contest winner, my friend, Jimmy Evans, sadly passed away before *Carolina Cruel* was published.) Of course, all characters are fiction and all ultimately have a life of their own.

And finally, on a much different note, I was midway through the writing of this novel when the terrible news came about Emanuel AME Church in Charleston, South Carolina, where nine members of that church were killed in cold blood. Suffice it to say that a fictional novel has no place in comparison to such a tragic event, but at the time, I couldn't help but feel that the Carolina Cruel of which I wrote is alive and well in certain societal segments, not only in my state but throughout this country and beyond. However, it was the fallout of that horrible crime that spoke to me even more. When the families of the nine showed such grace and forgiveness when confronting the killer of their loved ones, it moved me beyond words. And ultimately that's what I wish for every person to take away when faced with similar cruelties. Show the faith, courage, and love that the families of the Emanuel Church Nine showed, and we will make this a better world. From tragedy to triumph, that's the real power of the palmetto state. That's the South Carolina that I know.

Visit the author at lawrencethackston.com or riversturnpress.com for news, upcoming events and to offer your comments.